Please return/renew this item by the last date shown on this label, or on your self-service receipt.

To renew this item, visit **www.librarieswest.org.uk** or contact your library

Your borrower number and PIN are required.

Libraries**West**

Books by Andrew Lane

AWOL: Agent Without Licence
AWOL 2: Last Safe Moment

Young Sherlock Holmes
Death Cloud
Red Leech
Black Ice
Fire Storm
Snake Bite
Knife Edge
Stone Cold
Night Break

Lost Worlds
Lost Worlds
Shadow Creatures

Crusoe
Dawn of Spies
Day of Ice
Night of Terror

A.W.O.L.

LAST SAFE MOMENT

ANDREW LANE

Piccadilly
PRESS

First published in Great Britain in 2018 by
PICCADILLY PRESS
80–81 Wimpole St, London W1G 9RE
www.piccadillypress.co.uk

A CIP catalogue record for this book is available from the British Library.

ISBN: 978-1-84812-665-7
also available as an ebook

1

This book is typeset using Atomik ePublisher
Printed and bound in Great Britain by Clays Ltd, Elcograf S.p.A.

Piccadilly Press is an imprint of Bonnier Zaffre Ltd,
a Bonnier Publishing company
www.bonnierpublishing.com

Dedicated to Amber, Caitlin, Courtney, Beth and Sophie; because the last book was dedicated to the boys . . .

And with thanks to Emma Matthewson and Talya Baker, for the phenomenal editing work.

CHAPTER ONE

'This is going to hurt, isn't it?'

Kieron Mellor heard the slight tremor in his voice, and hated himself for it. Why wasn't he able to cope with this? After what he'd been through recently, it should be a walk in the park.

That's what he kept telling himself, but he could feel his heart beating fast in his chest.

'It won't hurt at all,' the man in the tattoo-and-piercing parlour said reassuringly. 'Just a pinprick. Well, two pinpricks. You'll hardly feel a thing.'

Kieron looked over the guy's shoulder at the shoppers passing in the mall. The piercing parlour was small – barely the size of his bedroom. With him, the man sitting on a stool facing him and the woman on the cash register, there was hardly enough room to turn around. Sam – Kieron's best friend – was waiting outside, leaning on the rail running around the balcony and staring down at the crowded expanse of mall.

Down below were the shops selling clothes, electronic goods, expensive handbags and furniture. Down below *them* was the food court. Up here on the top level were the cheaper places – a comic shop, a place that sold New Age figurines and packs of angel cards, a gents' hairdresser. And the tattoo and piercing parlour.

The man sitting patiently in front of Kieron wore a tight T-shirt and sported a luxuriant moustache that continued up his cheeks to join his sideburns. He also wore a leather cowboy hat. Tattoos of blue-and-gold fish scales covered his right arm from wrist to shoulder. On his left arm the tattoos were a work in progress: black curves that would be coloured in progressively at some later date. Kieron found himself wondering if the man tattooed himself. Was that even possible? Or did he go to another parlour or get the woman on the till to do it? And why wasn't it finished yet – had he run out of blue and gold ink?

'So,' the man said patiently, 'are we going to do this, or what?'

Kieron tried to calm his racing thoughts and his racing heart. 'Yes,' he said, then, 'Yes!' in a louder, firmer voice.

'And just to confirm – you *are* sixteen, aren't you? I have to ask. We don't pierce anyone younger than that.'

'Yes,' Kieron responded. He *wasn't* sixteen, but he looked as though he might be. He could see from the man's expression that he didn't believe him, but that it didn't matter. He'd asked, and Kieron had answered.

'Two snakebite piercings: one on each side, yes?'

'Yes.'

'OK.' He reached over and brushed underneath Kieron's lower lip with something that looked like a wet wipe and

2

smelled of antiseptic. 'I'm just going to make a couple of marks with a felt-tip pen. They'll wash off, but I want to make sure I get the piercings symmetrical.' He swapped the wet wipe for a pen, leaned forward and touched it twice to Kieron's face where he had wiped. 'There's nothing worse than lopsided piercings.' He looked critically at the placement. 'Yes, that should do it.' Putting the pen on a counter by his side, he picked up a device that looked like a small clamp. In fact, it *was* a small clamp, as Kieron found out when the man quickly fastened it to his lip over one of the marks. Steadying it with one hand, he scooped something else up.

Kieron closed his eyes and held his breath.

'Try not to flinch,' the man said. 'That thing on your lip has two holes in it – one on either side. I'm going to pass the needle through. The needle is attached to a stud. I'll remove the clamp, then pull the needle out. It'll leave the stud behind.' Kieron felt a sharp pain and a tug on his lip as the needle went through, then some fiddling as the man removed the clamp. He braced himself for a sharper pain as the needle was pulled out, but he hardly felt it. Maybe the wet wipe had some anaesthetic on it and it had just kicked in. A dull ache started up as the man leaned back and gazed at his handiwork.

'Perfect. You all right? Not going to faint?'

Kieron shook his head. He thought he could taste blood, but he wasn't sure.

'Ready for the next one?'

He nodded. Again the clamp was applied to his lip, but

3

this time he didn't even feel the needle going in, let alone coming out. As the man replaced the clamp on the counter Kieron touched the studs with his tongue – first left and then right. He felt a slight jolt as the tip of his tongue met the cold metal, like a very small electric shock. Experimentally he moved his lips and waggled his jaw. The studs had gone in higher up, so they didn't clash unless he deliberately rubbed his lower lip against his teeth.

'Finished. Don't eat or drink anything for half an hour. Come back in two weeks and I'll replace the studs with rings. All part of the price. Talking of which, if you could pay the lovely Maria there on your way out – thirty pounds, please.'

He stood, and moved past Kieron to a small washbasin. Kieron levered himself to his feet, feeling slightly woozy, and stepped over to where Maria already had her hand out expectantly. He fished around in his pocket for the cash he'd painstakingly saved up from the pocket money his mum gave him and handed it across. It was a lot, but he'd wanted these piercings for ages.

Outside, the cool air hit him. He could feel beads of sweat on his forehead.

'What do you think?' he asked as he approached Sam.

His friend frowned. 'Sorry, what?'

'Don't muck around. You heard me.'

Sam smiled. 'Yeah. Actually they look great. Better than I expected. What do you think your mum's going to say?'

'The question is, how long is it going to be until she even notices?' Kieron could hear the bitterness in his voice and hated himself for it.

4

'She's still doing overtime?' Sam asked.

'Every shift she can get. Then she spends the money she makes from the overtime on presents for me because she feels guilty about doing the overtime. What's that phrase – "vicious circle"? That's what we're trapped in.'

Sam nodded. He glanced at Kieron's piercings again. 'My sister told me about some guy she had come into Accident and Emergency. He'd had a piercing just like yours, except he'd already had the studs replaced with rings. Apparently he was eating dinner one night and got the fork caught in one of the rings. In his panic to get it out he ended up tearing his lip open. Nasty.'

Thoughts of Sam's sister Courtney made Kieron's cheeks feel hot. He knew he was blushing, and didn't want Sam to see. Trying to change the subject, he said, 'You're just jealous. Scare stories aren't going to put me off.'

'Hey, if you want to desecrate your own body, you go ahead.'

Kieron bristled. 'At least I'm desecrating the *outside* of my body. I've seen the amount of highly caffeinated energy drinks you chug every day. Your liver is probably making plans to move out even as we speak.'

Sam frowned. 'I think I saw that film. Or did I dream it?'

Gazing over the edge of the balcony, Kieron said, 'See down there? That's where we were sitting a week ago when we saw Bradley Marshall being attacked.'

Sam nodded. 'Just think – if we'd been at a different table in the food court, or if we'd decided to go somewhere else or left sooner, we'd never have got involved in all this.'

All this. Simple to say, but when Kieron thought back over what had happened in that past week he felt his head spin. One week ago he'd been a disaffected teen, watching the world pass him by and thinking about how boring and stale everything was. Now he could say that he'd helped an MI6 agent recover a stolen nuclear weapon and prevented several other nuclear weapons being detonated in cities across the Middle East and India. Well, to be fair, he *couldn't* say anything of the sort. He'd been sworn to secrecy by the agent in question, Rebecca Wilson – 'Bex', as she liked to be known – and nobody would believe him anyway. Apart from Sam, who'd shared the adventure with him.

'That reminds me,' he said, 'Bex is flying in to Newcastle later on today. We need to meet her.'

'I still can't believe you can fly from Mumbai to Newcastle,' Sam said. 'I'm having a hard time believing you can fly from *anywhere* to Newcastle.'

'Technically she had to fly from Mumbai to Delhi first, then catch a connecting flight to Dubai, then another flight to here. She said she wanted to confuse her trail, in case anyone was looking for her. But yeah – there's loads of flights from Newcastle. You can get to five different places in Lapland, if you want.'

'Brilliant. I'll remember that, come Christmas. My mum still has this strange desire to take me to see Santa Claus in his grotto in one of the big department stores. I'll ask her if we can go to Lapland instead.' Sam frowned. 'Hey – you didn't get the piercings to impress Bex, did you? I mean, that would be a little creepy. You've never even met her. In fact, correct me if I'm wrong, but you've never even *seen* her.'

'True,' Kieron said defensively, 'but with that kit we found when Bradley was kidnapped, I've pretty much been seeing everything she sees – at least when she's wearing her ARCC glasses. I've kind of shared her head with her.'

'Now that *is* creepy,' Sam said.

'It's all been very innocent,' Kieron protested. 'And no, I didn't get the piercings to impress her. I don't feel any need to impress her. I think of her more like a big sister.'

'That's even creepier,' Sam said, grimacing. 'I had to share a bedroom with Courtney when she was living at home. I've seen things you wouldn't believe. Never again.'

'Vietnam-style flashbacks?'

'Post-traumatic stress disorder,' Sam replied.

'Bex is going to want to see Bradley as soon as possible,' Kieron said. 'Is your sister in, or off working? It could get a little awkward otherwise.'

Sam was silent for a few moments before replying – probably replaying, like Kieron, seeing Bex's partner Bradley black out in Sam's sister's flat, face-planting on the carpet with a heavy thud. He'd recovered quickly, but not before they'd phoned for an ambulance. Ignoring his protests, they'd taken him to the local A & E, giving a fake name so that he couldn't be identified or tracked later. After an X-ray of his skull, an EEG of his brainwaves and an ECG of the electrical activity of his heart, the doctors had decided that they didn't know what had happened. 'Probably as isolated ischemic event,' one of them said, with the confidence of someone who'd considered all the evidence and come to a difficult conclusion. Kieron had been using the ARCC glasses while the doctor had been talking, and had quickly discovered from the Internet that an isolated ischemic event was just fancy medical talk for a temporary restriction of the blood supply to the brain. Basically, they were describing what had happened but using longer words. Kieron was keen to press for a full MRI scan of Bradley's skull, but Bradley himself at that point decided to walk out – or stagger out, as he couldn't quite keep his balance. Kieron and Sam had had little choice but to leave too, to make sure he didn't fall in front of a bus or something.

'Courtney's working a twelve-hour shift,' Sam said eventually. 'We'll have the flat to ourselves.'

'That's good. Courtney might be looking after Bradley, but she still doesn't know what he really does for a living.' Kieron probed the right-hand metal stud with his tongue again, fascinated by the feeling of something alien in his mouth. It felt huge – the size of a pea – but he knew that was just the sensitivity of his tongue playing tricks.

'What time is Bex's flight arriving?' Sam asked.

'About five o'clock.' Kieron checked his watch. 'We'd better get going.'

Sam smiled at him. 'What do you think Bex'll make of the piercings?'

'I told you, I didn't get them to impress her,' Kieron said quickly.

'You sure?'

'I got them because *I* wanted them! No, really, I did!'

Actually Kieron was feeling more nervous about meeting her than he liked to admit. They had shared so much together in such an intense way, and over such a short time, but he had never seen her face, and in so many ways they were complete strangers to each other.

'Ice-cream shakes first, for old times' sake?' Sam said, punching his arm.

He smiled. 'Why not?'

They got their shakes and headed out of the shopping mall and towards Newcastle Central Station. The Metro train to the airport took just under half an hour. They got some strange looks from the other passengers. Apparently two boys, one lanky with facial piercings and one shorter and stockier; both dressed in ripped black jeans and baggy black hoodies; one with dyed black hair hanging in front of his eyes and the other with dyed blue hair of an identical length; both drinking ice-cream shakes through striped straws, were an unusual sight. They certainly didn't look like typical airport travellers. They looked like what they were – greebs – although almost anyone looking at them would have called them 'emos' without realising the gulf of difference between the two tribes.

'Look at them, looking at us,' Sam said in a low voice. 'All dressed the same, in their suits and ties and their shiny leather shoes, with their expensive rucksacks that have never seen a mountainside or a forest in their lives. It's like they're wearing a uniform.'

'Yes,' Kieron said, amused that Sam failed to see the inherent irony, 'thank heavens we're dressed as individuals.' What he thought, but didn't say, was that the only forest they'd seen had been through the window of a bus, and the only time they'd ever seen a real mountain had been on TV.

At Newcastle Airport they followed the signs to arrivals. Kieron noticed that a couple of security guards tracked them for a while, checking on what they were doing. Sam had noticed it too.

'As if terrorists would dress like us,' he said dismissively. 'Stupid!'

'I think it's more likely they think we're smuggling drugs,' Kieron pointed out, 'or meeting someone who is.'

'That's just profiling – you can't target somebody based on appearance! I'm appalled! What about my human rights?'

'Yeah,' Kieron said, 'you tell them.' He paused, then added, 'You haven't got any of those highly caffeinated energy drinks on you, have you? I only ask in case they decide to strip-search you.'

'Very funny. Not.'

They stopped to consult a screen, hanging from a pillar, which provided a list of the anticipated arrivals. The next flight from Dubai was on time, landing in half an hour. Ignoring the security guards who orbited them at range, they settled down on the seating in the arrivals area to wait. Over to one side, the passengers arriving on various aircraft from far-flung destinations emerged, blinking, from an archway and were herded along a fenced-off section of flooring before joining the throng of excited relatives and uniformed chauffeurs waiting to greet them. Some of the relatives held balloons and tiny flags; the chauffeurs had signs with the names of their passengers written in marker pen on them. Like some sort of capitalist obstacle course, the last thing the arriving passengers had to go through was a duty-free area selling various bottles of spirits, perfumes and multi-packs of cigarettes.

'Who designed these seats?' Sam demanded to know as he squirmed around trying to get comfortable. 'You can't lie flat on them – the armrests stop you. I could have done better in TED classes back at school.'

'I think that's the point,' Kieron replied. 'They don't want people stretched out, dribbling and snoring. Makes the place look untidy.'

'But this is the one place you'd *want* to do that! If you've got a four-hour gap between arriving and departing, what else are you going to do? Sit upright with your arms folded, staring straight ahead?'

Kieron looked around. 'I think you're supposed to buy expensive stuff in the shops to pass the time.'

About five minutes before Bex's aircraft landed, he took the ARCC glasses and earpiece out of his pocket and slipped them on. The glasses looked just like anything you could get from an opticians, but the lenses were not only clear glass, they acted as miniature computer screens, projecting information and relaying to the wearer whatever was being seen by the glasses they were linked to – which, in Kieron's case was Bex. She wouldn't be wearing them on the flight of course – there were rules about having transmitting equipment switched on when the aircraft was in the air – but he suspected she'd put them on as soon as it landed. He was right – seven minutes later he heard a bell-like chime in his ear and the glasses sprang to life. A rectangular screen, partially transparent, so he could still see the arrivals hall through it, appeared in the centre of his field of vision. It showed the back of an aircraft seat, with a built-in screen displaying a crude world map with a silhouette of an aircraft sitting right over Newcastle. Given the relative scales, the aircraft pretty much obliterated the whole of the UK.

Kieron's discreet earpiece suddenly poured static into his ear, followed by a woman's voice saying, '. . . now landed at Newcastle International Airport. The temperature outside is seven degrees Celsius, with a good chance of rain.'

That pretty much summed up Newcastle, Kieron thought.

'Please do not unfasten your seat belt until the captain has turned off the signs. Thank you for flying with us, and we look forward to seeing you again.'

'Not if I can help it,' Bex's voice muttered.

'Bad flight?' Kieron queried.

'Cramped seat, tasteless food, babies crying, but I had a lovely chat with the woman beside me . . . Kieron?' Bex said. 'Are you at the airport?'

'Is that Bex?' Sam asked. 'Is she there? Say hello for me.'

'Sam says hi,' Kieron said. 'Yes, I'm here. We're both here, in arrivals.'

'Great. I'll be out in a few minutes, assuming there are no queues at passport control.' She hesitated. 'How are you? Recovered from what happened at the . . . place where you . . . did that thing?'

She was being careful in case anyone was listening, but Kieron knew what she meant. She wanted to know if he'd

12

recovered from setting fire to a base used by neo-fascists and electrocuting one of them before the man could shoot him. That place, and that thing.

'Yeah,' he said, and actually it was the truth. It wasn't as if his mind was pretending it was all a dream or something; he knew what had happened, and he knew what he'd done, but he was proud of it. The memories hadn't caused any mental trauma that he could detect. 'Yeah, I'm fine. Really good, actually.'

'And Sam?'

Sam had been caught up in it as well – taken prisoner by the fascist organisation Blood and Soil in fact. 'He's OK. Just a bit grumpy.'

In his earpiece Kieron heard the voice of the stewardess say, 'Ladies and gentlemen, you can now –' The rest of her words were lost in the sound of several hundred people all trying to stand up at once and open the overhead luggage bins.

'– Bradley?' Kieron heard Bex ask.

'Sorry – I couldn't hear what you said.'

She raised her voice to be heard above the din in the cabin. 'I said, "How's Bradley?"'

'He's . . . OK.'

'Just "OK"?' He could hear the worry in her voice.

'Headaches, some blurriness of vision. Oh, and the blackouts of course.'

'I need to see him straight away.' Bex had stood up now, and was wriggling her way past other passengers to get off the aircraft.

'We assumed you would. It's twenty-five minutes back to town on the Metro, then a forty-five minute bus ride to Sam's sister's place. We can't use the van,' he added apologetically. 'If Sam gets caught driving it, we're really in trouble.'

'I am not taking the train, or the bus,' Bex said firmly, walking out of the aircraft into the connecting corridor that led to the terminal. 'I'll hire a car. Something anonymous.'

'Oh,' Kieron said. That hadn't occurred to him. 'Maybe we shouldn't have bought return tickets.'

He and Sam gravitated towards the barrier that separated the new arrivals from those greeting them. Every now and then he heard excited squeals as people who hadn't met face to face for years suddenly saw each other. His eye was caught by a young guy, hopping from one foot to another in anticipation as he scanned the faces of everyone coming through. As Kieron watched he saw an Asian girl come through the arch. She saw the young man, and the adoration on their faces as they ran towards each other made Kieron's heart burn. Would anyone ever feel that way about him?

'Do you think she might buy us something from that duty-free shop?' Sam asked.

'What?'

'Bex. She's got to go past all those bottles of spirits before she gets to us. Could you maybe ask her to pick us up a bottle of amaretto? I mean, surely we're owed something for saving the world?'

Kieron shook his head in disbelief. 'Of all the things you could ask for, you want amaretto?'

'Yeah. So? It tastes like marzipan. I like marzipan.'

'I am *not* asking her to buy us drinks, but if I did it would be something more sophisticated than amaretto.' He wondered what a freelance agent working for MI6 might drink. 'A ten-year-old single-malt whisky maybe.'

Sam snorted. 'You wouldn't be able to tell good whisky from the blended stuff they sell at petrol stations.'

The translucent image in Kieron's ARCC glasses indicated that Bex was heading towards what might be the arrivals arch as viewed from the other side. He moved to the far end of the barrier so he could catch her eye as she moved into the main arrivals area. He'd seen her a couple of times, in mirrors and windows, so he knew he'd recognise her.

For a few seconds his brain was paralysed by a bizarre double vision – he could see the faces of people coming towards him, looking tired from the flight but happy to have landed, at the same time as he was seeing the backs of their heads in the ARCC image. He struggled for a moment to make sense of what he was seeing, and where he was actually seeing it *from*. And then the people moved left or right, creating a gap, and he found himself simultaneously looking at a young woman who was looking back at him quizzically and looking at himself through her eyes. Or her glasses.

The 'him' that he saw shocked him – a skinny teenager with an acne flush on his cheeks and nose and black hair that hung in a fringe across his eyes. Did his clothes really hang off him like that? Were his boots really that clompy?

With an effort, he stared *through* the image at the girl. She was as tall as him, with brown hair pulled back into a ponytail, startlingly green eyes and a smattering of freckles across her nose. She had a rucksack slung casually over one shoulder and she towed a small, wheeled hard-shell suitcase behind her. She came to a halt in front of him. The corner of her mouth twitched into a half-smile.

He wanted to say something important, meaningful, but nothing came to mind. 'Hi,' just wasn't going to do it. Instead he found himself dredging up half-forgotten English lessons, and saying: 'Ill met by moonlight, proud Titania.'

What? He couldn't believe he had just said that. And to his horror he could see a look of disbelief appear on Bex's face. What had he done? But then her disbelief turned to a broad grin. 'What, jealous Oberon!' she responded. 'Fairies, skip hence!' After hearing her voice through an earpiece for so long with a background of static, he was surprised at how rich and deep it was.

Kieron took a deep breath. He hadn't blown it!

Sam, standing beside Kieron, frowned. 'Is that some kind of coded talk?' he asked.

'Just breaking the ice,' Bex said, removing her glasses and taking her micro-earpiece out.

Kieron extended his hand awkwardly, not knowing if she would expect to shake hands, but instead she abruptly stepped forward, let go of the strap of her rucksack and the handle of her suitcase, and gave him a quick hug. Her cheek pressed against his: warm and soft.

'I feel like I know you but don't know you,' she said, stepping back.

'Long-distance relationships . . .' he said. Over her

shoulder he saw the English guy and the Asian girl still wrapped in each other's arms. 'Hey,' he went on, forcing a casual tone into his voice, 'are you hungry? Want to grab a bite to eat?'

'As long as I can get a coffee and maybe a croissant from some takeaway place, I'll be OK.' She glanced at Sam, then stepped closer and gave him a brief hug too. 'You must be Sam. Thanks for all the help you've given us, and the risks you've taken.'

Sam shrugged, staring at the ground. 'Hey, no problem.'

'Let me take your suitcase.' Kieron took the handle and started pulling it towards a coffee kiosk. It took just a few minutes to get Bex set up with her coffee and croissant, then she led the way to the car rental desks. There were four of them, all different companies, lined up in a row. Kieron wondered why there had to be so many. Surely they were all offering cars for the same price – otherwise the more expensive ones would have gone out of business.

Arrangements complete, Bex headed towards the car park with Kieron and Sam in tow. Kieron caught up with her. 'False identity?' he whispered.

She instinctively looked around to confirm that nobody else was close enough to overhear them, then nodded. 'I have several. This one isn't known to my employers at SIS-TERR. I don't particularly want to alert them to the fact that I'm back in-country. Not until I've sorted things out, anyway.'

Sorted things out. A neutral way of referring to the fact that someone in the Secret Intelligence Service's Technology-Enhanced Remote Reinforcement team was a traitor, working with the extreme fascist group Blood and Soil. Bex obviously wanted to find some way of dealing with the traitor before letting SIS-TERR know that she was back. As far as Kieron knew, she was actually a freelance agent, along with her partner Bradley Marshall. Security-vetted and highly trained, but not officially a member of MI6, she and Bradley could do jobs for MI6 as needed and then conveniently disappear. A cheap and efficient way of managing an increasingly fractured and dangerous world, as far as Kieron could work out.

Once in the car park they headed for the area reserved for hire cars. All of them gleamed as if they were freshly washed – which presumably they were. Kieron stared enviously at the sleek black executive cars that they passed, but Bex stopped by a white Kia.

'Ooh,' Sam said. 'No Aston Martin for us. Agents in a Reasonably Priced Car.'

'Just get in,' Kieron growled.

Inside, Bex turned to them. 'Right – bearing in mind I've never been to Newcastle before, which one of you is navigating?'

'Me!' Kieron and Sam said at the same time.

Bex sighed. 'OK, it's like that is it? No fighting, children. Just tell me where I'm going.'

'My sister's flat,' Sam said from the back seat. 'That's where we've stashed Bradley.'

'Is your sister in?'

'No, she's at work.' He paused. 'She doesn't know what Bradley really does. She thinks he works in IT. We told her

18

that he got beaten up when he was trying to rescue a girl from being attacked in a park.'

'That's good. It's the kind of thing he would do anyway.' Bex started the car up and gave the controls a quick once-over. 'Didn't you say she was a nurse?'

'That's right,' Kieron said. 'She's been looking after Bradley – making sure there wasn't any permanent damage from the attack and the . . . the beatings.'

He was watching Bex's face as he said the words. There wasn't any change he could put his finger on – no wincing, no frown of concern. Maybe it was some shift in the light shining through the car's windows, but whoever was responsible for hurting her friend ought to watch out, he thought. She would be coming for them, and she would not be polite.

Except that Kieron had already electrocuted one of them, which ought to get him some brownie points. He smiled to himself.

'I appreciate what your sister has done, but I need to get Bradley out of there as quickly as possible,' Bex said. 'While I was waiting in Delhi and Dubai airports for my connecting flights I did some hunting around on the Internet. I've leased a flat in the city centre. We'll use that as a base for the time being.' She glanced sideways at Kieron. 'And by "us", I mean me and Bradley. We appreciate what you guys have done for us, but I can't put you at risk any more.'

Kieron's heart sank. He had known this was coming. 'Can we still visit?' he asked.

She smiled a soft smile. 'Yes, you can visit. But no parties, OK? I know what you teens are like.' Turning her attention back to manoeuvring the car out of its bay and then out of the car park, she added quietly, 'After all, it wasn't that long ago I was a teenager myself, although sometimes it feels like centuries.'

Between them, Kieron and Sam managed to navigate their way back from the airport to the side of Newcastle where Courtney lived. Bex was a good driver – not too fast, but aware of everything around her and able to take advantage of gaps and changes in traffic speed. She kept looking at the rear-view mirror and the side mirrors. Kieron wasn't sure if she was just driving cautiously or whether she was actively looking for anyone who might be following them. Maybe a bit of both. He suspected that the things agents learned in training became second nature after a while. They lived their lives perpetually watching out for things that were out of the ordinary: warning signs that their world might suddenly turn upside down.

A bit like being a greeb or an emo in a city that didn't like people who dressed or acted differently, he thought bleakly. Both he and Sam were well used to watching out for signs that any nearby teenagers might suddenly decide to pick on them, call them names, chase them down the street, confront them.

Eventually Bex parked at the side of the road, a few hundred metres past the block where Courtney's flat was located.

'Come on then,' she said, taking a deep breath. 'Let's see how he is.'

Sam led them inside and up the stairs to the flat where

20

his sister lived. He delved into his pocket and pulled out a bunch of keys. Kieron watched incredulously as he sorted through them, trying to find the right one.

'Just out of interest,' he said, 'how many places do you live in?'

Sam shot him a dark glance. 'Just my flat and this place.'

'So what are the rest of the keys for?'

'Just – things I've picked up along the way. Don't judge me.'

He finally found the right key. Opening the door, he entered. Kieron and Bex followed.

'Bradley?' he called. 'It's Sam. I've got Kieron and Bex with me.'

No answer.

'Bradley – are you there?'

Still nothing.

'Maybe he's gone out,' Kieron said cautiously.

Sam walked down the short corridor and pushed open the door to the lounge, Kieron and Bex just behind.

Late-afternoon sunlight shone through the large windows, illuminating Bradley's body, sprawled face down on the wooden flooring.

CHAPTER TWO

Bex gasped and pushed past Sam and Kieron. Crouching, she checked Bradley's neck for a pulse. She could feel the blood in his carotid artery pulsing beneath her fingers, but it was slow and weak. 'Fluttery' was the word they used in TV medical dramas. His breathing seemed shallow.

'He's alive!' she said. 'Help me get him into the recovery position.'

Kieron and Sam joined in, getting their arms under Bradley's shoulders and turning him onto his side. Bex lifted his eyelids. His pupils didn't seem dilated, and they reacted to the light. Part of her – the professional part – was relieved that he didn't seem injured: there was no evident blood anywhere, or any noticeable bruising. She glanced at the wooden floor. No blood there either. Maybe he'd just passed out. Another part of her – the part that cared for friends and family and didn't want anything bad to happen – was panicking.

The two boys were hanging back, unsure what to do. 'What's the matter with him?' Kieron asked nervously.

'I don't know. You said he'd fallen unconscious before.

Maybe it happened again – not that that's a good thing, but when we first got in here I thought he might have been attacked, or that he'd fallen and cracked his skull open.' She glanced around at the small but neat lounge – sofa and two armchairs, side tables, large wall-mounted TV screen, bookcase. An empty cup sat on one of the side tables. 'Maybe he got up to make a cup of tea, felt dizzy and passed out before he could sit down again.'

'Should we call an ambulance?' Sam said uncertainly.

'Definitely not.' She sat on the arm of the chair and leaned close to Bradley's ear. 'Bradley? Can you hear me? It's Bex.'

His eyelids fluttered, and his lips moved, forming words that Bex couldn't make out.

She put her hand on his forehead, checking his temperature. He didn't seem to have a fever.

Eventually his eyes opened fully, and he rolled over onto his back. He glanced sideways to where she sat. 'Bex? You're here?'

'Where else would I be?' She ruffled his hair. 'Honestly – I can't leave you alone for a moment without you getting into trouble.'

'And what about you?' he asked, trying to pull himself up into more of a sitting position. 'Nuclear weapons? Gunfights in Pakistan?'

She grimaced. 'Yeah – that wasn't on the original travel itinerary.' She watched him as he sipped the water again. He had more colour in his cheeks now, and he seemed to be gaining strength, but she thought his hands were trembling slightly. She turned to where Kieron and Sam were watching from over by the door to the kitchen. 'Guys, can you give us a few minutes? We need to talk, and it has to be private.'

Kieron nodded, and pushed Sam into the kitchen. Seconds later Bex heard the radio come on. It seemed to be some middle-of-the-road rock station playing what she thought was Chris Rea's 'The Road to Hell, Part 2'. Before the intro was over she heard Sam saying, 'Oh, come on – this is *old* people's music. Isn't there some screamo or darkwave station around we can tune into?'

'Maybe,' Kieron replied. 'It's a digital radio – there could be anything out there if we just rescan. If we *can't* find anything, I'll just plug my phone into the audio socket.'

Leaving them to it, she turned back to Bradley. 'Honestly now – how are you?'

He shrugged. 'Sometimes I think I'm fine, but then I over-exert myself and I fall over again.' He indicated the spot on the floor where he'd been found. Bex noticed that a mobile phone and a pair of glasses were still lying there, near where his head had been. 'Believe it or not, I was just standing there, wearing Courtney's spare glasses and holding the mobile up by the side of my head so I could see its screen reflected back in one of the lenses. Kieron had taken the ARCC kit so he could stay in contact with you, so I couldn't use that, but I just wanted to see if I could manage to focus on any reflected screen that close.' He grimaced. 'I guess we proved I can't. I don't know if it's the brightness, or the strobing, or a problem focusing my eyes, but a couple of seconds of staring at the thing and I was feeling dizzy. The next thing I knew, I was lying on the floor and you were bending over me.'

'Looking at a mobile screen up close isn't quite the same as looking at information in the ARCC glasses,' she pointed out. 'The technology is different.'

'I know, but it's close enough. I'll try with the glasses and see if they're any different, but I wouldn't hold out much hope.' He glanced towards the kitchen and started to open his mouth to call Kieron back, but Bex put her finger against her lips.

'Not right now,' she said. 'Wait until you've recovered a bit more.' She thought for a moment. 'We need to get you checked out properly. I know Courtney's a nurse, but I doubt she's an expert in neurology.' She grimaced. 'The problem will be arranging treatment without flagging up to our employers where we are. Let me think about it for a while.' Her brain suddenly caught up with something Bradley had said earlier. '"Courtney's spare glasses"? You sound like you know your way around this flat pretty well. Are you and Courtney . . . ?'

She expected him to deny it instantly, like he did any time she teased him about some girl he'd mentioned meeting, but this time he just looked at the floor and blushed slightly. 'You know what?' he replied quietly. 'I don't actually know. I mean, we've not talked about it, but there are times when I look at her, and she looks at me and it's like there's some kind of unspoken message passing between us . . .' His lips twitched into a half-smile. 'I think, yes, I'm developing feelings for her, and I hope she's developing feelings for me as well. Is that a problem?'

'Honestly?' Bex said. 'I don't know. It's not like we're in the kinds of jobs where we can each settle down and have two point four kids and point five of a dog.'

'Aren't we?' He gazed up at her from his slumped position. 'I know we never talk about the future, and we've been too busy having fun in the most exciting job in the world –'

'And serving our country,' Bex pointed out primly.

'Yes, that too. But are we expected to do that forever? Or until we die while carrying out a mission? What's the career plan here?'

'That's a good question.' And one she'd been thinking about on the flight back. 'We did kind of drift into this without an exit strategy. Maybe it's time we took a look at where we are and where we want to be. Especially given what we've discovered recently. Our future employment may be, let's say, *problematic*.'

Bradley shrugged. 'All I know is, I've had dates with a fair number of girls, and enjoyed myself, but this is the first time I've ever sat down on a sofa with one of them, watching TV, and thinking, "You know what? I like this!"'

'You haven't told her what you do, have you?'

Bradley shook his head. 'Of course not. I used our standard cover story – that I'm a freelance computer network engineer. And actually, it's not that far from the truth. I do know my way around computers.' He paused and smiled. 'I told her you're my boss and that you spend a lot of time travelling abroad, setting up computer networks for big companies and for UK embassies, and I act as your technical support back in the UK.'

A thought struck Bex. 'Where does she think you live?'

'I told her I've got a flat in London but I spend a lot of time travelling around the country staying in hotels. Which, again, isn't far from the actuality.' He grimaced, and looked away. 'This job we do is great, but it doesn't leave much time for meeting people. Courtney's the first person I've met that I feel terrible about lying to.'

Bex was about to say something she hoped might be reassuring, but suddenly, from the kitchen, loud music suddenly blared out. It sounded to her like several heavy metal rockers all playing different songs badly and at the same time.

'Sorry!' Kieron called as the volume suddenly reduced by half.

'We *are* getting old,' Bradley said. He squirmed until he was sitting properly, rather than being slumped on the cushions. 'There was a time when I was convinced that they couldn't invent a form of music I wouldn't listen to – well, excluding country and western of course. But they did, and that's it.' He sighed. 'We're talking around a subject that we really need to discuss, Bex.'

She nodded. 'The traitor in MI6. Yes, I know.'

'Did Kieron tell you about that meeting he and Sam spied on in the Baltic Centre – the one where the traitor turned up to give instructions to those Blood and Soil goons?'

'He did. At least we know the traitor is a woman.' She bit her lip. 'The problem is, there are a lot of women in MI6 – especially the bit we freelance for. I can probably think of fifteen women in various positions in or near SIS-TERR. And she would have been wearing a disguise, so whatever description Kieron gives us won't really be what she looks like.'

Bradley smiled slightly. 'The funny thing is, most people disguise themselves as something different. So we know that the traitor definitely *won't* look like Kieron's description. That might narrow it down a bit. If he says she's old then she's young. If he says she has red hair then her hair is blond, brown or black. If I ever have to go undercover, I'm going to disguise myself as a nerdy hipster with a beard and glasses. That'll fool everyone.'

Bex made a thing of feeling his forehead. 'I think you're feverish,' she said.

He smiled, and touched her hand briefly. 'I'm glad you're back.'

'So am I.'

'I've been thinking. You realise there are two things we *can't* do. The first is: we can't tell MI6 that someone in the SIS-TERR department is a traitor working with a neo-fascist organisation to somehow ethnically cleanse areas of the world. We don't actually have any proof, and we wouldn't be believed. Worse – just making the accusation will reflect badly on us, and we'll probably never work for MI6 again, and because we'd have to come out in the open to make the accusation, the traitor would know where we are and probably take some kind of action against us.'

Bex nodded. 'True.'

'The second thing is: we need to continue working for

SIS-TERR – at least for the near future. We need to pay the bills of course, but we also need to stay involved with MI6 so we can try and find more evidence as to who this traitor actually is.' He paused. 'I presume we *are* going to try to flush the traitor out? I mean, we're not just going to walk away and forget about them?'

'That traitor was responsible for having you hurt, which means I will pursue them to the ends of the Earth if I have to,' she said quietly but firmly. 'And, of course, they were colluding with a scheme that would have killed hundreds of thousands of people in nuclear explosions.'

'Thank you for putting their sins in that order.' Bradley thought for a moment. 'I guess we can stay below the radar for a little while. Hopefully that will give me a chance to recover to a stage where I can work the kit again.'

'Remember,' Bex said, 'we're not completely on our own. We have friends.'

Bradley glanced towards the kitchen. 'I thought you didn't want to risk the boys.'

'I don't. I was referring to Agni Patel.'

Bradley nodded. 'Ah yes – this mysterious businessman you met who steals weapons of mass destruction from various unfriendly countries so he can "destroy" them rather than, say, hang them on the wall so he can admire them on those long tropical evenings. Or maybe even sell them to terrorist groups.'

Bex felt a sudden need to defend Patel. 'Hey, I've seen his operation at work. He really is working to destroy those weapons, and he's spending a lot of his own money doing it.

He wants the world to be a better place. If it hadn't been for him, there would be large, glowing holes where Islamabad and four other cities used to be.'

Bradley shrugged. 'Look, if you trust him then I trust him. It's just that I haven't met him.'

'He's coming to England soon. We've arranged to meet up. I'll introduce you then.'

'Maybe he'll offer us a job.'

Bex opened her mouth to say something, then stopped herself. Actually Agni Patel *had* offered her – and Bradley – a job. After she and his team had returned from the wilds of Pakistan with the nuclear weapon that Blood and Soil had stolen from the Pakistani government and had intended to explode, and after it had become clear that Kieron and Sam had prevented the broadcast of the radio signal that would trigger the other four weapons, Agni had strongly urged Bex to throw her lot in with him. He had told her that he was impressed with her commitment and her talent, and wanted her on his team – and Bradley, if Bex vouched for him. She'd thought seriously about the offer, but she knew that she had to come back to the UK first – at least until she'd managed to find out who the traitor was. 'Who knows?' she said eventually.

Bradley sighed. 'I'm guessing you want me to move out of here,' he said. 'If I know you – and I do – you've probably already rented a place where we can lie low for a while. Obviously we can't go back to our own flats in London – that's the first place this traitor, or her Blood and Soil shock troops, will look for us. So you've found us an apartment.'

He frowned for a moment, thinking. 'You want it to be somewhere they won't think of looking for us, but because you're worried about my health you don't want me to be under too much stress from a long journey so it's close to where we are now. You also want to have easy access to motorways, railways and airports. So . . . you've found somewhere here in Newcastle! How did I do?'

Bex nodded, impressed. 'Your brain is obviously firing on *some* cylinders at least. Yes, I've found us a place in Newcastle city centre. It's a new-build apartment block. I've got a car downstairs – whenever you're ready, we can go.' She patted his knee. 'The fact that it's still close enough that you can visit your girlfriend is a convenient but unplanned bonus.'

'She's not my girlfriend!' Bradley exclaimed. A voice from the kitchen – Sam – shouted the words 'She's not his girlfriend!' at exactly the same time.

'Hey – I thought you were giving us a little privacy?' Bex called back.

'It's a small flat,' Kieron yelled, 'and the walls are thin.' He paused for a few seconds, then added: 'Can we come and see the flat too? Please?'

'Look, I don't think –' she started to say, but he interrupted her.

'We can tell you where all the best restaurants are, the best places to eat, the places to avoid . . . we can pretty much give you a full rundown on the area.'

She sighed. Local intelligence was always a good thing. 'OK then. Give me a hand getting Bradley down to the car.'

31

'Hang on a second,' Bradley said, standing up with some effort. 'I'll get my teddy bear.'

'Your . . . what?' Bex's expression was a picture of disbelief.

He went on defensively: 'Courtney bought it for me. It was a joke.'

'Does . . . does Teddy Weddy have a name?' Bex asked, barely able to control her smile.

'No,' Bradley answered, but Bex could tell from his expression that it did but he wasn't going to admit it.

While Kieron and Sam helped Bradley down the stairs – clutching his teddy bear – Bex went ahead and got the car. She felt a lot better now she'd seen Bradley. They didn't meet up that often when they were working – she was usually undercover somewhere else in the world while he stayed back in the UK, providing her with covert support, but he was a constant and comforting voice in her ear, and whenever they finished a mission she made sure she came back and spent a couple of days with him, relaxing and decompressing and having fun, catching up on movies, TV and gossip.

When she got to the hire car, Bex briefly bent down and pretended to tighten the laces on her trainers. Actually she was checking underneath for any objects that might have been attached to the underside of the vehicle. She had no reason to suspect that a bomb or tracking device had been placed there – as far as she knew, nobody apart from the four of them and Agni Patel knew she was even in the UK – but years of training and a couple of bad experiences meant that it had become a habit by now. Not a habit she liked particularly, but one that felt necessary.

If she and Bradley *did* manage to get out of the game, she wondered how long it would take for the habit to fade. Maybe it never would. Maybe she'd end up as a mad old cat lady, checking under her car at the age of ninety-six.

With Bradley in the front passenger seat and the kids in the back, Bex drove the hire car back towards the city centre. She'd memorised the directions, and soon they were approaching the new apartment block – which was located just to the north of the River Tyne and to the west of the railway station. The apartments were new but had been built inside the shell of an old warehouse.

'Very impressive,' Bradley said, craning his neck so he could look up at the redbrick building. 'I don't think I've ever lived anywhere this nice before.'

'Two bedrooms,' Bex said as she circled the place, checking in her rear-view mirror for other cars doing the same thing, and then, when she didn't see any, turned into the parking area through an arch in the wall at the back. Kieron and Sam looked around self-consciously as they got out of the car. Bex smiled to herself. They probably felt out of place. She would tell them some time that the key to operating undercover was to always look like you belonged, no matter how strange the location.

As they got out of the car, she gestured towards the boot. 'Kieron, Sam – can you grab my bags and bring them up, please?'

A door with an electronic security lock gave access to a lobby painted in an eye-wateringly bright white. Apart from two lifts, a set of modern-looking lockers for post and several potted plants strategically dotted around, the lobby was empty.

'How did you know the code to get through the security door?' Kieron wanted to know.

'The management company emailed it to me when they'd confirmed that I'd paid the deposit,' she replied. 'Everything was done remotely, without having to meet up.' Crossing to the bank of lockers, she typed a number into a keyboard off to one side and one of the locker doors *ping*ed open. 'They gave me this code as well.'

'What's in there?' Kieron wanted to know.

Bex reached in and pulled out a bulky envelope. 'The keys to the flat.'

Bradley frowned. 'Given the impressive tech level of the lobby, I thought the front door of the flat might be voice-activated,' he said.

'Or it scans and recognises your retina,' Kieron added.

'Or your brainwaves,' Sam threw in.

Bex stared at them and slowly shook her head. 'You guys have been alone together for too long.'

They took the lift up to the top floor. The door to their apartment was down a stark white corridor.

Bex nodded towards a corner of the ceiling just opposite the lift door. 'We can put a small Bluetooth camera up there,' she said quietly to Bradley. 'Just so we can get some warning as to who's coming and going.'

The door to the flat opened onto a spacious wood-floored apartment with a large window overlooking the Tyne. The furniture was chunky, heavy and comfortable. Off to one side Bex noticed an expansive kitchen area separated from the living area by a breakfast bar.

'I could be happy here,' Bradley said, gazing around appreciatively.

Kieron had gone straight to the stereo, while Sam had headed for the LCD screen on the wall.

'Hard-disc storage,' Kieron said approvingly.

'4K display,' Sam murmured. 'Just imagine what we could do with this and a decent gaming platform.'

'Hands off,' Bex said, trying to sound fierce but actually, inside, feeling strangely warm. It was like watching a bunch of brothers she never knew she had. 'This is our new work headquarters, not a kids' playground.'

'Free-standing claw-foot bathtub,' Bradley called from a doorway that Bex assumed led to the bathroom. 'And fizzy bath bombs.'

'Mine!' she said quickly. 'Dibs on the first bath. I've been travelling all day.'

By the time she'd had a long, hot, deep bath – with bath foam, of which she found there were several varieties – towelled herself dry and then dressed in relatively clean clothes from her suitcase, the boys were sitting in front of the TV, watching YouTube videos, while Bradley was moving slowly around in the kitchen.

'I'm making a cup of tea,' he said. 'I was waiting until you got out of the bath so I could use the ARCC kit to put in an online order for a food delivery.'

'That is a complete misuse of high-tech security equipment.'

He stared at her for a moment. 'I presume you don't want to go out shopping?'

'Good point. I'd rather we all stayed together, out of sight. I've got several credit cards under various identities that we can use.'

Sliding a cup in front of her, Bradley walked into the main area of the apartment. 'Kieron – could I have my ARCC glasses and earpiece back again, please?'

Kieron looked . . . unhappy, Bex thought. 'Is there something I can do for you?' he asked. 'I mean, I really like using it, and I'm very good.'

Bradley waggled his fingers. 'Mine,' he said simply. 'Give.'

Kieron nodded, slid his hands into one of his many pockets and retrieved the glasses and the earpiece. 'I wasn't going to keep them forever,' he muttered as he handed them over. 'Just for a while longer. Until you were better.'

'I've got to get back on the bicycle sometime,' Bradley said, taking them. 'And that means you have to get off.' He sat in a comfy armchair, hesitated, then slid the glasses on and slipped the earpiece into his ear. He glanced up at Bex, who was watching. 'Here goes,' he said, and touched a hidden button at the side of the frame.

From where Bex was standing, she couldn't see any response in the glasses, but they were designed that way. Nobody looking at them could tell that the wearer was looking at something projected by tiny lasers onto the inside of the lenses.

Bradley frowned in concentration. His right hand reached up and started touching things that only he could see. His tongue poked out slightly from his mouth and he licked his lips nervously. 'You've played around with the settings,' he said.

'Sorry.' Kieron was sitting on the edge of his seat, hands clasped as if he wanted to launch himself forward and snatch the glasses away from Bradley. 'I meant to change them back.'

'Don't worry,' Bradley said, distracted. 'I think I can – *ouch*!'

'What is it?' Bex said, stepping forward.

Bradley's face contorted into a pained grimace. 'I think – *ouch! Ow!*' He swept both of his hands up to his face, knocking the glasses. They flew off over his head. Eyes screwed shut, he put his hands over his temples and leaned forward, pressing hard. 'Sorry – everything suddenly went blurry, and I felt a sudden sharp pain between my eyes. It was like someone had shoved a knitting needle right through my forehead.' His voice sounded strained. More than that, he sounded frustrated.

Bex sympathised. She knew how badly Bradley wanted to be able to get back to work. 'Go and lie down,' she said firmly. 'Kieron – you help him. Sam – there are some painkillers in the front pocket of my rucksack. Can you get them and a glass of water and take them in to Bradley.'

'I can do it myself –' Bradley said, trying to stand up.

'Just do it.'

As the three of them headed away, Bex retrieved the ARCC glasses from the floor behind the chair before someone stepped on them. She stared at them bleakly. She could operate them of course – not as well as Bradley, but she knew how they worked and what they could do, but she couldn't use them to do the job they were supposed to do. If *she* was using these ones, then who was going to use *her* glasses on a mission? There had to be two of them in the team!

'What's the problem?' Kieron asked from one of the bedroom doorways. He sounded concerned.

'Whatever's wrong with him is affecting his ability to use the ARCC equipment,' she said. 'I don't know if it's neurological or psychosomatic. We need to get him looked over.' She held the glasses up. 'But I also need to see if MI6 have sent through any messages. It's been a while since we checked in, and I should give them an update.'

Kieron walked across the living area and took the glasses from her. She noticed that he was holding the earpiece. He must have taken it from Bradley's ear. 'Look – you sit down. I'm used to the kit. I've used it more recently than you. I'll check for messages, and then you can talk me through any response.' As she hesitated, he went on: 'You've been travelling, you're probably jet-lagged and you haven't stopped since you landed. Just sit down and have your cup of tea. You don't have to look after all of us. Let me look after you.'

It was the mention of jet lag that did it. Bex had been keeping it at bay, trying to pretend that it didn't exist, but she'd not slept a wink on the flight, and by now she'd been awake for longer than she wanted to think about.

'OK,' she said. 'I give in. Just this once.'

As she sank into the chair that Bradley had recently vacated, Kieron sat on the sofa and slipped on the glasses.

His hands immediately sprang to life: moving in the air as if he was assembling some complex invisible machine. Watching him, Bex found herself amazed at the ease with which he used it. Bradley was competent, but Kieron seemed almost . . . intuitive.

'Right,' he said. 'I've got the classified email program up and running. It needs a separate password obviously.'

'TAG-LOL-GID,' Bex recited automatically. 'It's a randomly generated set of three single-syllable sounds. It avoids people using the names of their pets or the road where they used to live. All of those things can be researched.'

His fingers twitched. 'Got it. Right – OK! Wow – no spam!'

'Of course not. You've accessed an MI6 server. It's separated from the public Internet, and it's got all kinds of firewalls.'

'I know – I've been taking a look at them. Very impressive.' He paused, reading. 'There are a couple of queries about how your mission is progressing –'

'Where do I start?' she muttered.

'And an email with a new mission! It says you should confirm receipt and give an estimate on when you can start.'

'Who's it from?'

'There's no name – just what looks like a job title: "Dep-Director, SIS-TERR".'

Bex took a deep breath. She'd have to debrief her bosses on what had happened in Mumbai of course – although as she was supposed to have been undercover, luckily they were used to waiting until she was clear so that she could update Bradley. But this new assignment – was it real, or was it a trick to lure her and Bradley out of hiding?

'What's the mission?' she asked.

Kieron nodded. 'According to this,' he said slowly, 'there have been several deaths of members of staff in something called "The Goldfinch Institute".' His fingers danced in the air. 'Yes – there's a link to more information on it. The Goldfinch Institute is apparently a research facility based in Albuquerque but with facilities around the world. It manufactures highly classified weapon systems for the British Army, MI5, MI6 and SIS-TERR in the UK, as well as the CIA, the NSA and the FBI in America.' He paused. 'Hang on – I'll move back to the email. OK, the briefing note says that the deaths appear, on the face of it, to be natural, but the fact that they all occurred at roughly the same time is raising suspicions on this side of the Atlantic. What this Dep-Director wants you to do is to go to Albuquerque and covertly investigate to see if there is any threat to British interests. Basically, find out if these deaths really are natural or whether they might be murders.' He frowned. 'Albuquerque. That's in America, isn't it? Somewhere down south? New Mexico . . . ?'

'New Mexico,' Bex confirmed absently. 'Your geography is surprisingly good.' Most of her mind was consumed with poring over the contents of the email that Kieron had read out. Investigate deaths at a classified American research institute? She and Bradley had done similar things in the past, but never in America. In fact, there were rules in place in the intelligence community that specifically prohibited members of what was known as the '5-Eyes Community' – the USA, the UK, Canada, Australia and

New Zealand – from spying on each other. It was fairly common knowledge that the Americans at least flagrantly ignored that prohibition, while everyone else pretended not to notice, but for her to be asked to operate in the USA . . . it must be important. And that meant it was the kind of thing that she really shouldn't turn down. And the money would be good, which was what they were particularly short of at present.

'I didn't learn that at school,' Kieron replied. 'I know it's in New Mexico because my favourite band record their albums in a studio there.'

'Lethal Insomnia?' she said hesitantly.

He smiled. 'You *do* listen. Sam said you don't, but I knew he was wrong.'

'Anything else?' Bex asked.

'A couple of attached files – looks like autopsy reports on the dead staff members – plus some maps of the area. Oh, and there's a budget. If you need to go above a certain amount of money then you need to seek approval. And that amount of money is –' he gasped – 'a *huge* amount! I'm not surprised you can afford an apartment like this!'

Bex shrugged, feeling strangely defensive. 'It's not that much, in the scheme of things,' she said. 'We've got to pay for all our own travel, and sometimes we have to go undercover, so we have to stay in good hotels and buy stuff to back up our story, like . . . wristwatches and . . . er, cars.' Even as she said the words, they sounded weak. 'And there's danger money as well. It's a risky job. If something goes wrong, the British government will claim they know nothing about us and leave us to our fate. That's one of the reasons MI6 uses freelance operative teams like us – we're eminently deniable.'

'Yes, but –' Kieron's eyes were wide behind the glasses – 'this is an *incredible* amount.'

'We have to sort out our own pension schemes and healthcare insurance,' Bex said in a small voice.

'My mum could buy her own flat for this amount of money.' Kieron's tone wasn't accusatory – more like sad. Maybe even wistful. The kind of tone that someone might use if they were describing the perfect Christmas present – one they would never, ever get.

'Look –' Bex said, wanting to try to explain the realities of the world to Kieron, but he interrupted her before she could get the words out.

'Oh!'

'What is it?'

'Apparently there's a time limit on this mission. It needs to be completed within a week, which means that you have to accept it or reject it pretty much within the next hour or they'll pass it to another team.'

'That,' she said, 'gives us a problem.'

Kieron nodded. 'Bradley can't help you.'

'But if I reject the mission then SIS-TERR will go to a different team, and we're not going to be top of the list for the *next* mission that comes along. If we're out of action as a team for too long then we'll slip off the list altogether.'

'There's only one answer then,' Kieron said. Maybe it

was the lenses of the ARCC glasses, but his eyes seemed very wide.

Bex nodded. 'Fancy doing some temp work?' she asked heavily.

CHAPTER THREE

Kieron felt a rush of excitement, but he kept his voice strictly neutral. 'If you need my help,' he said, 'then I'm more than happy to provide it.'

'Don't give me that,' Bex said, laughing at him. 'You'd cut off your own little finger for the chance to use the ARCC kit again.'

He tried to arrange his features into a wounded expression. 'Not *my* little finger. *Sam's*, maybe. And only his *left* little finger.'

Bex got up from her chair. 'I've got to check on Bradley, and then I'm going to arrange some kind of medical evaluation for him that doesn't depend on some kid's sister who he has a crush on.' She smiled to take the sting out of the words. 'Make yourself useful – put together a dossier on the Goldfinch Institute for me.'

As she vanished out of the living room, Kieron's fingers were already moving over the virtual keyboard that only he could see. He set searches going on the Goldfinch Institute on not just the normal Internet, but also on the dark web, where all kinds of illegal software could be found and illegal things bought using virtual currency, and on the various highly classified British government databases that the kit could access. Within a few minutes he had pulled together a virtual dossier of information, starting with the company records that were available online, going through blueprints of the facility's buildings in Albuquerque and staff lists, and ending with a list of the various top-secret projects that the institute was working on for various clients. They seemed to spend a lot of time developing weapon systems, he discovered – not just guns, missiles and bombs but also non-lethal weapons: things designed to stop rioting crowds or bring down armed criminals without causing them any damage. Well, no lasting damage, anyway. Going sideways from some of the information he'd found, chasing links to mainstream sites like Wikipedia, Kieron discovered that there was a surprisingly big debate within the non-lethal weapon community. Some people were happy with the term 'non-lethal' while others wanted it replaced with 'less-than-lethal' on the grounds that non-lethal weapons sometimes killed people, despite the best efforts of the people firing them. Kieron couldn't see the point. If you were going to do that, he thought, then why not rename 'lethal weapons' as 'more-than-wounding weapons', on the basis that sometimes when you fired a gun or dropped a bomb people *didn't* die? It was a pointless discussion.

He pulled the various bits of information he'd found into a dossier, then used the capabilities of the ARCC computer – actually a chip somewhere inside the glasses – to index it and provide a table of contents. It even produced a one-page summary, just to make it really easy.

He'd just finished when Bex came back into the room. She was talking on her mobile.

'Thank you for that – I really appreciate it. Yes, someone will be here to let you in. Don't worry. Thanks – goodbye.' Putting the phone back into her pocket, she said, 'I've arranged for a doctor to come and take a look at Bradley. Because she's private, and because she's charging us an arm and a leg, there won't be an information trail for SIS-TERR to follow if anyone there wants to find us.' She laughed. 'I think she thinks that we're criminals and she's coming to treat a gunshot wound.'

'Even so,' Kieron offered hesitantly, 'I could always wipe her computer records from here, using the ARCC equipment.'

'You can do that?' Bex asked, apparently amazed.

'This kit can do pretty much anything, as long as it's got a satellite link and can access the web.'

'Wow.' She sounded impressed. 'Let's hold back on that for now, but keep it in mind. Any luck on producing a fact-file for me on the Goldfinch Institute?'

'Yeah – do you want me to send it to the printer, or do you want to look at it on the glasses?'

'The glasses, please. Never good to leave secret information lying around where anyone might see it – including random doctors who get invited in.'

With what he recognised as a slight pang of reluctance, Kieron took the glasses off and handed them to Bex. She slipped them on.

'You manipulate the information by –' he started.

'It's OK – I've done this before,' she said. She waved a hand, but he wasn't sure whether she was shushing him or accessing the ARCC system. 'Bradley and I worked on this together after we left university. We set up a start-up company to fund it, but we got bought out by MI6. They wanted to keep the technology to themselves. That's how we got involved in the missions – they wanted to keep us close by to act as technical consultants, but we knew more about how to use it than anyone else, so they started giving us things to do.'

She was quiet for a few minutes, and Kieron watched as she moved information around and navigated between virtual screens. Apart from Bradley, in the Newcastle shopping mall the first time Kieron had seen him, and Sam a couple of times, Kieron hadn't had the chance to watch someone using the ARCC equipment – especially the way it was meant to be used. Bex's gestures were fluid and precise, like a dancer's. He wondered how he looked when he was using it. More like a performing bear, he suspected.

'Oh. Oh no.'

'What is it?' he asked, leaning forward. 'Is the equipment working OK? Your head isn't hurting, is it?'

'It is, but not for medical reasons.' She abruptly removed the ARCC glasses and put them on the arm of the sofa. Her face was creased into a frown. 'I found something in the information that I really don't like.'

'Sorry.'

'Not your fault, Kieron.'

'What is it?'

She paused for a few moments, marshalling her thoughts. 'The idea was that I would travel to Albuquerque under some kind of false identity with my end of the ARCC equipment – the covert end – and investigate the Goldfinch Institute secretly to find out how and why these deaths have occurred, right? Probably put a Trojan virus on their computer system from a USB thumb drive that would hoover up the information we want. Meanwhile, Bradley – or, more likely, you – would provide support and feed me information.'

He nodded. 'Right.'

'The trouble is, there's a name I recognise on the Goldfinch Institute staff list. Tara Gallagher. She's apparently Head of Security at the Institute, working directly for the boss – Todd Zanderbergen. She used to be with MI6. We shared an office for two years. She'd recognise me straight away. And even if I was in disguise, it's too much of a risk.'

'Maybe it's another Tara Gallagher,' Kieron suggested.

'No such luck. I checked her date of birth and her staff photo. It's definitely her. She looks older, but then I guess I do as well.' She paused, remembering. 'We weren't close and we never kept in touch. I'd heard she'd gone into the army, and then a while later I heard that she'd been recruited into the Royal Marines. I guess she retired and went into independent security. Good choice for a technology company – she's fearsomely intelligent.' She sighed. 'I suppose that blows the whole plan out of the water. There's no way I can go out there now. It's just too risky.'

'What about Bradley?' Kieron asked. 'Can he go? I mean, if he doesn't actually use the glasses at *this* end – the ones that actually project the information – then he should be OK, shouldn't he?'

Bex shook her head decisively. 'I'm not taking the risk of him having another fit or blacking out while he's undercover. No, I'll have to tell MI6 that I'm scrubbing the mission. They can give it to someone else.'

'If they do that,' Bradley said from the doorway of his bedroom, 'then we can say goodbye to our jobs. They'll ask why, you'll have to admit that I'm ill, and that will spook them. There's other teams jockeying for top slot. If this job goes to one of *them*, then we become redundant – figuratively and probably literally. You know what they say – you only turn a mission down once.'

'Yes, but –' Bex started to say.

'We need to keep on top of the pile,' Bradley carried on, not waiting to hear what she had to say, 'especially if we want to identify this traitor in SIS-TERR. We can't let them get suspicious, or think that anything is wrong.'

Bex stared at him. 'So what do you suggest?'

Bradley shook his head. 'I hadn't got that far. Get me better quickly perhaps?'

'Maybe I could go,' Kieron said quietly.

'Or maybe recruit someone else we know,' Bradley went on. 'Someone with security clearance we can work with.'

'I could go,' Kieron said again.

'We could maybe recruit a medic who could go *with* you,' Bex mused, looking at Bradley. 'They could make sure you're OK while you're working, and treat you if there's a problem.'

'Or I could go,' Kieron repeated, louder. 'You're not listening to me.'

Bex sighed. 'We were listening to you,' she said. 'We just didn't want to hear what you were saying.'

Bradley shook his head. He was still holding onto the door frame with both hands. 'No – it's better that I go.'

'Can you do me a favour?' Bex asked him. 'Can you just release your grip on that door frame?'

There was a long silence before Bradley answered. 'No,' he admitted. 'If I do that I'll fall over.'

Bex nodded. 'I thought as much. Your knuckles are very white. Your whole body weight is being supported by your hands, isn't it?'

He paused. Kieron assumed he was trying to think of a response that didn't give away the fact that he was seriously incapacitated. 'Maybe,' he said in the end.

Kieron was marshalling a killer argument in his head that would completely nail the discussion when his mobile rang. 'Sorry,' he said, pulling the mobile from his pocket, 'I should have – oh.' The words on the screen suddenly registered in his brain. 'It's my mum. I need to take this.'

'James Bond's mum never phones him when he's on a mission!' Sam's voice floated in from somewhere behind Bradley.

Kieron swiped the screen to accept the call as he headed into the bathroom for privacy – and to avoid any more embarrassment. 'Hello? Mum?'

'Kieron? You could answer your phone more often, you know? I've left seven messages!'

'You left three messages,' he pointed out. 'And one of those was you telling a barista in a coffee shop somewhere that the coffee beans he'd used for your latte were burned. I think you'd pocket-dialled by accident.'

'They *were* burned,' she said defensively. 'He tried to tell me the coffee was supposed to taste that way, but I wasn't having it.' She suddenly seemed to remember that she was supposed to be the one on the offensive. 'Anyway, where are you? I haven't seen you for days!'

'That's because you come home late and leave early. We hardly overlap.' Before she could get all apologetic and he could hear the tears lurking somewhere behind her voice, he quickly continued: 'Not that it matters – I'm fine on my own. Well, not really on my own. I've got Sam.'

'Just Sam?' she asked. 'Not that I've got anything against him – I love him to bits – but there's something unhealthy about two goth teenagers spending all their time together. That's how high-school massacres start. I know – I've read it in the newspapers.'

'We're not goths,' he said patiently, for what seemed like the millionth time, 'we're greebs. And we're not going to go round any local Newcastle schools shooting people. Not even with foam bullets fired by springs from brightly coloured plastic guns.'

'But you have got other friends, haven't you? And by "friends", I mean people other than those groups of kids you see hanging around the bus station.'

'Actually,' he said, 'some of those kids in the bus station *are* my friends, and the only reason we hang around there is that we don't like coffee and they won't let us in bars.' Before she could go on, he added quickly, 'And, yes, I do have other friends. I'm round their house now, playing on the computer.' Not too far from the truth, he thought.

'Oh – anyone I know? What are their names?'

'Bex and Bradley,' he said, then immediately started cursing himself. He'd been so tied up with trying to mollify his mother that he'd given out their real names!

'Bex and Bradley. I don't know them, do I? Are they from school?'

'No,' he said, still trying to think of a way of diverting the conversation. 'I only met them recently.'

'And this Bex – short for "Rebecca", I assume? Are you . . . *interested* in her. I mean, more than just friends? Do we need to have a conversation about this?'

'It's not like that,' he said. He felt a slight twang of anxiety somewhere inside his heart. It wasn't like that with anyone – that was his problem. The closest thing he had to a girl he liked was Sam's sister Courtney, and not only was she too old for him but she was apparently interested in Bradley. Which was fine. 'You needn't worry – we can save *that* conversation for another time. Or just not have it at all – I've been doing biology for years at school. I know all about it.'

'It's not the biology I'm worried about – it's the sociology.' She paused, and Kieron imagined her shrugging. 'Well, I hope this Bradley and Bex are decent people. Maybe you could arrange for me to meet their parents. Who knows – we might get on.' A different, strange tone crept into her voice, and Kieron understood with a slight shock that he must be becoming an adult without realising, because he recognised it as self-pity. 'It's not as if I have many friends around Newcastle.'

'That's a good idea,' he said reassuringly, but without the slightest intention of following through. 'But why don't you and I try and spend an evening together. We could go out for a pizza, and maybe see a movie. There has to be something we can both watch without one of us wanting to throw up.'

His mum laughed, as he'd hoped. 'Hey, now that you've grown out of *Thomas the Tank Engine* I think I can cope. I don't mind superhero movies, or action thrillers.'

'Let's do it then,' he said, and he was surprised to feel a warm, affectionate glow in his chest.

'I'll clear an evening,' she said. 'Look, you take care of yourself. You're very precious to me. And you're growing up so fast. I'm scared I'm going to miss whole chunks of your life.'

'Love you too.' Before his mother could get all mushy, he said hurriedly, 'Gotta go. Let me know when you want to do the pizza-and-movie night.'

'I will. Make sure you shower, and change your clothes, and brush your teeth properly. Girls don't like boys who smell of sweat or whose breath stinks.'

And then she was gone. He took a breath, trying to steady himself. He felt as if he was somehow balancing on a thin wall, trying not to fall. One side of the wall was childhood, which he'd enjoyed but grown out of, and the other side was adulthood, which scared and fascinated him in equal measure.

Eventually he slipped the phone back into his pocket and went to join the others.

Bradley had sat down by now, and Sam had joined him on the sofa. Bex was still sitting where she had been when he left. She looked . . . angry. Frustrated.

'You're right, Kieron,' Bradley said. 'It has to be you that goes to America to investigate the Goldfinch Institute.'

Kieron felt a swelling sense of happiness and, yes, nervousness. He tried to keep the elation from his face as Bradley went on:

'There are a great many reasons why it *shouldn't* be you, and we've gone through most of them in the past few minutes, but in the end it all comes down to three simple facts: the mission needs to be undertaken so that SIS-TERR don't start getting suspicious about us; Bex's cover would be blown because she would be recognised instantly by this Tara Gallagher; and I can't provide Bex with the technical and operational support she needs – not until I'm better.' He looked as if the words pained him. They probably did. 'So that leaves us with one simple alternative – you go, and Bex goes with you. She provides the support via the ARCC kit, and you do the investigation.' His gaze flicked across to Bex, who had her arms crossed and was staring at the wall, then back to Kieron. 'But at the slightest sign that anything is going wrong, we pull you out. Understood? No heroics.'

'No crashing trucks, starting fires or electrocuting people,' Sam added.

'Not helping,' Kieron told him. He looked back at Bradley. Bearing in mind the conversation he'd only just had with his mother, he said hesitantly, 'I know my mum doesn't spend much time in the flat, but even so, she's going to realise that I'm not around. And I mean *really* not around, not just "out with Sam" not around. "In another country" not around.'

Bradley opened his mouth to say something, but Bex interrupted. 'We've talked about that as well,' she said. 'You mentioned that your favourite band were rehearsing and recording their new album in Albuquerque?'

'Lethal Insomnia,' Sam added helpfully.

'Yes – Lethal Insomnia.' The way she said the band's name made it sound as if there were invisible quotation marks around it. 'We thought we could invent a fake competition which you've supposedly won. Maybe we can say it's something through a website, or something you entered when you saw a flyer in their last album. We'll tell your mother that the prize is an all-expenses-paid trip to Albuquerque to see Lethal Insomnia rehearsing their new album. Studio access and tour, three nights in a hotel, all food paid for, plus flights there and back. How could she possibly refuse you permission to go? It's the opportunity of a lifetime.'

'She's not stupid,' Kieron pointed out. 'She'll know that any online competition where a teenager goes to America by himself is likely to be fake.'

'You're right,' Bradley said. 'We thought we'd make the trip for two. Chances are that your mother won't be able to take the time off work – you've told us about all the overtime she does – but even if she thinks she can, we can get inside her firm's computer system using the ARCC kit and create some work crisis that means she needs to stay in Newcastle.'

'She'll just say I can't go.' Kieron's initial elation was collapsing like a slowly leaking balloon. 'Not by myself.'

Bradley nodded. 'But what if we tell her that Bex will go as well, in the guise of someone from the publicity company who ran the competition? She'll be looking after you all the time, as far as your mother knows.'

Kieron ran the plan through his head. 'I guess it might work,' he said cautiously. 'She'd have to meet Bex of course. She wouldn't just let me go to America with some woman she'd never seen.' He glanced across at Bex. 'And you'd need to stress that this trip would be educational – not just fun. You know – experiencing the sights and sounds of another country, gaining an insight into the music business. That kind of thing.'

'Maybe,' Sam said, thinking as he was talking, 'Bex could tell her that there's even a possibility that the visit could lead to a job working on the band's publicity or something here in the UK. You know how she's worried that you're never going to get a decent job.'

'Can we fly first class?' Kieron asked hopefully.

'In your dreams,' Bex snorted.

'But it *is* a competition. Winners of competitions usually get treated to first-class travel, and limousines, and all kinds of luxury stuff.'

'I refer you to my previous answer.' Bex's expression was serious. 'That cover story goes out of the window the moment you say goodbye to your mother. After that, we'll assume false identities and we'll just be two travellers flying to New Mexico.'

Sam cleared his throat. 'Actually,' he said, 'I was going to ask about that. If Kieron's mum isn't allowed to go – for obvious reasons – maybe I could take her place. I mean, I've seen these competitions. *My* mum cuts them out of magazines and enters them all the time. Our kitchen table is littered with coupons and entry forms. They all say the same thing: "The winner *and a friend* will travel to" wherever it is.' He glanced around expectantly. 'Well, I'm the only friend he's got. Can I come?'

Bex shook her head. 'I hate to break this to you, Sam,' she said, 'but this is actually *work*. We're not *really* going to see this band recording their album. It's not actually a competition.'

'Oh,' he said, crestfallen. 'I just thought –'

'Don't think. You're staying here.'

'OK.'

Bradley raised a hand. 'I had a thought about what happens when you get there,' he said. 'Let me run this past you.' He paused, gathering his thoughts. 'We obviously need to be able to get Kieron inside the Goldfinch Institute itself, so he can take a look around. There's not a lot he – or you – can do from a hotel room, apart from talk to friends and relatives of the people who've died and maybe covertly access the autopsy reports, and we can do that from here. What if we give Kieron a reason to be there? What if we give him a fake identity as, oh, say a teenage computer nerd who's apparently invented a new way of breaking computer encryption, or speeding up processing, or something like that. He's flown out to Albuquerque to talk to the guy who runs the Goldfinch Institute –'

'Todd Zanderbergen,' Bex said.

'Yes, him. We'll need to construct the cover story carefully, and make sure Kieron sounds like he knows what he's talking about, but that's the kind of thing we do anyway.' He suddenly looked rueful. 'The kind of thing I *used* to do anyway.' He glanced over at Kieron. 'Ever done any amateur dramatics?'

'He was a tree once,' Sam chipped in, 'in a school production of *Hansel and Gretel*.'

'I did more than that,' Kieron pointed out, annoyed. 'I had a starring role in Bertolt Brecht's *Mother Courage and Her Children*, and I was also in Ayckbourn's *Ernie's Incredible Illucinations*. I've got a lot of stage experience. The only thing you've ever done is be the front end of the pantomime horse in *Cinderella*. And your head fell off.'

'It wasn't attached properly,' Sam objected.

'OK, that's all good,' Bex said firmly. 'We know what we've got to do: firstly, fake a website for this competition; secondly, send a letter to Kieron at his home address telling him he's won; thirdly, arrange fake passports and travel documents; fourthly, book flights and hotel rooms; and fifthly, if that's even a word, get in touch with Todd Zanderbergen and arrange an appointment with him. Oh, and sixthly: somehow find something that Kieron can take along and demonstrate that looks as if it might be some cutting-edge software.' She smiled brightly. 'All in a day's work for us.'

'And seventhly,' Kieron added, 'we need to craft some kind of Trojan computer virus and put it on a USB stick.' He frowned. 'Maybe we could put a non-disclosure agreement on the USB stick and ask this Todd guy to check it over. When he plugs the stick into his system it'll copy over. Simple.'

'I'll go low-tech and make some phone calls about the travel arrangements,' Bradley said.

'Are you sure you'll be all right doing that?' Bex asked, concerned.

He nodded. 'As long as I'm not wearing those glasses, I'm fine. And I've got a couple of unregistered "burner" phones I can use that can't be traced back to us. It's the software and hardware that Kieron's going to have to take into the Goldfinch Institute that I'm more worried about.'

'Actually,' Kieron said, 'I think I might have a solution for that. Give me half an hour to do some research.'

Bex and Bradley didn't look convinced, but were soon busy with their own tasks.

While Bradley went off to get the fake passports organised and Bex logged into her laptop to start mocking-up the fake Lethal Insomnia competition website, Kieron gestured to Sam to come and join him. 'The Goldfinch Institute is into non-lethal weapons,' he explained. 'Their big publicity thing is that they're trying to move armies and police forces *away* from lethal measures and more towards things that don't kill people. If we can persuade them that I've developed a really good non-lethal weapon, they'll be interested in talking to me.'

Sam looked sceptical. 'You're going to come up with a completely new type of non-lethal weapon?' he said. 'Something that nobody's ever thought of before? In the next half-hour?'

'It doesn't actually have to work,' Kieron pointed out reasonably. 'It just has to look like it *might*. And we don't have to actually invent it – we just have to find someone who already has, and then steal it from them so we can use it.'

'Oh,' Sam said, relieved. 'For a moment there I thought you were suggesting something impossibly difficult and incredibly risky.'

For the next half-hour the two of them swapped ideas, mainly based on things they'd seen in computer games. They fairly quickly abandoned the crude solutions that most police forces used – solid projectiles that acted like a punch to the stomach or Tasers that delivered an incapacitating dose of electricity to the nervous system. Anaesthetic gases were obviously beyond their capabilities – nobody would believe that a teenager would whip up a batch of anaesthetic gas in his garage. They discussed for a while the 'vortex ring guns' Kieron had seen Bex use in Pakistan – weapons that used explosively driven rings of compressed air to knock people over, or knock them out – but they were part of Agni Patel's arsenal, and Kieron was pretty sure that Bex wouldn't want him to reveal them.

'What about sound?' Sam suggested eventually.

'What?'

'Have you ever heard of the "brown note"?'

Kieron shook his head. 'Don't think so.'

'It's a theoretical musical note below the limit of human hearing that's supposed to have "an effect" on the body.'

Kieron was dubious. 'What kind of "effect"?'

Sam smiled. 'It's supposed to make you want to – how do I put this? – go to the toilet. Suddenly and uncontrollably.'

Kieron slowly shook his head. 'I'm guessing it's not called the "brown note" because it's like white noise but different?'

'Oh no. I've seen it mentioned on the Internet, and also on TV sometimes. Nobody's ever identified the note itself, but it would be the perfect non-lethal weapon. And it's the kind of thing you might find while you were mucking around with a synthesiser or a bass guitar and a big amp.'

'Yeah. I think we'll keep that one on the back burner. But thanks.'

'I suppose you've got a better idea,' Sam challenged.

'Actually I have.' Kieron paused. 'You know how the brain produces electrical brainwaves?'

'Yeah.'

'And you know that thing we did in physics, where you make ripples in a pond and then make more ripples the same size but one-hundred-and-eighty degrees out of phase, so the peaks of the original sound wave are cancelled out by the troughs in the new ones?'

Sam nodded thoughtfully. 'Yeah – it's the principle that noise-cancelling headphones use. They record the background noise of the environment you're in – like a train or an aircraft – and then play it back a few milliseconds out of phase so it cancels the original sound out.'

'OK.' Kieron leaned forward. 'What happens if you

combine the two? If you can record someone's brainwaves and then play them back out of phase?'

There was a long silence as Sam digested what Kieron had said. 'It might actually switch the brain off,' he said thoughtfully. 'I mean, for good. Stop your breathing maybe.'

'Or it might just suppress your conscious mind and put you into a trance.' Kieron stared into Sam's eyes, willing him to buy into the idea. 'Remember – this doesn't have to actually work. It just needs to sound like it *might*.'

'You know,' Sam said slowly, 'this might *actually* work. We could make a fortune from this!'

'Baby steps, Sam. Let's concentrate on the current priority – selling the idea.'

'OK.' Sam leaned forward as well, so that his forehead was millimetres away from Kieron's. 'How do you record someone's brainwaves?'

'Electrodes,' Kieron replied. 'Stuck to the scalp.'

'Easy in a hospital; difficult if you're facing a guy with a gun.'

'Right – so how do we make it portable and simple?' Kieron felt a growing sense of excitement rushing through him as fragmentary ideas started to join up in his brain. 'We have something like a hairnet, but covered in electrodes. It's all squished up into a ball. It gets fired at a person from a launcher, and the net unfolds while it's in mid-air and wraps around their head –'

'Or it's like a plastic mesh covered in electrodes that gets warmed up somehow when it's fired, becomes pliable, folds itself up around the target's head and then quickly

62

cools down to make a kind of cage.' Sam shrugged. 'They use stuff like that for face masks when they give people radiotherapy for brain tumours. They're moulded to the face, and then bolted down to stop you from moving your head.' He looked away. 'My grandad had one. He used to let me play with it. It was purple.'

'OK,' Kieron went on, 'however it's done, it wraps around the target's head. There's a wire connecting it to a device that records the target's brainwaves and plays them back out of phase, thus rendering them unconscious. It's genius!'

'It's certainly the kind of thing a teenager might come up with. You'd need to convince them that the maths works. You'd also need to show them some kind of prototype. Doesn't need to actually work – it just needs to look good.'

'So what do we need?'

Sam thought for a moment. 'Something appropriately medical. Electrodes, plastic, wires – and maybe an oscilloscope. Oh, and some maths that sounds vaguely convincing.'

'Where can we get that from?'

Sam considered. 'I think the kit itself can come from the neurology department of a hospital. They'll have that kind of thing – I mean, they must record people's brainwaves all the time.'

'So – a big hospital then?'

Sam looked dubious. 'I'm all for a bit of breaking and entering – you know that – but I'm not sure I want to take stuff from a hospital. I mean, what if they need it?'

'Good point. What if we just borrowed it, and then donated part of the money we're getting from SIS-TERR?'

'I could work with that.'

Kieron glanced around the room. Neither Bex nor Bradley were paying them any attention. 'I think,' he said slowly, 'that it's time Bradley took your sister out for a coffee.'

'I don't think so,' Sam said warningly.

Bradley looked up. 'Did I hear my name being mentioned?' he asked.

Kieron smiled. 'We're thinking of taking a little field trip,' he said. 'Want to come?'

It took a good fifteen minutes of arguing and explaining, but eventually the four of them – Kieron, Sam, Bex and Bradley – were outside, getting into the car.

'I still don't think this is a good idea,' Sam muttered as Bex started the ignition.

It took just twenty minutes to get to the Walkergate Hospital. They headed in to the main building and looked for the Programmed Investigations Unit, where Sam's sister was working. As they headed up in the lift, Bex took over the planning.

'Sam, Bradley – you head into the unit and look for Courtney. Tell her you wanted to check when she was finishing so you could take her for a meal to thank her for everything. I'll snaffle a porter's jacket and a wheelchair from somewhere. When you see me come into the unit, Bradley – you fake an attack of some kind.'

'Might not be a fake,' Bradley said. He was, Kieron had to admit, looking a bit pale.

'While Courtney is sorting you out, I'll come in with the

wheelchair as if I'm collecting someone. Courtney should be distracted enough that she's only looking at Bradley, but I don't want her catching sight of me by accident. I'll take a set of electrodes and an EEG machine. The great thing about hospitals is that everything is labelled so that new nurses can find stuff quickly. While you're stopping Courtney from turning around, I'll put the things on the wheelchair and get out of there. Clear?'

'Clear,' they all said together.

In the event, it all went like a dream. Courtney was alone in the PIU, as she'd previously told Sam and Bradley.

'What are you doing here?' she said, surprised.

Bradley switched into what Kieron assumed was his 'smooth pick-up routine'. 'We thought we could take you for dinner when your shift is over,' he said. 'As a thank-you for looking after me.'

'What – all of you?' she said, glancing at Sam and Kieron.

'Yes – all of us,' Sam said firmly.

Bradley smiled. 'They insisted,' he added. 'Bless them.'

'My shift's over in half an hour – do you want to wait here for me? We haven't got any patients in this afternoon.'

Kieron saw, out of the corner of his eye, Bex pushing a wheelchair through the doorway. Before Courtney could spot her, he nudged Bradley in the back.

Bradley raised a hand to his forehead and winced. 'Actually, I could do with sitting down. Those stairs . . .'

'Oh, you didn't take the stairs, did you?' Courtney fussed around him, moving him towards a bay with a bed. 'In your condition?'

'I thought I was better,' he protested.

As the three of them helped get Bradley to the bed, Kieron glanced over his shoulder. Bex had moved to a set of cupboards and was opening one. She pulled something out, then glanced at Kieron and nodded. She had it.

Now all they had to do, Kieron thought to himself, was get through dinner without acting suspiciously.

CHAPTER FOUR

'This isn't going to be enough though,' Bex pointed out, holding the net of electrodes she'd 'liberated'.

It was the morning of the next day, and they were all sitting around the lounge of the apartment that Bex had rented. Kieron and Sam were still enthused by the success of their covert mission to get the EEG brainwave electrodes, while Bradley was just looking wiped out by the exertion.

Kieron glanced over at her. 'It's a standard head-size – one size fits all.'

'That's not what I meant. You've got the medical-standard electrodes for placing on the scalp. That's great – but it's just a prop. Just set-dressing. You can't go into a high-tech corporation with a prop in your hand and an idea in your head. You need more than that.'

Kieron frowned, while Sam said, 'Like what?'

'OK – explain your idea to me again, slowly enough that someone not brought up with YouTube can understand it. Then I'll tell you what else we need.'

Kieron leaned forward. 'Sound is a wave, right? Just a pressure wave travelling through the air. Sounds you hear are caused by the increases and decreases of pressure against your eardrum.'

'With you so far.'

'Imagine those pressure waves on a graph, like mountains and valleys.'

She nodded. 'Keep going.'

'Now imagine that you can play another sound that's the exact opposite of that graph – wherever there's a mountain on one, there's a valley on the other. And vice versa.'

'They would cancel out,' Bex said, picturing it in her head. 'There would be no landscape – sorry, noise – at all. Everything would be flat.'

'Correct.' Kieron looked as if he was going to continue, but Sam jumped in.

'Brainwaves are like sound waves, except that they are caused by positive and negative electrical currents rather than the physical movement of air molecules. If you look at a graph of your brainwaves they look just like sound waves. The maths is the same.'

'So,' Bex said, following the thought process along, 'if you can find a way to project a brainwave into a brain that's opposite to the brainwave it's already experiencing, the two will cancel out. That's your theory? It has the benefit of simplicity, I suppose.'

Kieron nodded. 'That's it,' he said hurriedly, before Sam could interject again. 'The question is – how do you get the new brainwave into the brain?'

'And also,' Bradley murmured from where he was slumped,

eyes half closed, 'how do you know you'll switch the brain off temporarily rather than permanently?'

'Yeah, I've been thinking about that.'

Bex had to admire Kieron's acting skills. She suspected he wasn't anywhere near as confident as his tone suggested.

He explained his theory. 'We're not stopping the brain producing the brainwaves – we're just cancelling them out *after* they're produced. Going back to the sound-wave analogy, the tuba is still playing, it's just that you can't hear the music.'

'I hate tubas,' Bradley said quietly. Bex wasn't sure if he was telling the truth, making a joke or losing his grip on events. He straightened himself up a bit and went on: 'When you say you're cancelling out the brainwaves, does that include the signals that tell the heart to keep beating or the lungs to inflate and deflate?'

Bex relaxed. Bradley still knew what was happening.

'We're not saying it'll work,' Sam pointed out. 'We're just saying it has to *sound* as if it could.'

'And besides,' Kieron added, 'we've been researching this. We really have. The brain produces a whole complicated set of brainwaves – alpha waves, beta waves, gamma waves, delta waves, and probably others as well. Some of them are associated with conscious thought – those are the alpha waves. Some are more associated with autonomic bodily functions like heartbeat and breathing. Those are, like, the delta waves and stuff. We aren't planning to cancel them *all* out – just the ones that are linked to conscious thought.'

'"And stuff",' Bradley said, settling back with his eyes closed again. 'I like the tech-talk. It's very reassuring.'

'We're not planning on cancelling *any* of them out,' Sam reminded them all again. 'We're just *saying* that we can do it.' He pointed to the hairnet of electrodes that Bex held. 'That's the microphone and the loudspeaker combined, if you like. We're saying we can use that to record the waves that the brain is producing and then play them back but reversed.'

Bex tried to picture it. 'So – you fire a net like this over someone's head, then feed signals into it. Sounds complicated.'

'I've actually put together a flash animation of it in action,' Kieron said. 'It looks good.'

'I'm sure it does.' She thought for a minute. Sam tried to say something, but she held up her hand to stop him: 'OK – the problem as I see it is this: you've got your prop, and you've got your flash animation. That's enough to get you through the Goldfinch Institute's door. That's the lure, if you like. It attracts the fish. But look at it from the fish's point of view. Once it gets close to the lure and realises there's actually no worm there, it'll swim off. What's your worm?'

Sam just looked confused. 'I don't understand,' he said.

Kieron was keeping up though. He nodded slowly. 'You mean, if we just dangle the idea in front of them, they can say, "Cool idea, lads," then pat us on the head, send us away and use the idea themselves. We need to have something that they *can't* develop – at least, not in a hurry. Something they need us for.'

Bex nodded. 'You need a worm.'

Kieron and Sam swapped glances. Bex was impressed

by the way they seemed to almost share the same thoughts sometimes. They didn't need to talk – they just each knew what the other one was thinking. That was a close friendship.

'We need –' Kieron started to say.

'– some kind of mathematical simulation of brainwaves,' Sam continued.

'One that's connected to a simulated heart, respiratory system and so on,' Kieron went on.

'That way –'

Kieron again, continuing rather than interrupting: '– we can show that transmitting a reversed brainwave will cancel out the top-level brain functions while allowing the lower level ones to keep going.'

'We need a simulated person,' they chorused together.

'Correct.' Bex didn't know if it was correct or not, but it sounded convincing. 'So how do you get one?'

The two boys just stared at each other.

'Neural network?' Sam queried.

Kieron nodded. 'Something like that. Let me check.' He slipped the ARCC glasses back on and started to wave his hands around, accessing information from the ether.

Bex glanced over at Bradley. 'How are you doing, Brad?'

'Hanging on,' he said, eyes still closed. 'I get little peaks of energy, and then it all seems to fade away for a while.'

'Hopefully the doctor will be able to sort that out.' Bex tried to sound less worried than she actually was.

'When's she coming?'

Bex winced. 'Unfortunately I think it'll be after the three of us have left for America. Will you be all right to let her in?'

71

Bradley smiled. 'Maybe I'll invite Courtney over. *She* can let her in.'

Bex was about to say that she didn't want any strangers in the flat when she realised that this doctor who was coming to see Bradley was technically a stranger and Courtney wasn't. Before she could resolve the logical discontinuity in her mind, Bradley went on:

'Did you get in contact with SIS-TERR? Have you accepted the new mission?'

She nodded but then, realising that Bradley's eyes were closed, said, 'Yes – I sent them a message. Just a simple acknowledgement.'

'And what about our last job – the one in Mumbai? What did you tell them about that?'

Bex frowned. 'That was trickier. Obviously I couldn't admit what had really happened – Blood and Soil stealing the briefcase, me going after it, discovering that there were five neutron bombs set to explode across the Middle East and Pakistan, joining up with a multi-billionaire to locate the devices and then relying on two teenagers to block the signal that would launch them. I mean, that would just be stupid. Even if they *did* believe me – and frankly I barely believe it myself – they'd drop us like a hot potato.' She sighed. 'In the end I went back to the simple fact that my brief was to witness the handover of the case containing the information on where the last neutron bomb was located. I told them I watched it being handed over to two Westerners with close-cut blond hair. That's the truth, pretty much. They don't need to know about anything that happened after that.'

'Just so I know,' Bradley said. 'I didn't want to contradict you, if asked.'

Bex noticed that Kieron looked as if he wanted to say something. 'What is it, Kieron?'

'There's a researcher at Newcastle University who's doing research on the brain/body interface,' he said. 'He's trying to work out whether self-awareness is an inevitable result of linking a brain and a body up, or whether it's something else.'

'Self-awareness?' Bradley asked.

It was Sam who answered. 'Dogs are self-aware,' he pointed out. 'You put a dog in front of a mirror and it knows that the image is a reflection of itself, not another dog. You put a cat in front of a mirror and it thinks it's looking at another cat. Dogs are self-aware, as are elephants and dolphins. Cats aren't.'

'And people get paid to research this kind of thing?' Bex was impressed. 'We're in the wrong game!'

'Anyway,' Kieron went on, 'this bloke's developed a simulated brain that produces brainwaves just like a real brain does. He intends to connect it to various mechanical arms and sensors, like cameras, to see if it develops a sense of self. *That*'s what we need to take with us – the simulation. We can demonstrate it to this Todd guy at the Institute.' A frown crossed his face. 'There's one problem though. The research is being sponsored by the Ministry of Defence. They're hoping to develop ways of commanding aircraft and tanks using brainwaves rather than hands-on controls or remote control. The lab is separate from the rest of the university, and it's in a high-security environment.

We're going to have trouble getting in there and taking his simulation.' He shrugged. 'On the other hand, that does mean it's something the Goldfinch Institute won't have access to.' He smiled. 'It's a worm that nobody else is using to fish with.'

'That's not the only problem you'll have,' Bradley pointed out. He raised a hand and tapped his head. 'What if this simulated brain is actually a *real* brain – a real *intelligence*? Isn't that going to complicate things?'

'It's not,' Kieron said dismissively. 'It's a replica – like a synthesiser making an artificial noise that sounds like a tuba. It's not a *real* tuba, and it never will be. It's just a representation of one.' He looked over at Sam. 'That's right, isn't it?'

'I hate tubas,' Bradley said quietly. 'Did I mention.'

'And we're not planning on taking this researcher's entire work, are we?' Bex asked, ignoring him. 'I mean, this mission is important and all, but I'd hate to destroy a man's career.'

Kieron shook his head. 'We'll just take a copy. It's several terabytes of code, but I've got a portable hard drive that'll take it.'

Bex sighed. 'So – having just stolen one thing from a hospital, you now want to steal something else from a military research laboratory. You kids don't do anything by halves, do you? Where is this place?'

'About half an hour's drive away.'

Bex closed her eyes briefly. This was all getting far too complicated. 'And it's on a military base?'

'No – it's on university grounds, but the laboratory itself has alarms and security systems.'

'Then what's your plan for getting in and stealing this data?' she asked.

Kieron winced. 'That depends,' he said. 'Can we use your credit card?'

Kieron's plan involved driving out to a nearby electronics store. When Bex saw what he wanted to buy – a small drone with five propellers and a high-definition camera, operated by a remote control – she almost refused.

'This isn't Christmas!' she said, trying to keep her voice down so that she didn't attract any attention from the store clerk on the till. 'I'm not buying you toys!'

'Oh,' Kieron said, ignoring her as he kept on going down the aisle, 'I'll need a wireless USB transmitter as well. And we may as well get a 5TB portable hard drive. It'll save me having to go home.' He looked a little shamefaced. 'Anyway, mine's filled up with PDFs of comics I've downloaded. I don't want to have to delete them.'

A thought struck Bex. She glanced at the store clerk, then said, 'Hang on a second – why can't we access this researcher's computer with the ARCC kit and download the whole thing that way? It'll save the trouble of having to break in to a secure facility.'

Kieron shook his head. 'Two reasons. Firstly, because it's technically an MoD computer, it's stand-alone – not connected to any networks or anything, to avoid being hacked by the Chinese or the Russians. I can't use the ARCC kit to get into it. Secondly, the bandwidth of the ARCC isn't big enough to scoop up several terabytes of data in a hurry anyway. Even if I could connect up remotely, it would take hours to siphon off the data, and anything could happen in that time. The researcher might discover that we've linked in, some kind of alarm might trip, the computer might power down or even crash – anything. I can use the ARCC stuff to get past any password he might be using, or any encryption, but after that it's like trying to fit a swimming pool's worth of data into a bucket.'

'Hence –' Bex indicated his shopping basket.

Kieron shook his head. 'Exactly.'

Sam came around a corner and joined them. Spotting the drone, he said, 'Ooh – nice!'

'What's that behind your back?' Bex asked suspiciously, noticing the way he was standing oddly.

'Behind my – oh, this!' He brought his hand into sight. He was holding a box.

'What's that?' Bex asked.

'It's a game capture card,' Kieron said when Sam didn't answer. 'You use it for recording computer games you're playing so you can upload them to YouTube for people to watch.'

'And that's a thing, is it?' Bex shook her head. 'The latest in spectator sports – kids watching other kids playing computer games rather than playing the games themselves. It's even lazier than watching football rather than playing it!'

Kieron and Sam looked at each other in what to her looked suspiciously like pity. 'You wouldn't understand,' they said together. Under his breath Sam added, 'And why would anyone want to watch football?'

From the electronics store they drove directly to the university site. Kieron had thrown a rapid battery charger into the basket, and he used it to power the drone up while Bex drove.

The university was on a campus away from Newcastle, almost out in the countryside. It was largely open, and Bex drove cautiously around the ring road that encompassed it, waiting for Kieron to tell her where to stop. Students were everywhere – groups of them, couples holding hands and individuals rushing to get to lectures.

Bex glanced sideways at Kieron. He was watching the students with a wistful expression.

'Ever thought about going to college?' she asked quietly.

'I've thought about it,' he admitted, 'but I've got to get through my GCSEs first. And I don't know what I want to study.' He shrugged. 'And even if I *did* know what to study, I'm not sure whether I could take the lifestyle. I'm not, you know, the most *sociable* of people. I prefer my own company, and that of just a few friends.' He jerked a thumb towards the back seat. 'Like him.'

'Maybe Sam would go to college as well. And even if he doesn't, there'll be other people like you there – people who have –' she had been going to say 'social anxiety issues', but stopped herself at the last moment. It sounded too clinical, too harsh – 'a few really good friends, rather than a lot of casual acquaintances,' she finished lamely.

'Maybe.' He shrugged and looked away.

Bex wasn't sure whether to press him further, but before she could say anything he pointed out of the window. 'Down there,' he said, indicating a side road that led away from the university campus.

A few minutes later they found themselves at a car park with about half the slots occupied. An automated barrier separated the car park from the road, but it was raised and she drove straight through without any problems. She parked in a large enough space that she wasn't near any other cars, and was also shielded by a couple of trees.

Beyond a wire fence at the far side of the car park was a single-storey building. On top of the fence, coils of wire lined with razor-sharp spikes caught the light. Looking along the fence, Bex saw an entrance turnstile with a security-card reader. There was a camera pointed at the turnstile, presumably to record anyone going in or out.

'Are you ready?' Bex asked Kieron.

'Ready,' he confirmed. 'If you can just lower the window.'

She did so, and he held the drone outside. 'Sam – ready?'

'I am,' Sam confirmed. Immediately the drone started to lift off, leaving Kieron's hands and rising up into the air. Beneath it Kieron had attached the portable hard drive, using cable ties. He'd also adapted a long plastic strut from the drone's packaging to hold the drive's USB cable out ahead of it, like a lance. Or a stinger, maybe.

'You're not assuming that someone is going to let that thing in through the front door?' she asked. Actually, she'd already worked out what he was going to do – or, at least, what *she* would do under the same conditions – but she wanted to check that he'd thought it all through.

'It's warm today,' Kieron said, watching as Sam moved the

drone through the air, keeping it low and in the shadow of as many trees and shrubs as he could manage. 'The windows are open. You can see them. We should be able to get the drone in through the lab window.'

Bex frowned. As the drone hopped up, over the fence and down again, into the cover of some large green wheelie bins, she said, 'But if the window's open, the researcher could be inside. He'll see the drone the minute it comes in.'

'We've thought of that too,' Kieron said.

He reached back, over his shoulder. 'Give me the tablet.'

Sam passed over the tablet, which was controlling the drone, and on which the image from its HD camera was being shown, then opened his door and slipped out. Keeping low, he moved towards some cars that were parked over near the fence.

'Have you ever noticed,' Kieron said, distracted slightly by steering the drone around a corner, relying on the moving image from the camera to show him where to go, 'that whenever your car alarm goes off, you know it's *your* alarm and not anybody else's? Even Courtney, four floors up in her flat, can apparently tell her own car alarm from anyone else's. And she can get down those stairs in thirty seconds flat as well, before any thief has a chance to get away.' He smiled. 'Sam says he's seen her chasing car thieves down the road, chucking stones at them until they're out of reach.'

Outside, Sam had reached a particular parked car. He looked around, making sure nobody was watching, then reached down and picked up a thick branch that had dropped off the tree he was standing beneath. Bracing himself, he bought the branch back over his shoulder like an American baseball player preparing to hit a ball, then *swish*ed it rapidly forward. The branch smacked into the car's radiator grille. The peace and quiet of the car park suddenly vanished, replaced by the shrill electronic blast of the car's alarm. Sam edged back into the shadow of the tree, dropping the branch as he did so, then slipped back along the line of bushes to where Bex was parked.

'Give it a few minutes,' he said as he got back inside.

'That *is* the right car, isn't it?' Bex asked.

'According to the information I found on the researcher,' Kieron said, 'it's his car. For sure.'

'Let's just hope he hasn't sold it to a work colleague in the past few days.'

Kieron grinned. 'It's still his alarm,' he pointed out. 'He won't have forgotten it. Coming out to check will be like an automatic reaction.' He grew distant. 'My mum said that she could always tell when I was crying, even at nursery when there were maybe twenty or thirty babies there. If she turned up to get me and heard crying, she'd know if it was me.' The expression vanished from his face, replaced by excitement. 'Look – there he is!'

Indeed, a man in corduroy trousers and an open-necked shirt was running down the path that linked the research building with the security gate on the fence. He scrabbled in his pocket for his keys.

'We are go,' Kieron said, stroking his fingers across the tablet.

On the screen, Bex saw the image change. The drone had

been hovering low, beneath an open window, but now it was rising. As far as the camera could see, the room inside was empty. Kieron guided the drone carefully inside. Bex could see several large computers, as well as whiteboards covered with diagrams and equations and a bookcase filled with books and journals and files crammed full of papers.

The researcher had got through the security turnstile now. He turned the alarm off, using his key fob, and glanced around suspiciously.

Kieron manoeuvred the drone towards one of the computers.

'How do you know it's that one?' Bex asked.

'His jacket is on the back of the chair.' Kieron guided the drone towards the computer. The USB cable, projecting into the camera's picture from above, wavered slightly as the drone moved, but it headed for an empty USB port on the computer. 'And,' he added, 'it's the only one switched on.'

'How are you going to actually find the file?' Bex asked. 'I mean, you can hardly operate the keyboard with that drone, no matter how good you are.'

'Don't need to,' Sam said from behind them. 'The portable drive has an automatic back-up function. Makes it easy for people who aren't computer experts, like we are. You plug it in, and it hoovers up everything it can find.' He sniffed. 'I configured it on the drive here.'

On the screen, the USB plug edged forward as Kieron manipulated the drone's controls. It took a few attempts, but eventually he got the two of them touching.

'Now,' he said, 'let's hope those propellers can generate enough force to push it in.'

'And then pull it out again,' Sam observed. 'Don't forget that bit.'

In the car park, the researcher was now checking over his car, looking for any damage or broken windows.

'Got it!' Kieron exclaimed as the USB plug slid into the computer's port. 'I can't see whether the drive is actually backing up. Let's hope you configured it correctly.'

'Worry about your own side of things,' Sam grumbled. 'I did my job properly.'

'How long do you think the transfer will take?' Kieron asked.

Sam thought for a moment. 'Less than a minute,' he said.

With a last glance around, the researcher locked his car again and headed towards the security turnstile.

'I've just thought of something,' Sam said. It sounded as if he was trying to keep his voice light and casual.

'What's that?' Kieron asked.

'We won't actually know when the transfer has ended.'

Kieron swore. 'You said it'll take a minute! "Less than a minute," you said!'

'Hey, that was an estimate. I could be wrong!'

'Well, what happens if we disengage too early?'

Sam shrugged. 'Depends. We might end up with some of the files but not all of them. Or the drive might get corrupted.'

The researcher was through the security turnstile now, and had nearly got to the building. As he reached the door it opened and a man in a security guard's uniform emerged to hold it open for him. They exchanged a few words before the researcher went inside.

'I'm going to stop it now,' Kieron said.

'Wait!' Sam's tone was strident. 'Just give it a few more seconds!'

Kieron's fingers hovered over the tablet's surface. He was obviously torn between doing what he thought was best and what Sam was saying.

'Just a little longer!' Sam urged.

Bex shook her head abruptly. 'Get out now. If he gets back to his lab and sees the drone, we're done for.'

Kieron nodded. He touched the tablet's screen, commanding the drone to disengage. The camera display showed it pulling back, tugging the USB cable out without problem and revealing more and more of the computer and the laboratory as it retreated.

Alarms suddenly blared out from the building inside the wire fence.

Bex started the car.

Kieron drew a wide circle on the tablet screen. The drone rotated, showing a blurred view of the bookcases and the whiteboards before it stabilised with its camera pointed at the door.

The researcher stood in the doorway. His face was set in stunned, disbelieving lines, but his hand rested on an alarm box set beside the door frame.

'We're getting out of here,' Bex said, feeling the sudden pulse of adrenalin rushing through her bloodstream like wildfire. Her heart rate sped up, and she felt suddenly nauseous. The feeling passed quickly, as it always did. She threw the gears into reverse, put her foot on the accelerator and raised the clutch until the engine caught. The car moved smoothly backwards.

She glanced at the building. As she watched, the door swung open and several uniformed guards rushed out. They looked around uncertainly. One of them saw the car and shouted. Bex couldn't hear what he was saying, but his intention was clear. He wanted them to stop.

She glanced down at the tablet in Kieron's hands as she automatically put the car into first gear and started to accelerate away from their secluded parking slot in a curve that would take them towards the barrier. From what she could see in her hurried look, Kieron had successfully steered the drone through the open window. She could see blue sky, and a flat asphalt roof.

She turned back to check the barrier.

Which was coming down rapidly.

Her foot went down instinctively and she slammed the car into a higher gear. The car leaped forward, pressing Kieron back into the seat. From behind her, Bex heard Sam's muffled curse as, caught by surprise, he banged his head on the back of his seat.

The barrier was halfway down now – a thick black diagonal line drawn across the bright blue sky. In the rear-view mirror she saw the security guards running to intercept them. They'd triggered some emergency setting that had caused the turnstile to swing completely open.

The car was halfway out of the car park when the barrier crashed down onto its roof. The screech of metal on metal set Bex's teeth on edge, like biting down on a piece of tin foil. The car juddered, hesitated, then sprang ahead, skidding out onto the road in a curve that left smoking black rubber on the tarmac behind them.

'Slow down!' Kieron shouted.

'I will *not* slow down!' she shouted back. 'Why would you even think that?'

'Because of the drone!' he yelled.

Bex looked sideways. The drone was halfway between the building and them. Its USB cable had come loose from the cable-ties and was hanging down, waving in the wind generated by its flight.

'Sam,' Bex ordered, 'open your window. Kieron, steer that thing towards us. I'll go as slowly as I can, but I'm not going to risk getting caught. The guards will be phoning ahead – we need to get out of here, fast.'

She drove as slowly as she dared. If the security guards hadn't memorised their licence plate, and if she could lose them among a whole load of traffic on a major road, then they might just get away. They could ditch the car later as it would certainly have been caught on camera. For now they just needed to concentrate on getting away.

The drone hovered alongside them. It was going as fast as it could, and it wavered unsteadily.

'Bring it in through the window,' Sam shouted.

'I can't!' Kieron shouted back, panic edging his voice. 'If I try to steer it sideways I'll lose speed, and it's going as fast as it can just to keep up with us.'

Bex heard Sam's exasperated sigh above the noise of the engine and the wind whistling in through the open window.

She felt him scrambling around in the back seat. She glanced in her driver's side mirror to see if anyone was following them. For a second she saw a clear road, but then the view was obscured by Sam's head and chest. He was climbing out of the rear window!

'What the hell are you doing?' she called.

'What I have to!' he called back. He had one arm inside the car, hanging on, while he perched on the edge of the open window. Reaching up with his free hand, he grabbed hold of the hovering drone.

'Cut the motors,' he shouted to Kieron. 'I've got it!'

Moments later he had pulled himself back inside, triumphantly holding the drone. Two of the propellers had been knocked off as he manoeuvred it through the gap, but the all-important removable hard drive still hung underneath it.

'Can we please,' Sam said breathlessly, 'never do that again?'

CHAPTER FIVE

Kieron's mother was sitting on the sofa with a glass of wine when Kieron got back home. Her coat had been thrown casually over a chair and her shoes lay untidily on the floor, upside down and pointing in different directions.

She pulled her attention from the news broadcast she was watching and gazed quizzically at him as he walked in. He could tell from her slightly unfocused gaze that she'd already had a large glass of wine. Possibly even two. It was pretty much par for the course on those evenings when she wasn't working late. He couldn't find it in his heart to blame her. She worked so hard to pay the mortgage on the flat, and buy the food that she and Kieron ate and as well as his clothes, his mobile phone, his computer and everything else. Since his father had left, she'd had to take up all the slack on running the house, and that meant he hardly ever got to see her. It didn't make him angry – not at his mum, anyway. Maybe at his dad, just a bit. It mostly made him sad. It also made him determined to get a job (as soon as he could find one that didn't involve menial work in a shop) and contribute to the family finances, and help his mother to relax a bit. Maybe, he thought, Sam was right – maybe they could actually get someone interested enough in this non-lethal brainwave device to buy the idea off them.

'Kieron,' she said, 'what's happened to your lip?'

For a moment he didn't know what she was talking about. He raised his hand to see if there was some blood there, or a trace of food or something. His fingers brushed across the piercings in his lower lip, and a sudden jolt of guilt ran through him. He hadn't told her! He hadn't even asked her! It had all seemed so grown-up a few hours ago, but suddenly he was a kid again, trying to explain how the vase had got knocked over or the crayon pictures had appeared on the wall.

'Ah,' he said. 'Yes. I got some piercings.'

'I can see that.'

'I probably should have asked you first.'

'You *definitely* should have asked me first.'

He felt his cheeks growing hot with embarrassment. 'Sorry – I just really wanted them.'

The long silence that followed made him even more uncomfortable. His mother just stared at the piercings with a slight frown on her face.

'Did it hurt?' she asked eventually.

'A little bit,' he admitted.

'How did you afford them?'

'I saved up.'

'And did you lie about your age?'

He winced. 'Yes.'

Another long silence, then: 'They suit you.'

'Really?' He couldn't quite believe what he was hearing.

'They do. I mean, I wouldn't dress the way that you do, but if I did I'd probably get piercings just like that too.'

'They're called snakebites.'

'I'm sure.' She cocked her head to one side. 'Please tell me you haven't had any tattoos done.'

'No tattoos. I promise.'

'If you ever decide you want a tattoo, talk to me first. I'll tell you some personal horror stories.'

'You've got tattoos?' he asked, aghast.

She nodded. 'Had them since I was sixteen.'

Kieron couldn't believe this. 'Where?'

She raised an eyebrow, and he looked away.

'Never mind,' he said. Then, as things seemed to be going well, he decided to go for broke. 'Mum – can I go to America?'

'Sorry?' She shook her head. 'I thought for a moment there you asked if you could go to America.' She glanced at the glass in her hand. 'This stuff must be stronger than I thought.'

'No, I'm serious. Am I allowed to go to America?'

She sighed. 'Oh, Kieron, we've had this conversation. All the money I earn goes to keeping this flat, and on food and the essentials. I wish I earned enough to take us on holidays abroad, but I don't. Look, I'll see if there are any other jobs going around Newcastle that I could do – jobs that pay more money. That, or I'll walk into my boss's office and ask her for a raise. You never know – it might work. But don't pin your hopes on it, kid.'

'No, I didn't mean us going on holiday.' He flapped his hands, trying to make it look as if he was surprised and pleased about something. 'There was this competition. There were flyers in the local record shop, and a website. You had to come up with a title for the new Lethal Insomnia album. The title the band liked best would win, and the person who came up with it would get a free, all-expenses paid trip to America to see them actually record the album.' He paused for dramatic effect. 'And I won.'

His mother's eyes went wide and it looked for a moment as if she might spill her wine. She took a sudden gulp.

'You're serious? Of course you're serious! You actually won a competition.'

He smiled. 'Yeah, I did.'

'I'm so proud of you! I don't think I've ever won a competition in my life! I always thought we were an unlucky family, because nothing good ever happens to us. And a trip to America! I mean, a free copy of the album, yes, or a mention in the credits, or maybe even a VIP ticket for the next concert they do in England, but actually flying you out to America?' She fluttered her free hand in front of her face. 'I'm feeling faint.'

'Take a breath,' Kieron advised.

'This is going to be the most amazing experience of your life,' his mother said. 'You'll need new clothes, a new toothbrush and luggage! I think your dad took the big suitcases when he left – which is probably a good thing, otherwise I'd have killed him, chopped him into pieces and taken the pieces to the rubbish tip in them.' She reached out to touch Kieron's arm. 'Don't worry – I'm kidding. I wouldn't have wasted a good set of luggage on disposing of his body.' Her face, which had shed about five years as surprise and joy replaced her usual harried frown, collapsed into the lines that Kieron was all too familiar with. 'Oh, hang on. This isn't real, is it? It can't be!'

Kieron felt a wave of panic run through his body. What had they missed? What had given them away?

'I've heard about things like this,' she went on, her voice suddenly controlled and quiet. 'They call it "phishing", don't they? They explained it in the newspapers. People set up fake websites that lure in unsuspecting teenagers. Then when the kids are hooked they're told to go somewhere for what they think is an innocent meet-up, but they're kidnapped and horrible things happen to them. Look, Kieron, I'm really sorry to tell you this, but I think this is a set-up. You've been conned.'

The wave of panic receded, but only far enough that he could still sense it lurking in the background. 'I don't think so,' he said, trying to sound calm and reasonable. The last thing he wanted to do right now was to start an argument. That would only backfire badly. 'The competition is on the record company's website as well as the band's website – and they're a well-known record label, not some kind of fly-by-night operation. Look – I'll show you. Give me your tablet.'

His mother reached under a cushion on the sofa and pulled her tablet computer out. She handed it across to him with some reluctance, saying, 'These websites can be faked, you know? "Spoofed". They warn us about this kind of thing at work. We go on courses about it. One of the finance assistants fell for something like this a few months back. She was sent an invoice via email for ten thousand pounds. She checked out the company on the Internet, and they seemed legitimate, so she paid the invoice, but it was a trick. Someone else had done the work; she'd paid the wrong company. When the police tried to track them down, they'd closed the website and done a runner.' She reached out and touched his arm again. 'I'd hate for something like that to happen to you.'

'I haven't got ten thousand pounds,' he pointed out as he launched the browser and typed in the address of the fake website that Bex had mocked up. His mother was right – it was all too easy to do.

'You know what I mean. Bad things.'

Kieron handed the tablet back. 'Here – take a look.'

His mother frowned. 'Hang on – I thought I'd password-protected this thing.'

'You did. You always use my birthday as your password.'

She sighed. 'You are far too clever. I really don't know where you get it from. Certainly not your father.' She glanced over the website. 'It looks authentic, I suppose, but what do I know? These people are very clever. Kieron, I'm sorry, but I'm not convinced.'

Time to bring in the big guns. 'The email I got telling me I'd won said that they'd write to us confirming the details. Maybe the letter arrived this morning.'

'Do you want to go and check?' she asked, looking uncertain.

Kieron raced to the front door and picked up the letter that he had placed on the doormat when he'd arrived, ten minutes earlier. Bradley and Bex had written it an hour or so ago, and then printed it out and put it in an envelope. It had joined several other letters that his mother had left lying there. He knew all too well that she tended to let the mail build up, unopened, until it was a trip-hazard, and only then would she go through opening the envelopes and complaining in a low voice.

'Here. "Parent or Guardian of Kieron Mellor" – that's you, isn't it? You open it.'

His mother weighed the envelope in her hand. 'Good-quality paper,' she said. She slid a fingernail beneath the flap and opened it. Several sheets of paper were inside. She took them out and started to read.

'Very polite,' she murmured as she scanned the pages. 'It's not a form letter. Good grammar and spelling too. Those fake emails that come in telling you that someone wants to send you ten thousand dollars if you only provide them with your bank details and a ten-dollar handling fee are always really badly written. I often wonder if they do it deliberately, to filter out people who are too suspicious and leave behind the idiots who are likely to fall for the con. So – yes, it's from the record company, and it says you've won their competition to name the next album for the band Lethal Insomnia – first prize, an all-expenses paid trip to Albuquerque to meet the band and watch them recording the album.' She glanced up at him. 'What was your title? I hope it wasn't something horrible. I know the kind of music you listen to.'

Kieron's mind suddenly went blank. All of the preparation and planning, all of the effort in creating the website and the letter and making sure the story hung together and made sense, and they hadn't done the simplest thing – they hadn't actually come up with his winning entry! He had to think of something, quickly, or his mother would suspect it was all a ruse. He couldn't claim that he'd forgotten – how could he forget something that important? But what would Lethal Insomnia call their new album? What kind of title would make sense?

He quickly ransacked his brain for ideas, but everything he came up with was boring, stupid or obvious.

'Come on,' she said, 'you can tell me. Don't be embarrassed. After all, everyone's going to know about it soon.'

'*Saccades*,' he said suddenly. He had no idea where the word had come from. It had just popped into his mind.

'*Saccades*?' she repeated. 'What does that mean?'

'It's the medical term for the small, involuntary movements that the eye makes,' he explained, remembering a split second before speaking. 'When you're looking at something, like someone's eyes when you're talking to them, your gaze actually moves around randomly over a small area, taking in all kinds of other details that you don't even realise. I thought it was a good, interesting word, and there aren't any other albums with that name. That's the kind of thing you have to watch for if you're in a band: calling an album something like *Live in Newcastle* when there's already sixteen different *Live in Newcastle* albums out there.'

'Wow,' she said, looking impressed. 'You know so much more than I do. How do you cram all that knowledge into your head?'

'Sometimes I wish I couldn't,' he admitted, relieved.

His mother turned back to the letter. It was strange watching her face – she didn't move her lips, like Sam did when he read something, but her eyebrows moved up and down slightly, and her eyes opened wider and then narrowed as her brain processed and reacted to the words on the paper.

'Actually,' she said cautiously, 'this does look OK. The woman who wrote this – Chloe Gibbons, her name is; she apparently works in the publicity department at the record company – says that I can phone her any time. She says she appreciates how much of a surprise this is, and how it would raise suspicions in any sensible parent's mind, and she says that she'd be happy to come up to Newcastle, meet us for lunch and talk it through.' She nodded. 'I have to say, I like her already.'

'Chloe Gibbons' was of course Bex, and she was only just up the road, but she and Kieron had agreed that his mother needed the reassurance of meeting someone that was part of this apparent competition.

'So what do you think?' Kieron asked nervously.

'I think I'm going to give this Chloe Gibbons a ring,' his mother said, getting up off the sofa clumsily while still holding her glass of wine in one hand and the letter in the other, 'and see if she works weekends.'

'She works for a rock band,' Kieron pointed out. 'She probably works all kinds of hours.'

Kieron watched as his mother headed towards the kitchen. Part of him wanted to follow, just so he could hear at least one side of the conversation with Bex, but another part of him knew that it was best to let his mother have the lead on this. What was the phrase they used on TV sometimes, in pretentious documentaries? She needed to 'take ownership' of it.

He sat there nervously, hearing voices from the kitchen. He couldn't tell if his mother was angry, grateful, suspicious or amused. He thought about turning the TV up to distract himself, or finding some game on his mother's tablet to play, but he knew he wouldn't be paying attention to whatever was happening. He was too on edge.

Eventually he heard his mother saying goodbye. It was a few moments before she came back into the living room, and when she did her expression was serious. She sat on the arm of the sofa and stared at him for a few seconds. He forced himself to say nothing.

'Right – there's good news, bad news, and then more good news,' she said. 'The first lot of good news is this all seems above board, and this Chloe Gibbons is happy to travel up tomorrow and meet us for lunch somewhere near the station and explain more.'

'And the bad news?' Kieron asked.

'The bad news is that the only dates that the record company can offer are right in the middle of a new project I've got starting at work. It's a really unfortunate coincidence. Kieron – I won't be able to go. I'm sorry.'

'Does that mean *I* won't be going?'

She shook her head. 'Not necessarily – Chloe has said that she'll be going along anyway to make sure everything goes OK with the trip, and she's more than happy to look after you – if, of course, I agree when we meet tomorrow. Obviously I'm not going to leave you in the hands of someone I don't like or trust. I'm really sorry I won't be able to go – are you all right about flying out to America with just this Chloe woman?'

Kieron was more than happy to fly anywhere with Bex, but he put on a serious face and said, 'I think I'll be OK once I've met her. After all, I've got to grow up some time.'

'You already have,' his mother said sadly, 'and so fast.' She smiled. 'Let's order a takeaway to celebrate.'

'Hang on,' Kieron said, remembering, 'you said there was more news. What is it?'

'Oh – yes.' His mother grinned triumphantly. Kieron got nervous whenever he saw that smile. It was the expression she had whenever she thought she'd done something wonderful for him, like buy him a book that he knew he would never read or an album by a band he hated. 'I asked this Chloe person if, given that I wasn't able to come, perhaps you could take someone else as a guest. She sounded a bit surprised, as if it hadn't occurred to her, but she said yes, she supposed so, depending on who it was. I suggested your friend – Sam. I hope that's all right – I'd feel a lot better if you had a friend with you. It'll stop you from getting lonely. And of course it'll be really good for Sam. I know his family didn't have a holiday this year either.' Her face fell. 'Oh, I hope they don't think this is like charity or something. I'll stress that it's a free trip and you won it in a competition.'

'And this – Chloe – she was OK with Sam coming along?'

'She seemed fine with it. I'll go and give Sam's mum a ring. You wait here. Oh, and I'll order that takeaway. Indian OK with you?'

'Yeah, fine,' he said as she walked back into the kitchen. For some reason she always made phone calls out of his earshot. It had started when she and his father were splitting up, and afterwards when various companies kept calling to chase up unpaid bills, and it had just become a habit. Kieron was surprised to realise that he wasn't sure how he felt about Sam coming along. On the one hand Sam was his friend, but on the other hand he felt as if this was *his* adventure.

A sudden flush of shame made his cheeks burn. He wasn't being fair. Sam had been hurt by the fascist Blood and Soil organisation, and he'd risked his life helping Kieron and Bex. He deserved to come along. It was a shame they wouldn't be seeing Lethal Insomnia, but it would be good to have someone else his age to compare notes with, and play games with on the flight. He got the impression that Bex would be all business once they set out.

His mother's conversation with Sam's mother went well, from what she said when she came back. The takeaway arrived half an hour later, and they both shared chicken korma, lamb pasanda and saag paneer with keema naan and rice. They ended up talking about old times – Kieron's earliest memories – the time he broke his arm by running full tilt into a padded pole at a kids' indoor play place with his arm outstretched, the time he'd seen his first bumble bee and excitedly called out, 'Look, Mummy – there's a fly with its dressing gown on!' And there were some tears when his father came into the conversation. It was one of those magical evenings which happened by accident, but which brought him and his mother closer together – at least for a while.

Later, as Kieron chased the last of the korma sauce around the plate with a scrap of naan bread, he found himself looking at his mother as she checked her tablet for emails. She had lines at the corners of her eyes and corners of her mouth that he hadn't noticed before. A few strands of grey hair were visible as well, swept back over her ears. He was growing up, but she was getting old – bit by bit. Kieron had a sudden vision of their future – her, old and increasingly infirm, and him visiting her and doing those odd jobs around the flat that she couldn't do any more: getting her shopping and collecting her prescriptions. It wasn't a future he wanted. The prospect made him shiver. Where would he be then? Living in his own flat, somewhere in Newcastle? Maybe sharing a place with Sam?

He had to admit it – the future frightened him. There didn't seem to be an upside to growing up: it just meant you had more things to worry about and less energy and free time. He didn't want to get old. He just wanted to stay exactly the age he was forever.

His mother noticed his introspection. 'Cheer up,' she said in a voice slurred by the wine, ruffling his hair. 'It might never happen.'

'Oh, it's going to happen,' he said bleakly. 'I can't stop it from happening.'

Soon after that he realised she'd fallen asleep on the sofa. He cleared the plates away, covered her with a duvet and went to bed.

Sleep didn't come, and eventually he texted Sam to see if he was awake too. *Understand you're coming to America*, he typed. *Wasn't expecting that one.*

Neither was Bex, came the instant reply.

I think my mum caught her by surprise, Kieron texted back.

Do you mind? It seemed like an innocent question, but Kieron could feel Sam worrying, even through the blandness of the text messages.

No stealing vans and driving them around without a licence, Kieron texted back, deliberately reminding Sam of what had happened when Sam had got involved in Kieron's recent adventures.

No chance, Sam texted back, then, *If Lethal Insomnia are actually in Albuquerque while we're there, what are the chances we might run into them?*

Slim to none. Remember – we've got work to do.

You have, Sam pointed out. *I'm sightseeing. Tourist stuff. Bex has made it clear that I'm not to get involved.*

Are you going to be at this lunch tomorrow? Kieron asked. He waited for a response, but nothing came through. After ten minutes he assumed that Sam had fallen asleep in mid-conversation, as he often did. Ten minutes after that, he was asleep as well.

He slept late the next day, and eventually his mum woke him up by opening the door and shouting 'Get dressed – we've got to meet Chloe.' He quickly pulled on the same black jeans, black T-shirt and battered black boots he'd been wearing the day before. When he came out of his room his mother pushed him towards the bathroom, then pulled him back and said, 'Are you wearing fresh clothes?'

'Yes,' he said.

Her eyes narrowed suspiciously. 'All your clothes look the same, so it's difficult to tell.' She sniffed. 'And I can't tell over the smell of the deodorant you've sprayed on. All right, I'll believe you. Go and brush your teeth.'

They drove from the flat into the centre of town and parked in a central car park. Bex – or Chloe, as Kieron had to keep reminding himself – had booked a table at a decent mid-range Italian restaurant.

The greeter who welcomed them and took them to their table recognised Kieron's mother. He smiled at her and nodded, and she smiled back at him. Kieron wondered how often she ate there. Then he wondered who she ate *with*. Then he shuddered, and stopped wondering. She was his *mother*. She didn't have dates.

Sam and *his* mother were already there. Sam's mum was almost the exact opposite of Kieron's: blonde rather than brunette, large rather than slim, and dressed casually – tracksuit bottoms and a T-shirt with a thin waterproof jacket over the top rather than tight jeans and silky blouse. The two women hugged briefly while Kieron and Sam exchanged embarrassed glances.

'Does it get any worse than this?' Kieron murmured.

Sam shrugged. 'Depends. Are a bunch of kids from school going to come in and start laughing at us for being here with our mums?'

'Ah,' Kieron said, 'I've worked out a plan in case that happens. We just find out who the alpha-male or alpha-female is in the group, then quietly tell one of the waiters that it's their birthday. I guarantee, fifteen minutes later the lights will go down, a small iced cake will be bought out with a sparkler stuck into it, and they'll start playing some cheesy birthday song on the music system. It always happens. Then who's going to be embarrassed?'

Sam stared at him sympathetically. 'Been here before for your birthday then?'

Kieron shuddered theatrically. 'Too many times.'

They both looked up as someone arrived at the table, assuming it was the waiter again, taking drinks orders, but it was Bex. She looked . . . efficient, Kieron thought. Just like a publicity assistant should look. He wondered whether she'd brought the trouser suit with her from Mumbai or she'd gone out and bought it five minutes ago. She held a folder by her side.

She didn't even glance at Kieron or Sam. Instead she looked from Kieron's mum to Sam's mum and back again. 'Mrs Mellor?'

Kieron's mum half stood and shook hands. 'That's me – but, please, call me Veronica,' she said, 'and this is Holly. She and I were pregnant with these two at the same time. We were in adjoining beds in hospital.'

Bex shook hands with Sam's mum. 'I'm Chloe,' she said; 'Chloe Gibbons.' She turned to look at Kieron, then Sam. 'And which one of you is Kieron?'

Feeling strangely like he was in some kind of stage play where everyone knew their lines but him, Kieron held a hand up. 'It's me.'

'Congratulations, Kieron.' Bex sat down, a professional smile and not a flicker of recognition on her face. 'You and your friend – Sam, is it? – you're going to enjoy this trip so much. It'll be the adventure of a lifetime!'

Kieron suddenly realised with a slight shock that Bex – in her guise as Chloe – was wearing the ARCC glasses. They were thin and almost invisible. He wondered if Bradley was on the other end, feeding her information, but kicked himself. Bradley wasn't physically capable of operating the kit – that was the whole reason for this elaborate charade. Perhaps she just felt more comfortable – more like she was undercover – when she was wearing them.

'Thanks for coming all this way just to talk to us,' Kieron's mother said. 'It's a lot of trouble for you to go to. Where are you based? London?'

'Manchester,' Bex said. 'That's where the record company has its UK headquarters And I'm more than happy to be here to reassure you that this is all above board and these two will be perfectly safe in our hands.'

Kieron tried to move his head sideways to see whether she had an earpiece in her ear, but his mother punched him on the shoulder. 'Stop squirming.' She smiled at Bex. 'Teenagers – they just can't sit still. I don't envy you – having to look after these two on a long flight. How long is it actually?'

'Seven hours to Washington DC,' Bex replied, 'then another four hours on from there to Albuquerque.'

'And this *is* free, isn't it?' Sam's mother asked. 'I mean, we don't have to pay *anything*?' She sounded as if the concept was so incredible that she just couldn't believe it.

Bex shook her head. 'That's right – the record company takes care of everything: flights, food, accommodation. It's all part of the prize.'

'And the band – what are they called? Lethal Insomnia? – they're actually going to use the album title that Kieron suggested?' his mum asked.

The words *Don't ask her what it is!* started running through Kieron's mind. He'd not warned Bex in advance about the answer he'd had to make up on the spot the night before.

'It's a great title,' Bex said smoothly. 'And the band love it. It'll *definitely* be the title of the next album.'

Kieron wondered to himself how Bex was going to manage that. Perhaps she'd get him to use the ARCC kit to hack the record-company servers and change the name of the album just before it came out without anyone realising. And all the publicity material and advertising. More likely either his mum would forget, or he'd have to explain to her that someone at the record company had had a change of heart.

'Let me take you through the details,' Bex said, opening her folder and pulling out a sheaf of notes. For the next twenty minutes – punctuated only by the waiter arriving and taking their order and then bringing their food – she went through what Kieron realised must have been something she and Bradley had created overnight, but which seemed totally professional and realistic – flights, hotels, dates, times . . . everything. The main thing he remembered was that the weather in Albuquerque was going to be hot – very hot – but dry – very dry. Oh, and they'd be staying in a hotel. An actual hotel.

'Do you know the first thing I'm going to do when we get there?' Sam asked, leaning across to him.

'What?'

'Head down to the local mall.'

Kieron stared at him. 'What's the point? We spend half our lives at the mall *here*.'

'Yeah, but this is an *American* mall!'

Hearing their names, they both turned around to hear Bex saying, 'What about passports? Do they both have them?'

They'd discussed this the day before – Bex had been confident that they could get hold of a fake passport for Kieron if necessary, but he'd told her that he still had one from a school trip a few years before. Sam had been on the same trip.

Both of their mothers said, 'Yes,' at the same time.

'What about visas?' Kieron's mother asked.

'It's all done electronically,' Bex said smoothly. 'If you can give me their passport numbers, dates of birth and places of birth, I'll get that organised.'

By that time they'd finished their main courses and

were drifting into dessert territory. In her guise as Chloe Gibbons, Bex engaged Kieron and Sam in conversation, asking them about their likes and dislikes, their lives, and what exactly they liked about the music of Lethal Insomnia. Kieron couldn't fault her professionalism. She'd obviously been researching the band; she knew their names, which instruments they played and everything.

'I have to ask,' Sam's mother asked as she finished the last spoonful of her lemon torte, 'do you actually *like* this music? I mean, we're older than you, but you're older than *them*.' She indicated Kieron and Sam with her thumb. 'Which side of the fence do you fall?'

'I *have* to say,' Bex answered smoothly, 'that I love the music. I have to say that because I'm the publicist, and that's what I get paid to say.' She leaned theatrically across the table. 'But to be honest, I prefer something a bit smoother; less spiky. More of a tune. And where you can actually hear the words.'

The lunch broke up shortly after that, with Bex saying that a car would pick the boys up at six o'clock in the morning, two days later. She left – supposedly to catch her train – and while the two mothers were saying their goodbyes, Sam looked at Kieron and muttered, 'Well, I have to say, undercover work is a lot more boring than I'd expected.'

'Yes, but the food is good,' Kieron pointed out.

CHAPTER SIX

They flew out from Heathrow Airport on the lunchtime flight.

For Bex international travel was always dead time, a pause between more interesting things, but it hadn't occurred to her that neither Kieron nor Sam had ever flown before. The whole experience was new to them, from the check-in (which was quick and painless), through the security checks (annoying and embarrassing, especially when Kieron had to take his boots and belt off because some pieces of metal somewhere in the massive built-up soles and the buckle set off the security scanner) to the wait in the departures lounge (tedious). Watching them experiencing everything afresh almost made her re-evaluate the whole process of travel. Almost.

'Why is there a smoked-salmon and seafood bar?' Sam asked as he looked across the crowd of travellers who were sleeping or sitting and staring blankly into space.

'What?' Bex asked, looking up from the ebook reader she'd bought with her. She'd loaded it a while back with all those novels that people were supposed to read but never did.

Right now she was fighting her way through James Joyce's *Ulysses*. 'Fighting' was the operative term. Each difficult phrase she deciphered was like a piece of hard-won ground in an interminable war of made-up words and complicated sentences. She was half inclined to jack it in and move on to something simpler, like *War and Peace*.

'Over there,' Sam said. 'Look. There's a kind of fast-food counter right in the centre of the concourse. It's like a burger bar, except that they're serving smoked salmon, oysters and prawns.'

Kieron shrugged. 'Maybe people like it.'

'Yeah, but you don't find that anywhere else. Why would people in an airport want to eat seafood?'

Bex searched her mind for reasons, but failed to come up with anything. She'd passed it a hundred times without noticing. 'I'm guessing,' she said, 'that it dates back to the 1950s, when intercontinental travel started became something for ordinary people, not just the super-rich. Passengers wanted to have an experience that made them feel like they were special.'

'Yeah,' Sam said, 'but seafood? How special is that?' He frowned. 'I hope I don't end up sitting next to someone who's been there. I'll be smelling prawns for the whole flight.'

'I could check it out on the ARCC glasses,' Kieron said, reaching into his jacket.

Bex hit him on the arm with her ebook reader. Gently. 'Do *not* do that. I don't want us to attract any attention, and I don't want you using the ARCC equipment unless it's in furtherance of the mission. No playing around.'

He scowled, but he brought his hand out. 'I was just trying to help,' he muttered.

Once they boarded the aircraft, they had seven hours of tedium ahead of them. They had three seats together, with Sam by the window and Bex on the aisle.

'Is that so you can quickly leap into action if anything bad happens?' Kieron asked her as they strapped themselves in.

'No,' she said patiently, 'it's so I can get to the toilet without having to clamber over you two.' Actually, it *was* so she had freedom of movement if there was trouble. The chances of any terrorist activity were slim, especially flying out of Heathrow where security was intense, but she wanted to be in a position where if anyone looked as if they were trying to take the battery out of their laptop and ignite it, or set fire to their chemically treated underpants, she could do something. Not that she wanted to – especially not in the case of chemically treated underpants. But at least she had a clear line of sight up and down the aisle. That made her feel more secure.

A rogue memory from years ago struck her, and she smiled. On one of her first trips to America Bex had been sitting diagonally across the aisle from a man who, she'd noticed at check-in, had a glass eye. Halfway through the flight she had got the distinct impression that she was being watched. Bex trusted her sixth sense. She wasn't sure whether there *really* was such a thing as a sixth sense or whether it was just the other five senses picking up on something that was just beneath the level of conscious detection, but previous intuitive feelings had turned out to be true, so she was inclined to listen when unexplained alarm bells started ringing in her head. So she had casually put her book down, stretched and looked around as if she was searching for a stewardess. The man with the glass eye, sitting diagonally behind her across the aisle, was staring right at the back of her neck. He didn't even try to look away. Bex stared back at him, frowning, to see if he'd get embarrassed, but he just kept staring. And then she realised: the man had fallen asleep, but his glass eye was still open and staring at her. As she turned back to her book, she'd reflected that it made sense. It wasn't as if the light in the cabin was going to keep him awake.

'What's so funny?' Kieron asked.

'Just remembering something,' she said.

Kieron and Sam had both bought their hand-held game consoles, so they spent most of the time playing – either individually or networked together. Kieron fell asleep a couple of hours after take-off, while still playing his game, and he gradually slid sideways until his head ended up on Bex's shoulder. She debated pushing him away, but she didn't want to wake him up. And besides, he looked so young and vulnerable, with his eyes closed and his hair hanging across his face.

How had she got herself into this situation with Kieron and Sam, she wondered as she stared down at him? This had not been part of the career plan that she and Bradley had worked out. Each individual step had made sense at the time, but the end result was that she was embarking on an undercover intelligence mission in the company of two teenagers. This was not standard operating procedure for agents.

They *had* proved themselves in action though. She had to admit that. They were brave, and they were resourceful. And they were her last, best hope of exposing the traitor within MI6's SIS-TERR organisation.

Kieron woke up two hours later. His entire body language changed as he moved from the relaxation of sleep to the sudden realisation that he had his head on a girl's shoulder, from totally unselfconscious to very tense and awkward in a few seconds. Bex quietly leaned back and closed her eyes, pretending to be asleep as well. Kieron surreptitiously moved his head off her shoulder and straightened up. She left it a few minutes, then ostentatiously yawned and said, 'How long was I asleep for?'

'I don't know,' he said. 'I wasn't paying attention.'

She found herself wondering if he had a girlfriend. Or a boyfriend: either was fine. He and Sam weren't together, obviously – they were just good friends – but he never talked about seeing anyone else. Girls made him nervous though: that was obvious by the way he wouldn't look directly at Bex when he was talking to her if he could help it, and the way sometimes, if he wasn't talking to her, he'd surreptitiously look over at her, checking her out.

She hoped he wasn't developing a crush on her. That would be awkward.

There were movies on the in-flight entertainment system. Bex had thought Kieron and Sam might want to settle down and watch them, but actually they were bland things – comedies or dramas that had nothing in them that kids would find disturbing. Kieron had apparently downloaded a whole load of horror films onto his games tablet, but he didn't seem to be in the mood to watch them. That was probably just as well – there was a family seated in the row behind them, and Bex didn't want the young kids looking through the gaps between the seats and seeing the kind of horrible stuff that teenagers these days seemed to like watching. The in-flight entertainment system did, however, have a channel where you could watch the aircraft's progress on a crude map, and Kieron seemed to become almost hypnotised for a while by the way the aeroplane icon slowly inched its way across the Atlantic, leaving a dotted line behind it.

'Why's the pilot taking such a long route?' Sam asked, leaning over and glancing at the screen.

'What do you mean?' Bex asked.

Sam traced the path of the aircraft – a curve that led up from London, passed over the tip of Iceland, peaked over Greenland, then descended to hit the eastern coast of Canada. 'He's going miles out of his way,' Sam pointed out. 'He could have gone in a straight line. It would have been a lot quicker.'

Bex stared at him. 'Do you do geography at school?' she asked.

'Yes,' he said defensively. 'Why?'

'The Earth is a sphere, right? A ball. You've seen globes with all the continents marked on?'

'Ye-es.'

'But the map on that screen is flat, isn't it?'

'Yee-es.' Sam had an expression on his face that suggested he was expecting some kind of trick or punchline.

'Well, the curved surface of the Earth has to be distorted to make it look flat on the map. If you plotted the aircraft's course on an actual globe, you'd find it was actually the shortest route between England and America. It's not a completely straight line – that would take it right through the Earth's crust – but it's the closest thing you can get on the surface of a sphere. It's called a Great Circle.'

'Oh.' Sam shrugged. 'Who knew?'

'Well,' Bex said carefully, 'pretty much everyone, I thought.'

They changed aircraft at Washington Dulles Airport, after a landing so gentle it was almost undetectable. It wasn't Bex's favourite airport, not by any means. Too impersonal, no decent shops and no decent restaurants. You'd think that the main international airport of the capital city of the most important nation in the world would try to be a little more impressive, but no.

It impressed Kieron and Sam, though, if only because they recognised the control tower from the Bruce Willis action film *Die Hard 2*. Which they referred to as 'that old action movie', making Bex feel really old.

The second leg, from Dulles to Albuquerque, was on a smaller jet with two seats on either side of a central aisle, rather than the 3-4-3 configuration on the aircraft that had bought them in to Dulles. Kieron and Sam both had window seats, and because this aeroplane flew lower for much of the journey, they spent most of the time with their faces pressed against the Plexiglas, staring at the terrain passing underneath.

Half an hour out from Albuquerque, Kieron invited Bex to look out of his window. 'Isn't that amazing?' he breathed.

Bex gazed out. They were passing over a broken landscape of vaguely reddish rocks – either the Sangre de Cristo Wilderness in Colorado or the Pecos Wilderness in New Mexico, she thought, remembering the research she'd done on the journey before setting out. In the unlikely event that the aircraft might have to make an emergency landing, it was always useful to know where you might be. Not that it had ever happened to her, but there could always be a first time. The thing was to make sure that it wasn't the last – at least not for the wrong reasons.

Below the aircraft, away to one side , she saw what looked like a massive discontinuity in the ground: a rough line where everything on one side was several hundred metres above everything on the other. Along the cliff-edge she could see an apparently endless line of huge wind turbines, spinning slowly. The low sun cast their shadows long across the landscape.

'Impressive,' she said, and she meant it.

'This is the best trip I've ever been on,' Kieron murmured. 'Whatever happens, thank you for agreeing to bring us.'

Albuquerque airport shared its runways with the US Air Force's Kirtland Air Force Base, so there were several sleek fighter jets on the tarmac when they landed. Predictably, Kieron and Sam spent their time comparing notes and trying to identify them. *Boys*, Bex thought with a surprising but not unwelcome twinge of affection. It didn't matter that they were both emos with a massive disdain for governments and the military: show them some actual hardware and they'd be talking about maximum airspeed and armament. It was the same trading-card mentality that led to things like Pokémon and Yu-Gi-Oh! Bradley would have been the same.

The airport buildings – well, the civilian ones anyway – were cool and spacious, influenced largely by the artwork and the dwellings of the local Navajo people. It didn't look like England, and it didn't smell like England, and the boys were entranced. They in turn attracted a lot of strange glances from the Americans retrieving their luggage at the same time. The hairstyles and the clothes that helped Sam and Kieron blend in in Newcastle town centre – at least, to an extent – made them stand out among the shorts, T-shirts and baseball caps that seemed to be de rigueur for the typical American teenager. Bex mentally cursed. She should have anticipated that. Drawing attention was something she tried to avoid whenever possible, but these two were about as subtle as a pair of pandas in a supermarket. She had to get them into something more suitable, and quickly.

'Are we going to the hotel?' Kieron asked as they walked out of the terminal towards the area where the rental cars were parked. The air was warm and smelled of dust and aircraft fuel. The sky was an incredibly clear blue. 'Only Sam thought –'

'We're going to the mall,' she said, cutting him off. 'I need to get you into the kind of clothes that a teenage technical genius would wear. Something smart but casual. Sam too.'

'Why me?' Sam asked, affronted.

'Just in case you're seen together,' Bex said, thinking quickly. 'We don't want anything that looks too odd, like an emo and a tech entrepreneur together.'

'We're not emos,' Kieron grumbled. 'We're greebs.'

'Whatever. You're going undercover – remember?'

Albuquerque was a smallish city, and the airport was close to the centre. It took less than twenty minutes to drive along wide roads and past low, one- or two-storey buildings, in which Mexican restaurants and car dealerships seemed to alternate, to a mall that was actually just across the road from their hotel. Bex parked the hire car out in the open and started to lead the way towards the shops, but she realised after a few moments that neither Kieron nor Sam were following. She turned, to find them gazing in wonder into the distance. She followed their gaze, trying to work out what it was that had paralysed them.

'What's the matter?' she asked eventually, giving up.

'Mountains,' Kieron said. 'Look.'

She looked. There were, indeed, mountains, rising up from the edge of town.

'Yes, the Sandia Mountains,' she said.

'We've never seen mountains before,' Sam explained, still staring. 'We've got things called mountains in England, but they're really just hills. These are *real* mountains.'

Bex shrugged. 'Seen one mountain, seen them all,' she said. 'Come on, let's go.'

The mall was buttressed at each end with a large department store. Bex took the boys inside the mall through the food court and then along rows of smaller shops towards the nearest, found the men's department, then selected appropriate clothes for each of them – casual shorts, T-shirts and baseball caps, like the teens in the airport had been wearing, and slightly more formal lightweight jackets, cotton shirts and pressed jeans for any business dealings.

'I'm not wearing this stuff,' Sam protested.

'Then you can go home,' Bex said firmly. 'I can exchange tickets and send you right back. You've done the journey out – you can find your own way back with no trouble, I'm sure.'

'But –' Sam held up the garish shorts – 'no greeb would be seen dead in stuff like this!'

'You're not a greeb while you're here,' Bex pointed out in a low voice. 'You're undercover, remember? Pretending to be something else. *Somebody* else. And the main point about being undercover is that you don't *want* to be found dead.' She took a deep breath. 'If you don't like the clothes, you're *really* not going to like the next bit.'

'What next bit?' Kieron asked suspiciously.

'The bit where the two of you get your hair cut.' Before their stunned expressions could turn into howls of protest, she said quickly, 'I spotted a barber's shop across the car park. You can keep it long, but we've got to find a way to make sure that it fits in with the clothes. Long but neat, in other words. And those piercings are going to have to come out.'

Fortunately they were too shocked to actually say a word.

117

They both just closed their eyes for a few moments, and nodded.

'I think we both knew it was going to come to this,' Kieron said, his expression pained.

Sam nodded. 'Undercover opportunities for greebs are fairly limited. We talked about this before we left. If we've got to conform to go undercover, then so be it. Bring it on. Dress us up however you want.'

'Didn't Courtney and her friends used to do that to you when you were little?' Kieron asked. 'I'm sure she said there are photographs of you in a dress that they'd forced you to wear.'

Sam shrugged. 'Don't have to force me, these days,' he said off-handedly. 'Come on – let's get this over with.'

The barber was an elderly black man who'd had his shop since before the mall was built. 'They wanted me to sell this ol' place,' he told Bex as he cut a wincing Kieron's hair, 'but I told them no. So they changed their plans and built around me – left me here on the edge of the car park. Which is a good place to be. The ladies, they shop, an' their husbands come in here for a trim or a shave an' a chat. You guys ain't from around here, are you? That accent – Australian, ain't it?'

Afterwards she led the two shell-shocked teens back past the car to the mall again. 'Come on,' she said. 'Let's get some ice cream. I saw a place in the food court selling flavours I didn't even know existed.'

After Kieron had demolished his black-walnut-and-honey ice-cream sundae and Sam had finished his lavender and green tea with shortbread crumble – both covered with several different varieties of chocolate and caramel sauce – Bex shepherded them both back to the car. It had been sitting in direct sunlight for several hours, and Bex felt sweat breaking out all over her body the moment she slid into the driver's seat. She quickly clicked the air conditioning on, and drove to the hotel.

She'd booked into a mid-range Marriott – one of several in the city. She had one room; the boys were in one down the corridor. 'Unpack and rest for an hour or so,' she told them. 'Then we'll get an early dinner and plan on what we're going to do next.'

Dinner was steak and pasta in the hotel's restaurant. The ice cream didn't appear to have dented either Kieron or Sam's appetites.

'Do you think Lethal Insomnia are staying in this hotel?' Sam asked, gazing around at what, to him, was probably a very upmarket place to eat. Bex had to admit that he looked good in his new clothes, and with his hair shortened and tidied. Kieron too. They 'scrubbed up well', as her mother would have put it.

'I doubt it,' she replied. 'I didn't notice any TVs thrown out of top-floor windows or expensive cars floating in the swimming pool.' At their blank looks she added, 'It's a rock 'n' roll thing. From before you were born. Right – let's get down to business.' She glanced at Kieron. 'We need to get you into the Goldfinch Institute. You've got something to show them – this idea for a non-lethal weapon that you and Sam have come up with – but that's for once you're in there. The first step is to actually get through the door.'

'I've got an idea about that too,' Kieron said. He glanced around, much like Sam had done a few moments before, but with less awe and more nervousness. 'Do you think we might be being – you know – bugged? Listened to?'

Bex shook her head. 'Nobody knows we're here. I've made sure of that. What's your idea?'

'I use the ARCC kit to hack into the Goldfinch Institute computers. They'll have all kinds of firewalls protecting the internal, top-secret stuff, but their outward-facing admin server is likely to be only lightly protected. It has to be, otherwise it wouldn't let emails in and out, allow them to synchronise calendars and so on. So I'll sneakily create an appointment in the calendar of the guy in charge . . .'

'Todd Zanderbergen,' Bex said.

'Yeah, him. I then turn up at the main reception desk expecting to see him. His PA will be surprised, because she didn't think he had any appointments, but there's unquestionably one in there.'

'Won't they be able to check that it's only just been added?' Bex asked.

Kieron shook his head. 'I can fake the timestamp so it looks like it was created a month ago. They'll assume it didn't show up until the last minute because of some kind of IT problem. So – I go in and talk to him. Then what do I do? Ask about these dead scientists and people who'd been working for him? That's going to make him suspicious, isn't it?'

'OK – two things. Firstly, if you're supposed to be trying to go into business with him you're entitled to ask about anything that concerns you. It's called "Due Diligence" – you thoroughly check a company out before you sign a contract. Say you've noticed that he's been recruiting an unusually large number of staff recently. Ask him what happened – did lots of people resign? Did he fire people?'

'We *know* why he's recruiting,' Sam pointed out. 'Some of his staff have died.'

'Yes,' Bex explained patiently, 'but when you're interrogating someone, you never let on that you know stuff about them. You try to look innocent – see if they tell you what you already know or try to lie.'

'Is that what I'm doing?' Kieron looked impressed and slightly daunted.

'Don't worry,' Bex said reassuringly. 'I'm your backup. I'll be with you every step of the way.'

After dinner they went to Bex's room. Kieron slipped the ARCC glasses on, ready to go to work.

'Hang on,' Bex said, holding up her hand. 'Make sure you don't use your own name when you make the appointment. Use the name Ryan Allen.'

'That's me, is it?' Kieron asked. 'I was wondering if I had an alter ego, like Clark Kent or Bruce Wayne.'

'More like Barry Allen,' Sam muttered. At Bex's questioning glance he added: 'He's the Flash's alter ego. He's a geek.'

'Right,' she said, understanding the reference but pretending she didn't, just for effect.

Kieron frowned, the movement making the ARCC glasses ride up on his nose. 'But what happens if they spot the appointment early? I mean, Todd Zanderbergen's PA is probably going to go through his diary when she gets in in the morning. She'll see it, and she might worry about the fact that she hadn't prepared for it. Isn't she likely to be suspicious?'

Bex shook her head. 'If she's any good – and I can't imagine Zanderbergen employing anyone who isn't – then she'll prepare a briefing pack for her boss on anyone coming in for a meeting – who they are, what they want, where they come from, maybe even some suggestions as to what the benefits to the Goldfinch Institute might be of making a deal with them.'

'So she'll go on the Internet and check me out,' Kieron said with an edge of worry in his voice. 'And she'll find out that there's no information about me.'

'Oh, but there is.' Bex smiled. 'Before we left, Bradley put together a complete dossier on Ryan Allen. I'm going to spend the next couple of hours seeding it around the Internet – not obviously, but scattered around in databases and stuff. There'll be information out there on where Ryan Allen went to school, what his local paper wrote about him when he won a science prize, all kinds of little things. Nothing obvious – there's quite a few people who don't have a digital presence at all – but enough to satisfy their curiosity.'

Kieron nodded. 'You've done this before,' he observed.

'It's what I do. These days most of our jobs are as much about the digital information that's out there as they are about disguises and adventures. More even.'

Bex watched while Kieron used the ARCC kit to infiltrate the Goldfinch Institute's servers and place a spurious appointment in Todd Zanderbergen's calendar. His hands moved gracefully and expertly through the air, moving data around and altering it. He really was a natural at this, she thought admiringly. If she was going to be using that same kit to provide information to *him* when he was in the meeting the next day, then she was going to have to get some practice in. Maybe a couple of hours while the boys were asleep. She'd trained herself to get by on only about five hours a night – she might as well use the rest of the time to prepare.

'Right,' Kieron said eventually. 'That's done. I'm in for 11 a.m. tomorrow.'

'In that case, go back to your room and get some sleep. Rest, and I'll see you for breakfast at about eight.'

'Chances are I won't sleep,' Sam muttered. 'Jet lag.'

'Jet lag won't really affect you, flying west across the Atlantic. It'll hit you when we fly back though,' Bex said. She rooted around in her handbag and bought out a container of pills. 'Take one of these, both of you.'

'What are they?' Kieron asked suspiciously.

'Melatonin. It's a hormone the body produces naturally at night. It gets your body ready to go to sleep. We're eight hours behind the UK here, so your brains think it's now morning and you've stayed up through the night. Take the melatonin and you'll be fooling your body into resetting its clock.'

'OK.' Kieron took the container tentatively. 'If you're sure.'

The two boys went to their room, and Bex set to work, using the ARCC kit to scatter little traces of Ryan Allen's life around the Internet, just difficult enough to find that anyone looking would be persuaded that they were actual facts rather than constructed bits of fake data. It took her three hours, but it was useful. It had been a while since she had used the equipment – Bradley was the expert – but the mental muscle-memory was still there. By the time she'd finished she felt confident that she could support Kieron as well as he'd done for her in Mumbai and Pakistan.

Still wide awake, she decided to go for a drive. It was good practice to reconnoitre in advance if you were going on a mission. Discover the ways in and the ways out. Work out your options for in case anything went wrong. So she left her room, walked out to the hire car and drove away from central Albuquerque, along wide and gently curving roads towards the desert that surrounded the city. Night had fallen, and rather than turn the air conditioning on she rolled the windows down and let the breezes and sounds of the resting city come to her. The heat of the day had faded to a comfortable warmth now, but the scent of desert flowers was still marked, along with the smell of kerosene drifting across from the Air Force base. Through force of habit she checked her rear-view mirror every thirty seconds or so to see if there was ever a set of headlights that remained stubbornly behind her, but the cars she saw all turned off the road after a while, their drivers heading to their own homes, to restaurants, cinemas or bars. There was no reason for anyone to be following her, but it was like indicating before making a turn: something her brain automatically did without her having to tell it. A survival instinct.

The Goldfinch Institute was located some ten miles north of Albuquerque, on a route that she noticed with a smile eventually led to the town of Roswell. The boys would love that: Roswell was where the fabled Area 51 was supposed to be located: the military base which housed the hangars where a crashed alien spacecraft had allegedly been kept and evaluated by the American military since the 1950s. Rubbish of course, but it was a legend that just wouldn't die.

The Institute itself was a mile down a spur road off the main highway. There were no signs for it: if you were heading for the Goldfinch Institute it was because you wanted to go there and already knew where it was. A subtle intelligence test, of sorts. Bex slowed down and parked on the dusty hard shoulder just before the turning, in the shadow of a massive advertising hoarding telling her all about the health benefits of some miracle juicer. She checked the car's satnav. The spur road was marked, but according to the map it led nowhere: no houses, no towns, nothing. Her original intention had been to drive down and check out the main gates and the fences – drive around the Institute if possible and take some photographs – but she decided against it. There was a very good chance there would be CCTV cameras trained on the road, and number-plate recognition software that would note her car's details for later analysis. Maybe even low-light, image-intensifying cameras that could get a good image of her face, even in the dark. It wasn't worth taking the chance.

She was just about to turn around and head back to town, get a few hours' sleep, when she saw a light down the spur road. On instinct, Bex turned her own headlights off. For a while the light seemed to just bounce around, illuminating the dusty tarmac and the scrubby cactus-like bushes that lined the route on either side, before it resolved into the twin beams of a car's headlights. The sparse starlight, and the splash back from the beams, soon revealed the bare lines of a sports car manoeuvring along the road towards her.

At the junction with the main road, the car slowed down before turning. Bex sat quietly, not moving. Maybe it was a late worker, heading home, or maybe it was the Institute's security guards on patrol. Either way, she didn't want them to know she was there.

The car accelerated into a turn, heading back the way Bex had come, towards Albuquerque. When its lights caught the advertising hoarding and reflected momentarily back, illuminating the driver, Bex felt the breath catch in her throat as she recognised Tara Gallagher, her old friend from MI6 training. She was older, and she'd dyed her hair red, but Bex would have known her anywhere. They'd spent too long together in muddy ditches and in dimly lit bars for that.

The car rounded the corner and sped away. Tara's head didn't turn. She hadn't seen Bex.

It took fifteen seconds before Bex felt she could breathe again. What were the odds that she and Tara would end up at the same remote road junction in a foreign country at the same time of night? Was that an omen, or was it a warning? Bex wasn't sure, but as she drove back to town – slowly, so she didn't run the risk of overtaking Tara and giving her old work colleague (and, she admitted to herself, one-time friend) a possible view of her face – she turned the unlikely encounter over and over in her mind. One way or the other, she decided, it was a bad sign.

Tara's car had either got to town way ahead of her or had turned off, perhaps down a side road leading to some exclusive development of ranch-style houses, and Bex got back to the hotel without incident. She checked the car park carefully before parking, and used her key card to enter the hotel through a side entrance rather than the main lobby just in case someone was watching. She got to her room, undressed and brushed her teeth and was asleep within moments. She didn't dream.

The next morning she met the boys in the restaurant for breakfast. It took a few moments for her to recognise them: automatically she'd been looking for them in their emo – sorry, *greeb* – guises, but they were neat and tidy, in the clothes she'd bought for them the day before. They'd even washed their hair and shaved the few hairs they had – 'bum fluff', her mum would have called it – from their chins. She felt strangely proud.

Breakfast was the standard American buffet arrangement, and they'd stacked their plates up with bacon, mushrooms, scrambled egg, sausages, hash browns and refried beans. Kieron had even balanced several slices of cheese on top of his pile, while Sam had poured maple syrup over his.

'It's OK,' she said reassuringly, 'you're allowed to go back as many times as you want. You don't have to carry the absolute maximum away on your first visit to the buffet bar.'

They stared at her, wide-eyed.

'*Really?*' Sam asked.

'Really,' she said.

While the boys ate everything on their plates and then went back for more, Bex contented herself with a coffee and toast. After they'd all finished their breakfast, she looked at Kieron.

'Ready for this?' she asked.

'As I'll ever be,' he said.

She smiled. 'You'll be fine.'

Bex slid the ARCC glasses across the table towards him – not the special VR ones that he was used to wearing, and which she had used the night before to seed his new identity across the Internet, but the ones *she* generally wore on missions. The undercover ones. The ones that looked like ordinary glasses, but which had concealed cameras and microphones in the frame that would transmit everything Kieron saw and heard to her, wherever she chose to base herself.

'Put these on,' she said. 'They'll make you look even more like a tech-savvy teenager than you already do.'

As he placed the glasses on his nose, she passed him the tiny earpiece that would slip inside his ear canal and relay everything she said to him, undetectably. She smiled. 'Come on – let's go. We've got an undercover operation to complete.'

CHAPTER SEVEN

As Kieron and Bex drove from the hotel to the Goldfinch Institute – Sam having decided to go back to bed – Kieron spent the first ten minutes trying to get used to the fact that his glasses weren't showing him anything – there was no video feed. Everything was reversed now. Bex had access to the Internet and lots of secret databases; he had nothing.

'Are you OK?' she asked, and he had the bizarre experience of hearing her voice normally and also, slightly tinnily, through the earpiece buried inside his right ear canal.

'Honestly – trying to get used to it,' he said.

'Me too,' she confided. 'I can see the road ahead directly of me, and also through your glasses. It's like watching a 3-D movie with the glasses on backwards: really disconcerting. It's been a long time since I wore *these* glasses in anger.'

Kieron watched the traffic as they drove through Albuquerque. Most of the cars looked familiar – except they seemed larger and shinier – but the trucks! They were massive things, with huge cabs with blacked-out windows and silver exhausts that ran up the side of the cabs like chimneys. And there were adverts everywhere he looked. Adverts for hair products, painkillers, law services and anything else you might want. There were even adverts for candidates in the elections for the local sheriff: photographs of pleasant-faced men with big smiles and big hats, all promising to fix whatever law-enforcement problems existed in the city.

After a while they left the city behind and they were driving through dusty desert. Glancing to his left, Kieron noticed something moving parallel to them. It took a few seconds before he realised that it was a train, but one that had to be ten times longer than any train he'd seen in England. And it had no passengers – just an apparently endless line of cargo containers all joined together. He couldn't see the engine at the front, or the far end.

'This place is incredible,' he murmured.

Bex turned the car off the main road and headed down a narrower track. Five minutes later a cluster of buildings appeared on the horizon. Bright sunlight reflected from blue glass panels that seemed to cover every surface. Each building was wider at the bottom than the top – like pyramids made of glass with the tops cut off. A forest of antennae covered their roofs. No, hang on, Kieron thought, amazed: there *were* some antennae, but they were set among what looked suspiciously like a *real* forest. Thin saplings with leafy tops rising up out of a sea of shrubs.

'Is that . . . ?' he asked.

Bex slowed the car down to a crawl, then took one hand off the wheel and waved it around, accessing the feed from

Kieron's glasses. She must have been zooming in on what he was looking at, because she suddenly said, 'It's like a garden. There's grass, and benches to sit on, and some big shades so people can keep out of the sun.'

'The Goldfinch Institute really cares for its staff,' Kieron observed.

Bex sped the car up again. 'Unless it's all for the use of the man in charge – Todd Zanderbergen.'

'Do these ARCC glasses have reactive lenses?' Kieron asked. ''Cos the sun reflecting off all that glass is really bright.'

'No, but even if they did it would be best not to use them,' Bex answered. 'People don't trust you if they can't see your eyes. Even if you're lying to them, they're more likely to believe you if you're not wearing sunglasses. Strange, but true.'

The buildings got closer and closer, looming up over the horizon like some bright, shining citadel. Kieron felt his stomach start to knot with tension. This was suddenly becoming real.

A three-metre-high chain-link security fence appeared. Coils of razor wire had been strung along the top. There would be no getting over that in a hurry. And even if it was possible, another fence rose up three metres behind it. Each fence had signs warning anyone who got close enough that they were electrified. The desiccated corpses of various birds lined up along the base of the fences – crows mainly, Kieron thought, but a few hawks as well – just served to reinforce the warnings. Overkill? Perhaps.

131

They continued along the road as it curved to follow the fence. After a few minutes they came to a gap blocked by waist-high metal sheets set into the ground. They seemed to glow in the sunlight. The air itself shimmered above them, indicating how much heat they had absorbed. A security cabin sat just inside the fence with a small tarmacked car-parking area just outside. A few metres to one side, a row of turnstiles with small boxes at eye level allowed staff to enter and leave the premises.

Bex drove the car up to the metal panels. Kieron checked out their reflections in the shiny metal. Both he and Bex looked calm and professional, he was relieved to see.

A uniformed security guard armed with a handgun strapped ostentatiously to his waist stepped out. He wore sunglasses and carried a clipboard, and his uniform looked as if it had been cleaned and ironed just moments before. He held up a large hand. His other hand was on the handle of his gun.

'Please turn off your engine, ma'am. What is your business here today?'

Bex lowered her window and was about to say something when Kieron put his hand on her arm.

'Let me handle this,' he said. Lowering his own window, he waved a casual hand at the guard. 'Ryan Allen,' he called. 'I have an appointment with Mr Zanderbergen.'

The guard checked his clipboard. 'Mr Allen?'

'That's what I said,' Kieron said loudly.

'Could you step out of the car, please?'

Kieron waved his hand dismissively. 'It's cool in here, and

it's hot outside. I'm from England; I don't do "warm", let alone "hot". Let me in, or don't let me in. I have something your boss wants to see.'

The guard's expression didn't change, but his body language suggested he was getting tense. He pulled a walkie-talkie from the back of his belt and spoke into it. Soon he said, 'OK, if you could park up on the tarmac, they'll send a buggy for you.'

'"Buggy" sounds very open,' Kieron called back. 'I told you – I don't like the heat.'

The guard held his hands up apologetically. 'I'm sorry, sir, but it's security. No choice in the matter.'

'Don't push it,' Bex said softly. 'You're in. Get out and wait for the buggy. I'll park up and wait for you.' She paused, and smiled. 'Oh, and well done. That was perfectly managed.'

'Wish me luck,' he said, getting out of the car. The dry heat of the desert seemed to suddenly hit him in the face. He felt a prickle on his forehead as if he should be sweating, but there was no sweat. It evaporated instantly. He supposed that might be an issue if he spent too long outside – he'd be dehydrating without realising it. He'd have to watch that.

'You don't need luck,' Bex's voice said in his ear as he swung the car door shut. 'You'll be brilliant.'

He stepped up to the barrier. The security guard stared at him impassively from behind his sunglasses. Kieron smiled at him.

After a few minutes a golf-buggy appeared from behind

one of the glass buildings and raced towards the barrier. The guard vanished back inside his cabin and no doubt pressed a button, because the metal plates suddenly retracted into the ground. Stepping out of the cabin again, the guard gestured to Kieron to walk inside the fence.

'Quick,' he said.

'What happens if I'm not quick?'

The guard's expression didn't change. 'The barriers spring back up and they cut you in half.'

'You're joking, right?' Kieron said, but he wasn't entirely sure so he got a move on. As he entered the Goldfinch Institute's grounds, he heard the plates slide up behind him. He thought one of them just brushed against his heels, but he wasn't sure.

The golf buggy swung around so that it was side-on to him. There was no driver. Kieron glanced around, wondering if he was the victim of some trick, but the guard was looking at him in exasperation.

'It's automatic,' he called. 'Just get in; it'll take you where you need to go.'

'Are you sure?' Kieron asked. 'Because I've seen this in films, and it never ends well.'

The guard just stared at him.

Kieron climbed into the passenger side and waited. After a few seconds the cart started off.

It took him along the side of the glass buildings and then down a glass-walled canyon between them. The breeze of its passage cooled Kieron down, for which he was grateful. He hadn't been lying about not doing well in the heat.

Eventually the cart came smoothly to a halt beside a set of sliding glass doors in a glass wall.

Kieron entered the glass building. Or the lion's den, as he couldn't help thinking of it. He noticed that a security scanner had been built into the door frame. What was it scanning for? he wondered – guns, explosives, or maybe any high-tech equipment. Like the ARCC glasses.

Inside the air was cool, and the sunshine was muted by what he now realised was the floor-to-ceiling mirrored glass. A long reception desk was occupied by a red-haired young man working on a computer. He was wearing a tracksuit. Several very plush chairs dotted around looked more like exotic mushrooms than anything a person might sit comfortably in.

'I'm beginning to sense a theme,' Bex's voice said in his ear.

Kieron started to say something back, but he stopped himself just in time. There was only one person in the reception lobby, but he didn't know how many others might be watching him on CCTV. This place struck him as being obsessed with security, albeit in a very discreet way. Instead he smiled at the man.

'You're Ryan Allen and you have an appointment,' Bex prompted.

'Ryan Allen,' he said. 'I have an appointment.'

The man looked up from his computer and nodded. 'Good morning, Mr Allen. I'm sorry,' he said, 'but there has been some confusion. Your appointment *is* in Mr Zanderbergen's diary, but it seems to have been overlooked somehow. I can only apologise. Mr Zanderbergen's personal assistant will be down momentarily.' He gestured towards a water dispenser at the end of the reception desk which, Kieron saw with slight surprise, was filled not with water but with a pale amber liquid. 'Please – help yourself to some iced tea while you wait.'

'Thanks,' he said, 'but where I come from, tea is served hot and with milk.'

'Nice one – the exaggerated Brit persona is working well,' Bex said in his ear.

Kieron stood where he was, looking around. Soon he heard a soft chime, and a previously invisible door opened in the wall to one side of the desk. A woman dressed in a severe turquoise business suit strode out. She was a redhead. Kieron was beginning to suspect that Todd Zanderbergen had a thing about redheads.

'Mr Allen?' She approached with her hand held out. 'I'm Judith. My apologies for the slight delay. Mr Zanderbergen *is* expecting you. Please come with me.'

Kieron shook her hand and followed her to what he realised was a lift. 'Thank you.'

'Tell them what a lovely building they have,' Bex said in his ear.

'You have a lovely building,' he repeated as the lift doors closed.

Judith smiled. Perfect teeth. 'Thank you. We're very proud of it. We're carbon-neutral and we recycle all the water. Nothing is wasted.'

'Lovely,' was the only thing he could think of to say.

Judith glanced up at the ceiling of the lift. 'Eight,' she

said clearly, and the lift started to move. Looking around, Kieron could see no controls at all: no buttons, no switches, no indicators. Everything was apparently voice-controlled.

'What do we do if something goes wrong?' he asked.

Judith glanced at him. 'We say "Help" in a clear, calm voice.'

'OK. That's reassuring.'

With a few moments to think, rather than just react, Kieron felt his nerves coming back. He glanced around, looking at the lights in the ceiling, the mirrored glass walls, anything to distract himself from his worries.

'Calm down,' Bex said in his ear. 'You're doing fine.'

Kieron tried to control his breathing. He'd almost mastered it when the lift door slid open to reveal a carpeted working area where people dressed in a whole variety of ways – from jeans and sports gear to chinos and even suits – occupied computer-equipped desks that seemed to be arranged randomly rather than in rows or groups. Rather than chairs, they sat on inflatable balls coloured in pastel blues, pinks and greens. Everyone had hair that was arguably some shade of red, from bright orange to deep burgundy.

Seeing his surprise, Judith said, 'Our philosophy here at the Goldfinch Institute is to let people be themselves, not to regiment them. We find they work better that way.'

'I like it already,' Kieron said. 'And the . . . the seating arrangements.'

'Orthopedically designed to minimise back strain,' she said. 'Please – come with me.'

'Those computers aren't standard ones,' Bex said in his ear. 'I can't find the specifications anywhere online.'

'And what about those computers?' Kieron asked as Judith led him through the random arrangement of desks. 'They don't look like anything you can buy in the shops.'

'Well spotted.' Judith smiled a tight, professional smile. 'We make them ourselves. Nobody else can buy them. They're about five years ahead of anything that's available to the general public.'

Kieron desperately wanted to take a look at the computers, see what they could do, but Judith led him towards an office in the centre of the floor space that was entirely walled in glass. Inside, a man who looked only about five years older than Kieron was standing at a desk high enough off the ground for him to use the computer keyboard without having to sit down. No inflatable ball for him. A red-headed woman wearing a black business suit stood over to one side, watching Kieron as he approached.

'That's Tara Gallagher,' Bex said. Kieron could hear something in her tone, but he wasn't sure what it was. 'She's Zanderbergen's Head of Security. Watch out for her – she's clever, remember.'

Before Kieron could react, Judith knocked on a glass door set into a glass wall of the fishbowl office, opened it and gestured to Kieron to enter.

The man standing by the elevated desk turned around. He wore black jeans, ripped at the knees, and a T-shirt with a band logo on. As he turned towards Kieron, Kieron noticed that it was a Lethal Insomnia T-shirt.

'Mr Allen – welcome to the Goldfinch Institute! I'm Todd Zanderbergen. Call me Todd.'

'Please, call me Ryan. Cool T-shirt, by the way. I'm a big fan.' He turned back to Judith, standing in the doorway. 'Thanks for your help.'

She smiled, as if they shared a secret, and closed the glass door.

'You know they're local?' Todd held out his hands in feigned astonishment. 'How cool is that? They're in town recording their new album at the moment. Totally crowdfunded, but you probably knew that.' Todd grabbed Kieron's hand between both of his own and shook it enthusiastically. 'Oh, and this is my Head of Security, by the way – Tara Gallagher,' he said, grinning as he nodded towards the woman in the black suit. 'She's here to make sure I don't give away all my company secrets. I'm terrible – I just love talking about what we do. Apparently that's bad business practice.'

'Stay calm,' Bex's voice murmured in Kieron's ear. 'Just talk in generalities.'

Tara walked over and nodded at Kieron. 'A pleasure,' she said, shaking his hand.

'You're English,' Kieron said.

She nodded. 'I moved to the USA a few years ago. Can I get you a drink? Water, maybe?

'Yes, please, that would be great.'

'Look, I have to be honest,' Todd said as Tara moved away to type something into the keyboard on the desk, 'there's been some kind of miscommunication. We kind of lost your details somewhere along the way. We know you're here for a meeting, but we're a bit confused as to

139

why. I know you've come a long way, and I'm going to make as much time available as you need, but it would be great if you could give us a quick run-down of what you're expecting from us.'

'Normally,' Tara said, moving back to stand beside Todd, 'we'd expect security clearances to be sent over, along with an agenda.'

Bex's voice said in Kieron's ear, 'Tell them you sent everything well in advance, and you're surprised they've lost it all. Sound impatient.'

'My people sent everything in advance,' Kieron parroted, trying to sound as if the words were just coming to him unprepared. 'I have to say, I'm surprised that you haven't got it.'

Todd flashed Tara a quick angry glance. Just for an instant, and then the anger was gone and he was smiling again. 'I can only apologise. Data gets lost sometimes. Misfiled, deleted, who knows? People make mistakes, much as I try to discourage that kind of sloppiness. So – we know you're interested in non-lethal weapons. That's great, because it's our bread-and-butter work. What specifically are you here to talk about?'

Bex started to say something, but Kieron had already started speaking and couldn't stop. 'I've . . . got a design for a non-lethal weapon that can cause instant unconsciousness,' he said.

Todd held up his hands. 'Let me stop you there. Look, I don't want to waste either of our time. We've tried that. It's the Holy Grail of non-lethal weapons – being able to knock out terrorists who've taken hostages before they can blow up their hostages. If we crack that, it'll make our fortunes – well, in my case, my fifth fortune, but who's counting? We've checked out all the anaesthetics, but none of them works fast enough, or is safe in high doses. Believe it or not, we've evaluated over forty different analogues of fentanyl without finding anything we could use. You would not *believe* the number of monkeys we killed doing the tests. Rendering rioters or terrorists unconscious just isn't feasible.'

'The trick is not to use gases,' Kieron said, trying not to think about monkeys that had been gassed in the name of science. 'They're unpredictable and quite clumsy. I've been looking into something else entirely. Have you tried cancelling out brainwaves – in effect just switching people's brains off?'

Todd stared at him for a long moment. 'Interesting,' he said eventually. 'Tell me more.'

Kieron opened his mouth to answer, but Bex spoke in his ear. 'Not without a non-disclosure agreement. Tell him.'

'Not without a non-disclosure agreement,' Kieron repeated smoothly.

Todd nodded. 'Understood. Completely understood. I guess you've got one I can get my people to look over?'

Kieron pulled the thumb-drive from his pocket and held it up. 'On here, along with some other stuff you might like to see.'

'Sounds intriguing. Come on – give me a heads-up. What kind of stuff?'

In his ear, Kieron heard Bex saying, 'Tell him about the

neural simulator.' More quietly she added, 'After all, we went to so much trouble to get it.'

'I can take you through the theory later on,' Kieron said, 'but I've got a simulated brain that I've developed. The way the individual neurons fire together in groups simulates realistic brainwaves – alpha, beta, gamma, delta and so on.'

'Ooh – interesting. So this simulated brain,' Todd asked mildly, 'does it think? Is it, like, an artificial *intelligence*?'

Air hissed through Bex's teeth as she took a breath. 'That's a trick question if ever I heard one.'

'So what's the answer?' Kieron asked automatically, and then realised to his horror that he'd spoken to Bex out loud by accident.

Fortunately, Todd hadn't noticed. 'Well, that's what I want to know,' he said, nodding. He seemed to have assumed that Kieron's question was rhetorical. 'Come on – you can tell me that at least. I'll sign the non-disclosure agreement, no problem. I'm just curious.'

Kieron thought he could hear rustling noises as Bex waved her hands around, searching for any information that could help him. He felt like muttering, 'Don't worry – I've got this,' but he'd already nearly messed up once. He couldn't afford another slip. 'It's a simulation, not a replication,' he said eventually as Bex was clearly still searching. 'Although I guess if you think a driving simulator game is the same as driving a real car, then you might think that a brain simulator is the same as a real brain. You and I are cleverer than that though, aren't we? We know the difference.'

Todd nodded. 'Good answer. I guess your simulation produces brainwaves that are similar to *real* brainwaves though. That's the test.'

'Identical,' Kieron bluffed.

'OK.' Todd paused, musing. His face suddenly lit up. 'Hey, look at this!' he said, rushing across his office and grabbing something from a glass display table on the far side – a high-tech weapon, like something from a sci-fi film, with a stock, a handle and a trigger but with a flat circular plate at the end of the barrel instead of a hole for bullets. The only thing that made it look military rather than like something an alien commando might use was its colour – matte khaki, so it didn't stand out from any background.

'What is it?' Kieron asked, intrigued.

'It's a microwave skin heater,' Todd said, hefting it. 'The US Army has a much bigger version, and when I say "much bigger", I mean it's the size of a truck. We've managed to miniaturise the technology, and we're discussing contracts now. It generates microwaves, just like your basic kitchen microwave, but the difference is that the wavelength means they don't penetrate beneath the first millimetre of the skin. Oh, and the other difference –' he smiled – 'is that this one doesn't operate in a casing.'

'So what does it do?' Kieron asked. 'Although I guess the answer is in the name.'

'That's right. The microwaves cause skin heating in that top layer of skin. It starts out feeling like ants crawling, and then it changes to an itching, then a gentle burning, then it's like someone's put a huge magnifying glass between you

143

and the sun, and the entire heat and weight of the sun is bearing down on you, scorching every inch of you. Entirely harmless, doesn't cause any permanent damage, but it's phenomenally painful. At the moment it's used for crowd control – breaking up rioters and the like – but we've made it into a one-on-one weapon. Say you've got a gunman who's taken a hostage, or a terrorist with a bomb strapped to their chest – this weapon can incapacitate them until they can be disarmed.'

'Without causing their finger to clench on the trigger?' Kieron asked, 'or the bomb to detonate?'

Todd shrugged. 'There are always bugs to be ironed out. That's what research is for. Which reminds me – the brainwaves you send back into this simulated brain to cancel out the actual brainwaves – are you just recording and repeating the original brainwaves, a half-cycle out of phase, or are you generating fresh brainwaves using, oh, I don't know, Fourier analysis or something?'

Kieron thought he could answer this one. He often spent time in the music studios at school, after lessons had finished, playing around with the synthesisers. Reading the manuals, and looking stuff up on the Internet, had given him a fairly good grounding in how signals were generated.

'Recording and replaying, obviously,' he said with as much confidence as he could muster. He delved into his memory, desperately trying to remember things he'd read. 'Fourier analysis reproduces a waveform by adding lots of different sine waves together, but there's an unpredictable processing lag. It's far easier just to record the brainwaves and play

144

them back.' He smiled disarmingly. 'The important thing, of course, is that we can demonstrate what happens when the brainwaves are cancelled out using the simulator. It's a practical demonstration that it's possible to just switch a brain off – temporarily.'

'The trick,' Todd said, staring at Kieron, 'is making sure you can switch it back on with no damage whenever you want.'

'That *is* the trick,' Kieron said. 'And that's where the non-disclosure agreement comes into effect.'

'Yeah, but you can give me a hint, can't you?' Todd smiled engagingly.

Fortunately, just at that moment there was a knock on the glass door. It was Judith, Todd's PA. She had a glass of water.

'For you,' Todd said as she entered and handed him the glass. Kieron took a grateful sip.

Trying to change the subject, he looked around. 'This might be a stupid question, but is there anywhere I could sit down? It was a long flight yesterday, and I didn't sleep very well.'

Todd shrugged apologetically. 'Yeah, I kinda don't like sitting down. I find I'm so much more energised if I have to stand up when I'm working.' He pointed towards his computer, on its elevated desk. 'Better for my posture as well. So many health benefits.'

Kieron nodded towards the people outside Todd's square working bubble, sitting on their inflated balls. 'Was there a palace revolution? Did the serfs refuse to adopt healthy work practices?'

'Careful,' Bex warned, quietly and privately, 'you don't want to alienate him.'

'Yeah.' Todd smiled, but the expression didn't seem to reach his eyes. 'I tried to persuade them, but it turns out if you try to force people to stand up all the time when they're working, it's a health and safety violation. Plus, they resign. So I had the stability balls bought in. They're almost as good.' He shrugged. 'Had to install coffee machines as well. The juice bar didn't go down too well. Apparently caffeine is more of a stimulant than wheatgrass.'

'Do you get a lot of staff leaving?' Kieron tried to make the question as innocent-sounding as possible, not wanting Todd to know that their task there was to investigate the strange cluster of deaths of Goldfinch Institute staff, but he heard Bex take a noisy breath through the earpiece.

'Might be a little soon to ask a direct question like that,' she said.

Todd glanced inquiringly at Kieron for a moment before answering. 'All organisations have some degree of staff turnover. We have our share of course, but I hope that the remuneration package and the staff benefits make us attractive.'

Kieron smiled back at him but said nothing.

'You want me to bring one of the balls in?' Todd asked. 'If you're not feeling too well . . .'

'I'll survive,' Kieron said. He took a sip of the ice-cold water. 'After all, I was sitting down all during the flight. My muscles could probably do with a little stretching.'

146

'Hey! I should have thought!' Todd brought both hands to his forehead theatrically. 'If you're here for a few days, do you want me to see if I can get you an invite to Lethal Insomnia's recording sessions? I'm, like, great friends with the studio manager. He promised to sneak me in, if I get some free time. Would you like that?'

A set of fireworks seemed to go off in Kieron's head. 'That would be – fantastic!' he breathed. Knowing that Lethal Insomnia were actually in the city at the same time as him had been driving him slightly crazy. It had been a useful coincidence that had allowed him to persuade his mother that going to Albuquerque was a good idea, but he'd hardly dared hope that his cover story – the one he'd told *her*, not the one he was busy telling Todd Zanderbergen – might actually come true. Suddenly it was difficult to take a breath.

'Calm down,' Bex said through his earpiece. 'Even from here I can see that you're trembling. The glasses are shaking. Remember – we've got a job to do here.'

'Could you – *would* you do that?' he asked Todd. 'I mean, that's a pretty huge favour for you to do for a complete stranger.'

'Hey – glad to help. Look, some companies take their business contacts out for dinner, or to sporting events, or to nightclubs. You look like you prefer a burger and chips to a steak, you don't look like you've seen the inside of a sporting arena, like, *ever*, and I'm thinking you're too young to get into a nightclub. Besides, it'll be such *fun*.' His smile stayed where it was, but his eyes were

147

suddenly hard, like polished pebbles. Kieron felt a chill run through him. 'Which reminds me – I have to ask: just how old *are* you?'

'Eighteen,' Kieron said.

'Liar,' Bex said, although only he could hear her. He ignored her – they'd rehearsed this.

'And yet you've managed to create your own highly accurate brain simulation, plus the software necessary to produce anti-brainwaves that can cancel out the normal brainwaves. That's very impressive for someone so young.'

Kieron gestured around. 'You've accomplished much more, and you can't be much older than I am.' He drank the rest of his iced water, trying to look calm.

'Nice save,' Bex murmured.

Todd shrugged. 'You've got a point. It's young people like us who have all the ideas, and the energy to develop and capitalise on them. Anyone over the age of thirty has pretty much done all the useful things they're going to do.' His face lit up, as if an idea had just struck him, but Kieron was beginning to get the measure of Todd Zanderbergen now. What looked like an improvised, intuitive attitude towards life was actually just an act. He suspected that the man thought very carefully about what he was doing, then made it *look* as if it had just sprung into his mind. 'Hey, here's a thought. While I'm organising the trip to see Lethal Insomnia recording their album, why don't you take a tour of the Institute? I'll get Judith to accompany you. See what we do, see what we're like, and then come back and we can discuss your non-lethal weapon concept.'

148

'That sounds great,' Kieron said. Actually, it *did* sound great, and it would get him away from Todd for a while. The man's apparently innocent but probing questions were making him edgy.

Todd turned towards his computer. 'Judith – come here, please.'

Kieron was about to comment on the voice-activated technology when he felt the empty glass being taken from his hand. He turned, to see Tara Gallagher standing beside him.

'Let me get rid of that,' she said. She tried to smile, but it wasn't very successful.

As she moved away, back towards the glass office door, Bex spoke in Kieron's ear: 'Don't be too flattered about the offer of the tour. It's a distraction to get you out of the way while Todd gets his people to check you out. Good thing we planted all that stuff on the Internet for him to find.'

Kieron noticed Judith approaching. Beyond her, he saw Tara Gallagher. She was now bent over one of the computer desks, fiddling with something.

'Don't look away!' Bex said, suddenly sounding tense. 'I'm just zooming in. I want to see what she's doing.'

Judith entered Todd's office and smiled at Kieron. He smiled back, trying to make it look as if he was paying attention to her while keeping the ARCC glasses pointed at the desk where Tara was working.

'Judith,' Todd said, waving a hand, 'can you give Ryan here a tour of the place? Show him everything.'

'Sure,' she said.

Over at the desk, Tara glanced over her shoulder towards Kieron.

'She's got your glass of water,' Bex said suddenly. 'She's just scanned it for fingerprints and DNA. They really *are* checking you out.'

CHAPTER EIGHT

From just outside the impressive security fence of the Goldfinch Institute, where she had parked the hire car, Bex watched and listened as Kieron dealt with Todd Zanderbergen's subtle attempts to question him.

The car's air con made it chilly enough that the hairs on her forearms were standing up, but whenever her hand touched the driver's side window she could feel the thudding heat of the sun bearing down on the car's metal skin. It was an odd juxtaposition. Still, at least the heat here was dry. Not like the humidity that she'd recently experienced in India and Pakistan.

Last week. She shook her head in disbelief. It had only been a week ago that she'd been in those two countries. And now she was in America. Sometimes she just wanted to sit back and wonder at this lifestyle of hers. One day she might be able to stop and settle down, but not yet.

As Todd instructed Judith to give Kieron the tour, Bex's thoughts whirled as she watched her old friend Tara Gallagher scanning Kieron's fingerprints and DNA on the Institute's computer system.

She understood that the news that he was being checked out so thoroughly would freak Kieron out, but she needed to tell him. Todd Zanderbergen was a charismatic man, and he'd already offered Kieron the biggest bribe a teenage emo could wish for by offering to take the boy to the Lethal Insomnia recording studio. There was a distinct risk that Kieron might get star-struck and give something away. She needed to remind him that there was danger all around, but she didn't want him panicking. It was a fine line to walk.

'I think it's safe to go on the tour,' she said. 'Give Zanderbergen the USB stick with the non-disclosure agreement. He'll virus-check it before he uploads the file, but the virus on the computer is more sophisticated than he's expecting. While he's checking you out, the virus will be modifying his system just a little bit. And while you're on the tour, I'm going to take the opportunity to head back into Albuquerque and do a little bit of investigating of my own. I hope that's OK.'

'You ready to go?' she heard the PA – Judith – saying to Kieron.

'Absolutely,' he said. 'It beats hanging around.' Bex realised that as well as answering Judith he was also talking to her. He was really getting the hang of working with the ARCC.

She made that little mental leap in her mind that allowed her to push to one side the things Kieron was seeing through the ARCC glasses and acknowledge what was happening in the real world around her. Everything was quiet, and her car was the only one on the tarmac area just outside the metal gates, but the security guard was standing outside his cabin, watching her. Maybe he was just bored.

With a slight pinch of her fingers she reduced the size of the virtual screen showing her what Kieron was seeing and pushed it to a corner of the lenses.

She put the car into drive and turned it in a tight circle, then accelerated away from the Institute.

'I'm going to check out the local coroner,' she said, not because she thought Kieron needed to know but because she didn't want him to think that the link was down or that she was ignoring him. 'Then I might see if there are any local newspaper archives I can check for obituaries, death notices and the like.'

Glancing automatically in her rear-view mirror, even though she was the only car on the narrow road, she saw that the metal plates that sealed the entrance to the Goldfinch Institute had slid into the ground. As she watched, a black car drove out. As it passed the security guard he made a strange little salute. Obviously someone important, she thought.

As Bex got to the interstate junction and headed towards Albuquerque, she looked in her rear-view mirror again. The black car had turned the same way. Not a surprise – the city was the biggest conurbation for some miles. Most of the Institute's employees probably lived there.

She checked in with Kieron briefly, glancing up to the corner of her vision. He was walking down a corridor, Judith just ahead of him. Bex wasn't sure whether he was concentrating on the PA's backside as she moved or whether it was just coincidence that his gaze kept on slipping down there. Typical teenage boy.

She moved her attention back to the road. Traffic was light, but she kept her speed low. The last thing she wanted was to draw the attention of any traffic cops. A pickup truck and a yellow school bus were ahead of her on the road, travelling slightly faster than her in the same lane.

She checked the rear-view mirror again. The black car was maintaining the same speed as her. That was probably just as coincidental as the fact that it had turned right at the junction.

Without really thinking about it, Bex eased her speed up, indicated and moved out to the next lane. Now she was travelling slightly faster than the pickup and the school bus and she began to creep up on them. As she overtook the truck, Bex looked in the mirror again.

The black car had sped up and changed lane. It was still behind her, pacing her.

Not looking like a coincidence any more. Intriguing. Intriguing, and slightly worrying.

She could see the black car passing the pickup truck now. Glancing ahead, she also saw that she was approaching the yellow school bus. She touched the brake lightly, just to slow herself down a fraction, and changed lanes again so that she was directly behind the bus, with the pickup truck a little way behind.

Seconds later the black car swung smoothly into her lane. It now sat between her and the pickup truck.

It was following her. She was fairly certain of that.

The best way to establish that for sure would be to leave the interstate and see if the black car did the same. The trouble was, if she then rejoined Route 66 her follower would know she'd spotted them. Worse, she would have given away the fact that she was watching for followers and didn't want to be followed. That in turn would cast suspicion on Kieron, because whoever was in that black car – or maybe their boss – would know that she'd dropped him off.

She had a problem. She couldn't just let the car keep following her, because she didn't want the driver to know she was going to the local coroner. That would raise just as many suspicions as if she let on that she knew it was following her. What to do?

A sign a little way ahead told her that a turn-off was coming up: a side road leading to somewhere called Los Lunas. Impulsively she indicated again and slid into the feeder lane for the exit.

Behind her, the black car did the same.

Steering one-handed, Bex called up the mapping function on the ARCC glasses. A secondary translucent window sprang to life, showing her the local area. A red dot identified her position. As she steered the car off the highway and onto the rougher local road she saw that there was a right-hand turn coming up ahead that eventually led to a Navajo reservation and, shortly after that, a left turn that wound back to Route 66. After that the road they were on kept on going all the way to Los Lunas, which seemed to be on the outskirts of Albuquerque.

She slowed down almost imperceptibly. As she'd intended, the black car started to creep up on her.

The right hand turn flashed past.

The road was badly pitted with potholes, and Bex's car juddered as she drove. She kept both hands on the wheel, making sure that she avoided the worst of the holes.

Just as she'd hoped, the other driver realised that he was catching up with her just before the left-hand turn came up. Without indicating, Bex abruptly jerked the wheel, sending her car into a slide that left an expanding plume of dust behind her. The black car momentarily vanished in the cloud. She pressed her foot hard down on the accelerator and her car sprang ahead like a greyhound released from a trap. She completed the left turn and started speeding back to the interstate. Behind her in her mirror she saw the black car going past the turn, continuing towards Los Lunas. If she was lucky, the driver would think she'd made a mistake, come off the interstate too early, then made a panicked manoeuvre to get back on – a panicked manoeuvre which he'd seen too late to copy.

Before the black car could turn around, come back and make that turn, Bex accelerated as fast as she could. Within moments the junction with the interstate appeared ahead of her. Instead of resuming her journey towards Albuquerque, she went under the highway, then rejoined it but heading back the other way, towards the Goldfinch Institute. That way, if the black car did get back onto the main road, it would be going in a different direction to her, heading into town and looking desperately to catch up with her.

At the Los Lunas exit Bex came off again, crossed back under the interstate and rejoined it, now heading *into*

Albuquerque, but hopefully a long distance behind the black car. If she kept her speed low she wouldn't catch up with it, and its driver would have no idea where she was.

It was a hell of a routine to have gone through to get rid of what might have been an innocent driver who'd just ended up accidentally copying every manoeuvre she made, but Bex was pretty sure it had been necessary. As one of her trainers had said, years ago: 'If something happens once, it's an event. If it happens twice, it's a coincidence. If it happens three times, it's enemy action.'

Tara Gallagher had been on that course with her. Strange, the way things connected up.

As Bex drove she put the cruise control on and checked again on Kieron. He appeared to be in a firing gallery, shooting non-lethal beanbags from a gun with a broad, short barrel. They zoomed away from him in a shallow arc, hitting a target like a hanging punchbag, making it swing back and forth. He looked as if he was enjoying himself, based on the way Judith was watching him and grinning.

Okay – time for some research.

According to the ARCC glasses, it was the job of the Office of the Medical Examiner to investigate any death occurring in the State of New Mexico that was sudden, violent, untimely, unexpected or puzzling. The OMI worked out of a building on the campus of the University of New Mexico in the centre of Albuquerque. Following the directions on the map function, Bex left Interstate 40 at a massive junction comprising lots of roads curving off in different directions. Within a few minutes she was parking in the OMI car park,

157

in the shadow of a modernist building constructed from white and orange stone.

As she opened her door to get out, a black car drove slowly past. For a moment her heart jumped, but then she realised it was a different make than the one that had been following her.

'Hi,' she said to the receptionist, who had glanced up with a professional smile when she entered the building. 'I'm sorry to bother you. I'm, like, a research student, looking into clusters of similar deaths – seeing whether they might be related to things like faulty air conditioning, areas of vegetation that have toxic spores, that kind of thing. Is it possible to get access to some kind of database that would help me?'

'You look a bit old to be a student, hon,' the receptionist said, raising a sceptical eyebrow.

'Post-graduate programme,' Bex replied. She wasn't even sure they had post-graduate programmes in the USA, but she'd heard the phrase and thought it was worth a try. 'Student exchange,' she added for good measure. 'I'm from England.'

The receptionist hesitated for a heart-stoppingly long moment, then nodded. This was obviously the kind of query she had to answer several times a week, and she had a script memorised. 'Sure, why not,' she said. 'A lot of our data is available to the public, and it's searchable. Everything is held electronically. Basically, the reports that the medical examiner produces are: a report of findings, which is a summary of everything, plus a full autopsy report, a toxicology report, if applicable, and a report of external examination. We do charge, unless you're a family member, and I'm guessing you're not. It's $1.50 per hour you spend on the computer, with a minimum of one hour. If you want to email documents to yourself, it's $7. Paper copies are $1.40 per page. Is that OK? We take all major credit cards.'

'Of course you do,' Bex said. This was, she reminded herself, America.

Ten minutes later she was sitting at a computer in a small cubicle in a room on the first floor, with a bored clerk giving her a quick lesson on how to use their database system. Five minutes later he'd left, and she started to type.

OK, she thought, her task was to look into deaths of Goldfinch Institute personnel. She didn't know their names, how they'd died or where. All she knew was where they'd worked *before* they'd died. Fortunately the system allowed her to search specifically on 'Employer'.

Fifty-nine people employed by Todd Zanderbergen had died in the past five years. That was a noticeable proportion of his workforce. Intrigued, she split it up by year.

Five deaths, eight deaths, four deaths, seven deaths . . . and thirty-five deaths. For the first four of those five years, Todd Zanderbergen had lost an average of six employees a year. In the last year he'd lost thirty-five. Unless a coachload of employees on the way to a company picnic had crashed and burned, that was *very* odd.

Changing the parameters of the search, Bex checked the causes of death over the same period. Yes, there *had* been a few car crashes, although not an unexpected number and no disasters involving coaches, plus a climbing accident, a couple of strokes, some deaths due to cancer, two murders and a suicide. Well, this *was* America she thought cynically. The largest cause of death however was heart attacks. That was hardly a surprise, however. Heart disease was the single biggest cause of death in the USA, and also in the UK. Bex's own mother had died ten years before of a sudden and unexpected coronary embolism. She'd been discovered by her father in their bedroom. She'd died while getting dressed: one sock on, one sock off, and a surprised expression on her face.

Unexpectedly thinking about her mother broke her concentration, and she leaned back in her chair for a moment, feeling a lump in her chest. She swallowed, pushing the memory away and trying to recapture the momentum she'd lost by checking in on Kieron. By now he was in a large, gleaming white laboratory, being shown a bizarre weapon that looked like a cross between a water pistol and a rocket launcher. A voice she didn't recognise was saying: '. . . And then we transmit an electric charge along the stream of water, powerful enough to temporarily incapacitate anyone it hits.'

Nice, she thought. That's next Christmas's presents sorted.

OK. She turned back to the computer and cleared her mind. Let's look at this from a different angle. What did those thirty-five people die of in the past year?

The answer was: heart disease. All of them. Every single one.

That wasn't just *odd*; that was positively *unusual*. It looked as if this mission that she and Bradley had been given actually had a point to it. There *was* something suspicious going on.

160

Bex considered emailing herself all the reports, but that would be a lot of data to go through – most of it irrelevant. None of the thirty-five deaths were listed as suspicious, which meant that the toxicology reports would be long, detailed and essentially useless to her. There was nothing to find.

Instead, on a hunch, she checked the place where each death had occurred.

They'd all occurred in the Goldfinch Institute itself. Every single employee who had died that year had actually died on company premises. None at home, none in a restaurant, or a gym, or a sports field. None while out jogging. Every single one of those people had died in that complex of blue glass buildings.

Surely that should have raised some suspicions? Someone should have investigated. But apparently nobody had.

She pulled all the data from the searches she'd made into one document and emailed that through to a secure and covert email address that she and Bradley used to share things when she was on missions and he was providing support. If she knew Bradley, he'd be monitoring it, but just in case she also sent a quick email to his regular account asking him to take a look and see if he could spot anything. It was mid-evening in England. Assuming he wasn't out on a date with Sam's sister, he might come up with something she'd missed.

Bex packed up, paid her bill at the reception desk and left. She had a feeling there was no more data there to find: if she wanted more, she'd have to look somewhere else.

When she checked the image from the ARCC kit, Kieron now appeared to be sitting in a small conference room watching some kind of company presentation. He'd got a milkshake from somewhere; she could see it in his hand. Every now and then it suddenly loomed up, obscuring most of the view from his glasses as he took a sip. Probably not wheatgrass, based on the fact that he seemed to be enjoying it, and it wasn't luminous green.

The video Kieron was watching momentarily caught Bex's attention. It showed what must have been some high-tech Goldfinch Institute piece of research: a man standing on a cliff-edge, probably somewhere out in the desert outside Albuquerque. He wore a flight suit and helmet, and he'd been strapped into a pair of wings shaped like a boomerang that extended out from his back, as wide as he was tall. Right in the middle of the wings she saw a jet engine with two protruding nozzles. As she watched, the man ran towards the edge of the cliff. He jumped, and the jet-engine came to life. Instead of falling, he flew!

'Project ICARUS,' a voice said on the soundtrack of the video. 'A developmental system allowing military personnel the freedom of powered flight on the battlefield.'

As Bex watched, the video showed the pilot looping the loop and conducting various aerobatic manoeuvres.

'And,' the voice continued, 'the ICARUS system is armed with eight small, high-velocity rockets, stored in the wings, for offensive and defensive use.'

The pilot adjusted his course so that he was flying parallel to the ground. Far ahead of him, Bex could see a large circular bullseye target, sitting surreally in the desert. Abruptly, several lines of fire leaped ahead of the pilot, linking his wings to the target. The bullseye exploded in flame as the pilot adjusted his course to avoid the blast, soaring triumphantly like some kind of superhero while the target blazed.

Impressive, she thought, as she pushed the images away into a corner of the glasses. The Goldfinch Institute seemed to have a lot of things going on in its research department. Kieron would be loving this.

Bex supposed that she ought to be heading back to collect him, but she could do with some food. Their hotel wasn't far away, and she'd noticed a coffee franchise in the lobby where she could get a latte and a croissant. She could also pick up a power bank from her room: the ARCC equipment didn't draw much power, but if she was going to have to sit outside the Goldfinch Institute waiting for Kieron to come out, then she might as well charge up her own glasses, just to make sure they didn't suddenly flake out on her. The great thing was, they didn't need a USB cable or anything – both sets of glasses and the earpiece charged electromagnetically when the power bank was near them. And, if she went to the hotel, she could check on Sam. Reaching her car, she quickly plotted a route through the centre of Albuquerque to the Marriott.

As she walked across the car park towards the hotel building she noticed several black cars parked there. Most of them were the wrong make, the wrong model or the wrong year to be the one that had been following her, but one car made her hesitate. It *looked* like the same car, but she wasn't sure. She glanced at the licence plate, but that wasn't much help: the car behind her had never come close enough for her to see its plates.

She shook her head in annoyance. There was no point getting paranoid. There had to be hundreds, maybe thousands, of cars meeting the same description. She couldn't let herself get spooked by every single one.

She went in through a side door, but not the one she'd used the night before. She hated falling into routines. Routines were what got agents killed.

When she reached her room she slid her key card into the lock. The green light came on, and she pushed the door open.

A woman stood in the centre of her room, and it wasn't the maid.

It was a redhead, wearing black trousers, black boots and a black jacket over a white blouse.

The woman looked surprised, but when she realised that Bex wasn't from housekeeping, her expression changed. The fake innocence dropped from her face, replaced by an icy detachment. She reached behind her back.

Assuming she was about to face a weapon, Bex sprang into instinctive attack mode. She flicked the key card at the woman, sending it spinning through the air. The woman tried to jerk her head away but the card caught her beneath her eye, drawing blood.

Bex had a split second to decide whether to run or fight. It didn't even take her that long: fight.

A folding metal and canvas stand was by the door, ready

for a guest to put their suitcase on it. Bex bent down, scooped the stand up and stepped forward, swinging it in an arc towards the woman's head. The woman fell backwards onto Bex's bed, but she used the bounce of the springs to propel herself back to her feet and towards Bex. Her fist swung up, hitting Bex beneath her jaw. Bex's head snapped back with a *click* she felt all the way through her skull. For a moment everything went red. She dimly felt the glasses falling away from her face and the stand falling from her hand.

In desperation, Bex clenched her hands together and punched outwards. She still couldn't see anything, but her fists met their target and Bex heard the woman hit the wall and slide down.

Her vision clearing, Bex looked around for a better weapon. Nothing: she'd packed her clothes neatly away in the wardrobe and her toiletries in the bathroom. Short of pulling the alarm clock / iPod dock from the bedside table and wrenching the power cable from the wall, she couldn't see anything of use.

The redhead – little more than a blur at the moment – had fallen into the space between the bed and the wall, but she seemed to be levering herself up. Bex kicked out, knocking the bed sideways. With her support taken away the woman fell back again. Bex yanked the duvet off the bed and threw it over her, just to slow her down for a critical few seconds. Before she could get up, Bex ran for the bathroom. Not to lock herself in though – all American hotel bathrooms could be opened easily from the outside, if you knew how. It meant that if a guest passed out or, God forbid, died in the shower, then staff could get in. But that meant redheaded attackers could get in as well. No, Bex wasn't going to shelter there. She was looking for a weapon.

She heard a scrabbling behind her, and muffled cursing. She slammed the bathroom door behind her and turned the lock. It wouldn't stop her pursuer for long, but it would give Bex a few more precious seconds.

She scanned the toiletries she'd meticulously arranged on the fake marble surface, frantically looking for something she could use. Nail scissors? Too small. Toothbrush? Too blunt. Antiperspirant?

Antiperspirant!

As the door burst open, slamming back against the bath, Bex scooped the canister up. Her fingers fumbled with it, almost dropping it in the sink, but she turned around with it in her hand just as the redhead bought her hand up to point at Bex's face.

Not a hand. A gun. A gun, pointed at Bex's face.

Bex pressed the nozzle on top of the can.

A fine mist of aerosol droplets lightly scented with jasmine sprayed into her attacker's eyes. She screamed, bringing her hands up to her face and dropping the gun. Bex bent to pick it up, and by the time she straightened up the woman was staggering back into the bedroom, wiping her arm across her eyes. She glared at Bex from bloodshot eyes, then turned and half ran, half fell out into the hallway. Bex's heart was racing. As she tried to get her breathing under control, she heard the woman stumbling against the walls as she tried to run unsteadily away. Seconds later a *bang!* echoed through the building as the fire-escape door was thrust open.

'What was that all about?' Bex muttered to herself, gazing around at the room that had, just moments before, been immaculate.

'Room party?' a shocked voice asked. She turned around. Sam stood in the doorway. His face was white.

'Don't worry,' Bex said. 'If it had been, I would have invited you. Come in – I don't want anyone else seeing in.' As he entered the room, she gave him a quick, impulsive hug. 'Sorry – I didn't mean for you to see this. Are you OK?'

He nodded. 'Yeah. I don't think she even saw me as she pushed past. I don't know what you did to her, but her eyes looked *terrible*.'

'Yeah,' Bex said, 'but on the plus side, they won't be sweating for a while and they're nicely fragranced.' She took a breath. 'Sit down. Let's catch up.'

'Well, I've been asleep all day,' Sam said, throwing himself into the small armchair over by the window. 'What's your story?'

Quickly she brought him up to date with the trip she and Kieron had made to the Goldfinch Institute, her journey back and the events in the hotel room. 'I'm guessing that someone at the Institute gave orders to follow the car and see where I went. Either the driver or someone else was instructed to search our hotel rooms for anything incriminating.'

'*Our* hotel rooms?' Sam squealed.

Bex nodded. 'Both rooms were booked at the same time, and we all arrived together. Normally I try not to leave a trail when I stay in hotels, but we're undercover – at least

167

Kieron is. We *had* to leave a trail. People need to think that we're real.'

'You mean this could have happened to *me*?' He gazed around in shock at the damage.

She shook her head. 'No – she would have knocked on your door and said she was there to make the bed up or something. If you'd answered, she'd have apologised and gone away. If you didn't answer, she would have picked the lock and searched the room without leaving any trace.' She thought for a moment. 'Either my room was first, or yours has already been searched. Actually she would probably have started with yours – Kieron's fronting up this operation.' A thought struck her. Kieron! She scooped the ARCC glasses up from the floor where they'd fallen and put them on. The earpiece was still in her ear canal, but her brain had been filtering out the noises from it.

Through the ARCC link she could see a conference table and, to her relief, Kieron's hands. Todd Zanderbergen was on the other side of the table. He was holding the rubberised electrode net, turning it over and examining it with interest. Tara Gallagher sat off to one side.

Bex would have liked to tell Kieron about the fight, and being followed, and pull him out while they considered their options, but Todd was talking.

'This is really great,' Zanderbergen said approvingly. 'Small, flexible and really well designed.' He scrunched it up. 'I guess your idea is that this is projected from some kind of launcher, like those beanbags you saw earlier, unfurls in flight and wraps itself around the target's head. Intriguing.'

He fixed Kieron with his pleasant and yet razor-sharp gaze. 'So, how do you guarantee that the net will unfurl properly and fit around their head rather than, oh, say, smacking them in the face? It seems a rather clumsy manoeuvre.'

'Well, that's a good question . . .' Kieron said. Bex could hear a slight tension in his voice. He sounded as if he'd been talking for a while and was running out of things to say.

'Sorry – I'm back,' Bex said. 'Tell him it's defined by distance.'

'Distance,' Kieron said with a notably relieved tone in his voice. 'It's defined by distance.'

'The launcher will have a laser rangefinder,' Bex went on. 'The net of electrodes will –'

'The launcher will have a laser rangefinder,' Kieron interrupted. 'The net of electrodes will be held together by an electrostatic charge.' Before Bex could speak, he kept going. 'At the right moment after it's fired, the launcher will communicate with the net using near-field wireless technology, like Bluetooth. The charge will flip, the net will be pushed apart and it'll wrap around the target's head.'

Todd nodded. 'Very clever. You've thought all this through. Can you demonstrate it?'

'That's why you need him,' Bex said.

'That's why I need you,' Kieron translated. 'I have the principle of the thing worked out from beginning to end, and I can demonstrate the way the reflected brainwaves will calm the real brainwaves. Putting it into practice – making a technology demonstrator – requires funding and support.'

'I need to get you out of there,' Bex said, then quickly added, 'Don't say this to him. But we need to extract you.'

'OK – let's talk turkey,' Todd said, leaning forward slightly. 'My legal people have read through your non-disclosure agreement, and we can live with it. Let's discuss terms.'

'Actually,' Kieron said 'let's not. I'm jet-lagged, and that means I'm not at my best for making deals. I'm sure you wouldn't want to take advantage of an exhausted kid. Can we meet tomorrow?'

'I'll clear my schedule,' Todd said. 'What about your car? Do you have to call it?'

'Interesting,' Bex mused. 'He knows I drove away. What else does he know?'

'I'll do it in a moment,' Kieron said.

'We need to go,' Bex said to Sam. 'Now.'

CHAPTER NINE

'Damn,' Bex said angrily; 'this is pointless.'

'What's the problem?' Kieron asked. 'We know Todd Zanderbergen's people put the USB stick into their computers. Didn't the Trojan transfer across, or was it detected by his anti-virus programs and eradicated?' He was sitting on her bed, watching her work the ARCC kit. Had he really looked that bizarre when he'd been operating it, he wondered?

He glanced at Sam, who had curled himself into the armchair. Bex sat at the desk. 'Do I really look that lame when *I* use the kit?' he murmured.

Sam nodded. 'Worse.'

'We'd assumed,' Bex said grimly, 'falsely, as it turns out, that the Goldfinch Institute were using a Windows-based operating system on the inside of the company as well as on the outside, in the admin areas. That's not the case.'

Kieron tried to remember what the PA, Judith, had said when he'd commented on the advanced design of the Goldfinch Institute's computers. *We make them ourselves. Nobody else can buy them. They're about five years ahead of anything that's available to the general public.*

'You know what?' he said. 'I think Todd's designed his own operating system. Not Windows, not iOS, not Linux and not Android.'

'Oh, "Todd" is it?' Sam muttered. 'Best friends now.'

'What does that mean?' Bex asked, gesturing to Sam to shut up.

Kieron considered for a moment, getting his thoughts in order. 'If our Trojan was like, say, a normal biological virus, then it would have been expecting a normal human bloodstream as its environment. Put it into a banana milkshake and it wouldn't be able to function. That's what Todd's operating system is: something completely alien to the Trojan.'

Sam licked his lips. 'I could demolish a banana milkshake right now.'

Kieron sighed. He'd been afraid of this, ever since seeing those computers. 'Then there's only one option, isn't there?'

Bex winced. 'I can't ask you to do that.'

Sam looked from Kieron to Bex and back again. 'What? What am I missing?'

Kieron felt his spirits fall. It was like that feeling of inevitable doom he always got at the dentist's surgery – the knowledge that what was going to happen next was going to hurt, and there was no way of avoiding it. He was on a road with only one destination. 'I'm going to have to sneak back into the Institute, log on to one of the computers and get the information we're looking for the old-fashioned way – by hand.'

Sam looked puzzled. 'OK – working backwards – how are

you going to get past whatever security your mate Todd has on his wonderful bespoke custom-built computer system? That seems to me to be a bit of a showstopper.'

Kieron thought back momentarily to his time in Todd Zanderbergen's office, gazing out at the people who worked for him, and his time touring the site. 'Todd's got what he thinks are a perfect pair of security measures,' he said, pulling his thoughts together as he spoke. 'The first one is that he has two layers of computers that aren't connected to each other – the administrative ones, which only communicate with the outside world, and the work ones, which are networked within the Institute but have no contact outside. That means a hacker or virus can get into the first layer, but no further. The second level of security is that the computers on the inside are all built by the Goldfinch Institute and run a unique operating system of his own design. Even if a hacker or virus *does* get in, it wouldn't be able to function.'

'The banana-milkshake problem,' Sam said, nodding.

'Indeed. And the strength of the security also provides its flaw. I watched as some of Todd's people arrived at their computers and started work. They didn't type any passwords in. Todd is so convinced that nothing or nobody can get to that second layer and use it that he hasn't implemented any security on it at all.' He sniffed. 'He probably dresses that up in some kind of caring, sharing language, saying that he wants all of his staff to have access to everything, so they feel trusted. In fact I think he said something like that while I was there.'

'OK,' Sam said, 'if you can get in and access his "special"

machines, then you can look for the information we need. How are you going to do that then?'

'Sam's right,' Bex said. 'I was wondering that too.'

'That's the trick,' Kieron said. 'Physical security at the Institute is managed using iris-recognition technology. The iris of each person's eyes has a unique pattern of blood vessels. Staff going in through the main fence and into the buildings are recognised by their eye-print. We just have to use someone's eye-print to get us in.'

'Uh,' Sam said, a wary expression on his face, 'if that means what I think it means, count me out. I've seen that film, and it didn't end well. Gross.'

'We're not going to cut someone's eye out and use it,' Kieron explained patiently. 'We're going to record their eye-print. Or, rather, we already have.'

'All that time you spent looking into Judith's eyes and smiling!' Bex said as the realisation struck her; 'you were letting the ARCC system get a good look at her irises.' She paused. 'Doesn't explain why you got such a good look at her bum.'

'What?' Sam said. 'You've got that recorded as well! Let me see!'

Kieron felt his cheeks getting hot. 'That was accidental!' he protested. 'I was behind her, and I was looking at the floor to make sure I didn't trip over anything.'

Before Sam could continue, Bex held up her hands. 'OK, be that as it may, I think I can see another flaw in your scheme. We might have a recording of Judith's eye-print, but what do we play it back on? You can hardly hold a laptop with a picture of an eye up to the scanner. Someone would notice.'

'The resolution's too low anyway,' Kieron said. His stomach felt filled with lead. 'Same applies to tablets, and to printout. The image has to be eye-sized, but 4K resolution.'

'So we're stuck,' Sam challenged. 'Unless you're going to chat this Judith up and persuade her to take you back in.' His face twisted, and he looked down at the ground. 'You get to do all the fun bits.'

'There's only one way I can think of to get an eye-print at the right level of resolution,' Kieron said quietly.

'I forbid it,' Bex said, standing up.

Sam glanced between them. 'I'm missing it again. Tell me!' As neither of them spoke, he suddenly slapped a hand to his forehead. 'Of course – the ARCC kit!'

'I repeat,' Bex said, low but forceful, 'I forbid it.'

'We have no choice,' Kieron pointed out, wishing he could just accede to her order but knowing that he couldn't. 'The glasses *I've* been wearing don't have the ability to project images on the lenses. That's so nobody I'm talking to, or standing behind me, can see the image reflecting from them, which would give away the fact that they're special. Only the glasses *you're* wearing can do that. And we both know that those glasses have the highest image resolution it's currently possible to get. They have to, because the images are so small. So – I take *your* glasses and use them to show Judith's retinal image to the scanners.'

'At least you can leave your ones behind,' Bex said reluctantly, 'so we can keep in contact.'

Kieron shook his head. 'Best if I take them as well.

There'll be a lot of data being flashed up, and I'll need a way of recording it. We already know I can't put a USB stick in Todd's "special" machines, or email myself a file from them, because they're bespoke systems behind a massive firewall.'

Bex made a frustrated 'tch,' sound as she thought the logic through, but she nodded.

'But that means,' Sam said, working through the chain of logic, 'that you'll have the glasses Bex would have used to give you operational support, as well as the ones you've been using. You'll be going in there with nobody at your back. And if you don't come out, if you get caught, we won't know what's up or what you've found out.'

'It's a risk,' Kieron said.

'An unacceptable one,' Bex insisted.

Kieron shook his head. 'We have to do this. It's the job.'

'Not your job! And I promised your mother I'd look after you.'

'You were undercover,' Kieron pointed out. 'Promises made undercover don't count. We have to do this. I've thought through all the options, and there's no other solution. We *have* to do it this way.'

He watched as Bex closed her eyes tight, as if she had a headache or was trying to brace herself for something unpleasant. 'OK,' she said eventually, and softly. 'Have it your way. Take both pairs. But be careful, be quick and don't take any unnecessary risks.'

'I'm a coward,' Kieron reassured her. 'I've spent most of my childhood running away from bigger, stronger kids, and kids who don't like the clothes I wear or the music I listen to. I would never take any unnecessary risks with my life. I'm not even keen on taking *necessary* ones.'

There wasn't much preparation. Sam suggested going out and buying some hair dye, or a red wig, so they could make Kieron look like everyone else who worked for Todd Zanderbergen, but Bex pointed out that they didn't have time, and besides, they probably had local contractors and workmen popping in all the time who had different-coloured hair. Sam joined them in the car, and Bex stopped at a drive-through burger place so at least he and Kieron had something to eat. She didn't have anything herself. Kieron thought he heard her mutter something like, 'I'd rather stick knitting needles in my eyes.' In fact, he thought it was the tastiest bacon cheeseburger he'd ever had.

The drive to the Goldfinch Institute took about half an hour. It was getting late, and they hit the tail end of the rush-hour traffic. Kieron used the journey to work with the ARCC glasses, making an enlargement of Judith's right eye and making sure that it showed up nice and clearly in the image in the lenses. She did, he had to admit, have beautiful eyes.

By the time they got to the patch of tarmac outside the gates, nobody was around. The sun had gone down, leaving a red and purple stain spreading upwards from the horizon. The light reflected off the glass bulk of the buildings, casting a fiery glow across the sand.

'What if people are working late?' Sam asked from the back seat.

'Judith told me that most of the employees have a special bus that picks them up in the centre of town and brings them out here, then drops them off again in the evening. That's apparently because Todd is trying to cut down on vehicle emissions, but an added bonus is that it means people all have to leave at the same time, so they can get a ride home.' He smiled. 'It also means that Todd knows that nobody is getting in late or leaving early. He's a bit of a control freak.'

'I bet *he* doesn't use the bus,' Sam said.

'No – he's got a Harley-Davidson bike.'

'Still,' Sam pressed, 'security guards? Cleaners? They might see you.'

'And they'll think I'm allowed to be there, on the basis that I obviously got past the eye scanners.'

Kieron took a deep breath. 'Having said that, if you guys hang around here for long, the guard will get suspicious. I'd better go.'

'Good luck,' Bex said. Sam just punched him in the back. 'I'll stay nearby, and I'll swing past every half-hour to see if you need to be picked up.'

Kieron got out of the car and walked towards the security turnstile, making sure that he was wearing one set of the ARCC glasses – the recording and transmitting ones – and holding the others – the ones that had the laser projectors to place images on the inside of the lenses. He turned and waved ostentatiously at the hire car, as if it was his mum who'd dropped him off. As he approached the turnstile, and as he heard the car drive away, with Bex beeping her horn in what hopefully sounded like a fond farewell, a security guard popped his head out of the cabin. It was a different guy to the one who'd been on earlier.

'You OK, sir?' he called. 'Working late?'

'Conference call with Europe,' Kieron called back, trying to approximate an American accent. 'They don't keep the same hours as us.'

'Really?' The guard looked puzzled. 'Why not?'

'Search me!' Kieron gulped as he realised that that was the very last thing he wanted the guard to do. 'Have a good evening!'

'You too, sir.' The man disappeared, and Kieron held the ARCC glasses in his hand up to the scanner, muttering a quick prayer under his breath. The scanner was just a simple weatherproof box with a circular grey rubber ring on the front designed to cup the eye socket. It also had the convenient side effect of concealing his head from anyone in the guards' cabin.

Nothing happened.

He pushed at the turnstile, in case it had released silently, but it didn't budge.

He panicked, and pulled the glasses away and then put them back against the rubber ring, just in case.

Still nothing happened. No click, no movement in the turnstile. He looked around for a keypad. Had he missed a keypad? Was there a code that needed to be typed in as well?

No keypad. Why would there be, when the person's eye was actually there, and the security guard could check that they weren't being forced to operate the turnstile by someone else?

What was he doing wrong?

He looked at the glasses in his hand, and suddenly realised. He'd been holding them up as if there was a face behind them, with the outward curve of the lens next to the scanner, but the projected image was on the *inside*, of course. Quickly he turned the glasses over, and pressed the inside of the lens against the rubber ring.

He heard a quiet *click*. This time when he pushed the turnstile, it began to turn.

Within moments he was inside the outer fence. The second scanner, on the second inner fence, worked just as quickly, now he knew what he was doing.

The second turnstile worked just as smoothly as the first, and he began to walk towards the nearest building. Nobody else was around, but he had the feeling that someone was watching him from behind the mirrored glass. Someone who was waiting for him to get within range before they struck.

He followed the same route the golf buggy had taken him that morning – down glass canyons to the central building, where Todd's office was located. He could probably do what he needed to do from any computer in any building on the site, but he felt safer on territory he'd already seen.

The door to the main block didn't swish open for him until he used the glasses for a third time, on a scanner just to one side. An additional level of security when most people had left, he supposed.

He walked past the deserted reception desk to the hidden doors of the lifts. When one slid open, he stepped inside and said, 'Fifth floor, please,' and then cursed himself for adding the 'please'. How British could you get – being polite to a lift?

When he stepped out on the fifth floor he consciously stopped himself from saying thank you.

Todd's glass-walled office was deserted – thank God. Kieron wondered briefly if he should actually use Todd's computer, but he might disturb something that Todd would spot. Best use another desk. As far as he could tell, all the staff hot-desked. There were no knick-knacks, photographs or even pens and pencils on the desks to disturb. They were completely characterless.

He sat on the nearest ball, and bounced a couple of times experimentally. On another day, in another place, he and Sam could probably have fun on those things, but not now and not here, he told himself sternly. Now that he had got through the security, he was beginning to enjoy himself.

The computer sat there, looking subtly different from anything he'd seen before. Maybe it was the aspect ratio of the screen – tall and thin, rather than short and wide. Or maybe it was the material the case was built from, which looked more organic than artificial – compressed hemp maybe, knowing Todd.

Tentatively he switched it on.

A scattering of tiny motes of light appeared on the screen, swirling in apparent random motion that slowly resolved itself into a movement towards the centre. There they formed an image of Todd Zanderbergen's face and the words *Goldfinch Institute – Secure System*.

He glanced at the desk. Keyboard, yes, but no mouse. In its place sat a circular grey pad. Probably a trackpad. Wireless, apparently, as it had no cable – just like the keyboard. If he ran his fingers across it, a pointer should appear on the screen. Should.

The picture on the screen had changed now to something that looked like a blend of the Windows, iOS and Android home screens: icons set against a background that seemed to show a close-up of a rock face complete with cracks and patches of orange lichen.

He scanned the icons. They seemed to be fairly standard – file explorers, word-processing programs, spreadsheets and so on. So far, so basic.

Experimentally Kieron played around with the computer, moving the pointer (crosshairs rather than an arrow) testing the trackpad and opening up various programs. The underlying logic of the system was no different from any other operating system he'd ever used: the cake was the same, even if the icing and decoration were different.

It took him about half an hour to find his way to the Goldfinch Institute's personnel records. They took the form of a fairly comprehensive database containing all the information one might possibly want to know about every person who had ever worked there and several things that nobody would ever want to know – name, address, date of birth, date of joining the company, date of leaving the company (if appropriate), salary, passport numbers, driving licence, criminal convictions, credit score, race, sexual orientation, status and number of partners and of children, favourite colour, score on several popular personality tests . . . Kieron had suspected Todd Zanderbergen had control issues, and this confirmed it. He seemed to want to know everything.

Swapping the passive ARCC glasses for the active ones, he quickly checked the information Bex had obtained from the medical examiner's office. Unfortunately he had no way of transferring the information from the glasses to the Institute's computer, so he had to type the names in by hand and check them against the database. It took him another half an hour, but eventually he had a list.

He scanned the screen intently.

Yes, the thirty-five employees who had died of heart attacks on the Goldfinch Institute premises last year were all listed. Very neatly, with no emotion. Kieron looked down the list of names – each one of which, he had to remind himself, was a real person, with friends, relatives, loved ones. He searched for any common thread, any similarity that might explain why they all died in the same way at the same place and time.

And he discovered something. Actually, two things.

The first was that each one of those thirty-five employees was listed as having died not at the Goldfinch Institute premises in *Albuquerque*, which is what the medical examiner's records had said, but at one of the Institute's research laboratories – specifically one just outside Tel Aviv, in Israel. Kieron hadn't even realised the Goldfinch Institute *had* a facility in Israel. It hadn't been flagged up on any of the information he'd researched for Bex a few days before. But that's where they'd all died.

The second one – and this took a while to spot – was that

each one had Eastern European heritage. It was the names that gave it away on some of them – lots of surnames ending in -ski, -vitch, -vic, -nvotny, –iak and suchlike. Once he'd spotted that, checking the others revealed that although their names seemed neutral, they had Russian, Polish, Czech, Hungarian, Lithuanian or some other Eastern European parents or grandparents but had changed their names, either through marriage or to fit in better in America.

Thirty-five deaths, all of employees of the same company, all of the same cause, all in the same place, and all with families originating from Eastern Europe. What were the odds? What did it all *mean*?

He leaned back in his seat, almost overbalancing when he realised that there was no back to it and he was sitting on an inflated ball. He regained his balance by flailing his arms around and throwing his weight forward so that he fell across the keyboard.

'Thank God there wasn't anyone around to see that,' he said.

'That,' a voice said behind him, 'is where you're wrong.'

It felt as if someone had poured freezing cold water from a jug, along with the ice cubes, down Kieron's back. He turned slowly. The stability ball squeaked as he moved, ruining the cool, smooth effect he'd been trying to achieve.

Tara Gallagher stood behind him, a security guard on either side of her. They were armed, and their hands were on their weapons.

'If I said I thought I'd left something behind and I'd just popped back to get it, would you believe me?' he asked. On the outside he was being flippant, but on the inside he was panicking. Not only had he been caught red-handed, but he had no way of letting Bex know what had happened. He had both sets of ARCC glasses.

That thought prompted him to remove the pair he was wearing and slip them casually into his jacket pocket, next to the other set. He didn't want Tara noticing anything strange about them.

'That depends,' Tara said unsmilingly. 'What did you leave behind?'

'A cufflink? My mobile?' He shifted on the inflatable ball. It squeaked loudly. 'My self-respect?'

'Oh, I'm not sure you had any self-respect when you first came in here,' she said. 'I told Todd you were too young and that this was some kind of set-up, but he didn't believe me. He was too enthralled by the wonderful product you were trying to get him to invest in.'

'If it helps,' Kieron said, 'I do think it'll actually work.' His mind raced, trying to find some way out of this situation.

'I'll be sure to tell Todd that. He can take the idea off your dead body and exploit it himself.' Finally she smiled. 'He'll probably want to name it after you. He's such a sentimentalist. I'll advise him not to though. Why celebrate the people you've had to crush in the course of business? They should rot in obscurity. Safer that way.'

'And does that apply to the thirty-five people of Eastern European heritage who died of heart attacks in Israel while working for the Goldfinch Institute?' Kieron asked. He didn't expect an honest answer, but he wanted to distract and delay Tara and the guards for a few precious moments.

She shook her head. 'You've watched too many movies,' she said. 'You think I'm just going to explain everything to you. I'm not.'

'But you're not going to kill me,' Kieron pointed out. Just past Tara he could see the lifts. The light above one of them had lit up, indicating that someone was using it. Maybe they were travelling to a lower floor, or maybe they were coming to the fifth floor, where Kieron, Tara and the guards were located. Maybe it was Todd Zanderbergen, arriving to gloat, or maybe it was someone else. He didn't know, but there was a chance it might provide a distraction. Just the faintest chance.

'*Why* am I not going to kill you?' Tara seemed genuinely interested in his answer.

'Because if you were, you'd have done it already. You're keeping me alive so that you can question me – find out why I'm here and who I'm working for.'

'You know the thing about non-lethal weapons?' Tara asked. Before Kieron could answer, she answered her own questions: 'They hurt. Some of them hurt a lot. Take the microwave skin heater you saw earlier. That one *really* hurts. You'll tell me what I want to know, and you'll do it very quickly; I have no doubt about that, no doubt at all.'

Kieron saw, beyond the armed guards, the lift doors slide silently open. Someone stepped out – a cleaner, holding what looked like some high-tech version of a vacuum cleaner. He obviously wasn't expecting the lights to be on. Blinking, he spotted the little group.

'Oh,' he said. 'Sorry. I'll come back.'

Tara and the two guards spun around, surprised. As they did so, Kieron stood up, grabbed the ball he'd been sitting on and threw it at the guard to Tara's left. Before it even hit he'd scooped up the wireless trackpad and skimmed it like a Frisbee towards the other guard. The ball hit the first man and bounced, unbalancing him, as the trackpad caught the second guard in the throat. He started choking.

No time to run to the lifts. Where could he go?

He did the last thing Tara and the guards expected. Instead of running for the lifts and stairwell, he ran in the other direction – towards Todd's office, in the centre of the building.

He got there just as he heard Tara behind him saying, 'He's trapped himself, the fool! Get him!'

He dashed across the office and scooped up the microwave skin heater from the glass display table. He wouldn't have thought to use it, except for Tara's mention of the weapon. Non-lethal, but extremely painful.

As he turned he saw the two guards rushing into the office.

He hefted the weapon, pointed it at them and pressed the trigger.

It only occurred to him then that it might not have had a power pack inside, or, worse, it could have been a model rather than the real thing, but his fears were unfounded. He knew that because the moment he activated it the two guards stopped as if they'd run into a brick wall. Their eyes widened and they started slapping at their clothes as if they were on fire.

Kieron stepped towards them, still firing. The weapon was easy to operate – almost instinctive. *Good design*, he thought. They backed away rapidly through the doorway. One man tried to go left while the other one went right, but Kieron herded them with the invisible beam of energy so that they both went in the same direction – towards Tara.

One of the guards tried to make a break for it, running away to one side, but Kieron used the weapon to make a wall of pain ahead of him. He quickly doubled back towards his friend.

It was like using a hosepipe to move sheep around, Kieron thought, and started to giggle.

The edge of the beam caught Tara, and she squealed.

Bit by bit, Kieron moved the two guards and the Head of Security to one side, giving him a clear run to the stairwell. He thought their skin was starting to go red, although that might just have been the pain, the exertion and the embarrassment of having a teenager shepherding them around. One of the guards tried to pull his gun, but Kieron had already spotted a dial near where his other hand supported the barrel of the weapon. He turned the dial, and the guard started screaming. When the man took his hand off the butt of his gun, Kieron turned the dial down again.

Tara's expression combined pain and fury in equal measure.

Kieron backed through the fire door into the stairwell. The moment the door closed, he sprinted down the stairs, still carrying the weapon. He had to get to the bottom before they did. He guessed Tara and one of the guards would take the lift while the other guard followed him down the stairs.

He passed the doors to the fourth, third and second storeys, expecting at each one to have someone jump through and try to grab him. Nobody did. He almost missed the exit due to the fact that Americans had first floors where English people had ground floors. He'd run past it and down the steps to the basement, wasting precious seconds, before he realised and went back.

The first floor housed the reception lobby. Instead of heading straight out through the doors Kieron went in the other direction, seeking a back exit. He assumed that Tara would have already notified the guard on the main gate to stop him, so he had to either find another way past the security fence or hide out somewhere and come up with a way to alert Bex to his situation.

A door next to the lifts led along a corridor to exactly what he wanted – another way in and out of the building.

And outside the door, in a covered parking area surrounded by blue glass walls and roof and with a tunnel leading to the outside, stood four Harley-Davidsons. Todd Zanderbergen's toys.

Kieron had ridden a motorbike twice before, both times on waste ground near where he lived in Newcastle. He vaguely knew how. He also thought he knew, from computer games rather than real life, how to hot-wire one. Quickly he put the microwave weapon on the floor, straddled one of the motorcycles and followed the three wires from the handlebars to a plastic firing cap. He pulled the firing cap apart and was left holding a piece of plastic with three square holes in it, with the wires leading away into the engine. He needed a loose piece of wire now. Glancing around, he cursed. This place was just too tidy. Trust him to try to steal a bike from a man with control issues.

But he did have the visitors' instructions Judith had given him earlier. They were held together by a metal staple. He pulled the folded bits of paper from his jacket and tore the pages away until he was just holding the staple. He straightened it, then bent it again into a curve.

And he rammed it into the two holes in the firing cap that would make a connected circuit.

As his thumb touched the ignition button on the handlebars something swished past his head and hit a glass wall with a loud *splat*!

Reflexively he turned his head to look. A football-sized mass of blue goo slowly slid down the glass, but it was drying as he watched, hardening into a distorted teardrop-shape, its surface turning into a crazy-paving of hard skin with still-liquid goo oozing between the cracks like lava.

He glanced sideways. Tara Gallagher stood in the tunnel that led out, to freedom. She held a massive bazooka-like gun in both hands: a tubular barrel large enough to fire tennis balls, with a chunky stock and a tube leading to a tank strapped to her back. Kieron didn't know where she'd got it from, but he knew what it was. He'd seen it demonstrated on the Goldfinch Institute video that he'd been forced to sit through in their conference room that morning. It fired a ball of quick-hardening plastic material. The intention was to incapacitate rioters bearing weapons; stop them from committing further acts of violence.

And they were using it against him.

Tara smiled wolfishly. 'Stick around, kid,' she said, and fired again.

Kieron jabbed his thumb on the ignition button. The Harley roared into life and he gripped the handlebars and twisted the accelerator hard. As the bike jerked and then leaped forward he saw a blue projectile emerge from the barrel of the weapon, trailing a tail behind it and looking like some kind of mutant tadpole from a horror film. The weapon bucked so hard in Tara's hand that the projectile shot past Kieron's head and splattered on the blue glass ceiling of the tunnel. It spread out into a thin layer from which blue tentacles started to descend before they set hard into icicle-like spikes. As he careened beneath them he heard them snapping like tiny bells.

The Harley seemed to buck beneath him like a living animal, and then he was speeding through the tunnel. It felt as if the motorcycle was in charge, not him. It was all he could do to stay in the saddle. The fact that he was half reclining in a kind of dentist's chair position didn't help.

The roar of the Harley's engine echoed back from the glass walls of the tunnel, filling the space with sound. Moments later he was out into the night, careering along between slanted walls of blue glass. Glancing left he saw another rider on another motorcycle, this one on some kind of platform a metre or so above him. He seemed to be leaning over, towards Kieron. His teeth were clenched hard and his hands were clamped on the motorcycle's handlebars with professional-looking skill. And then he realised. This

191

wasn't another rider; this was him, reflected in the slanted glass. He looked so competent, so aware of what he was doing, that Kieron felt a sudden burst of confidence. If his reflection could do it, so could he.

Looking right he noticed another reflection. Three Kierons, three bikes, all moving together like a formation team. All working as one.

Up ahead the two glass walls he was speeding between ended at a crossroads where four buildings met. Kieron cursed. There'd been a map of the Institute in the reception lobby earlier, but like a fool he hadn't thought to memorise it. Yes, the ARCC glasses had faithfully recorded the image, but he wasn't going to stop now and check for directions. He had to make a decision.

He slowed, and slewed the bike so that when it got to the junction he'd be facing left. Small stones sprayed up from beneath his tyres. He skidded out past the edge of the building and found himself staring straight down another glass canyon, heading who knew where.

A football-sized blue mass hit the building by his shoulder. Tara.

The goo splattered like a dropped bowl of porridge, sending tendrils in all directions. As he watched, it started to harden.

He twisted the accelerator and headed down this new channel. His engine noise, magnified, echoed back from the glass, deafening him.

Another junction up ahead – this one with just one alternative route, off to his right. Turn, or keep going?

Turning would take a precious few seconds but it would

disguise his course. If he kept on riding straight then Tara, when she came around the last corner, would see him and be able to report where he was heading, maybe set up a roadblock. He slowed, twisted the handlebars right and leaned with the curve. The Harley obeyed his instructions perfectly. He had exerted dominance.

He slid into the junction, ready to accelerate, but something was wrong. For a moment he thought that he was looking directly at his own reflection in a glass wall, but that wasn't it. This wall must be straight, not slanted, because the reflection wasn't tilted.

And it was still coming at him, even though he'd slowed for the turn.

It wasn't a reflection: it was another Harley. One of the guards must have taken another of Todd's bikes. Or been told to take it by Tara.

Kieron couldn't haul his bike back in time to keep going down the path he'd just come off. The bike was too heavy. He only had one choice.

He gunned the throttle again and accelerated straight at the oncoming bike.

The guard wasn't wearing a helmet. His features had contorted into a snarl, but Kieron wasn't sure if it was the speed of the air against his face that had forced it into that expression or whether he was just really, really angry.

The two bikes headed for each other at catastrophic speed.

At the last second, Kieron twisted his handlebars. His bike veered left and mounted the slanted glass wall. Like a trick rider, he was defying gravity, riding on the glass rather than the ground. It seemed strong enough to take the weight – for now. As the two Harleys passed each other in opposite directions, everything seemed to be in slow motion, and Kieron realised they were so close he could have reached out and tweaked the other rider's ear. And then they'd passed each other and time returned to normal speed. Kieron steered right and his bike obediently came back to flat earth again.

The other rider wasn't so lucky. Kieron heard a banshee screech of brakes, then a *crash!* so loud that it overpowered even the roar of the two engines. The bike had run straight into the wall, and the glass hadn't been strong enough to withstand this direct assault. As Kieron drove away he heard a distant *whoomph!* as petrol spilling from the tank ignited.

Now that there was nothing in his way Kieron could see that the channel between the buildings ahead of him ended not in another featureless glass wall but in a patch of open ground and a section of chain-link fence. It was a glimpse of freedom. Yes, he still had the two fences to negotiate, but that was a problem he could worry about in, oh, say, thirty seconds' time. His task now was to get there, alive and in one piece. One problem at a time.

The ends of the two buildings forming his channel were just three bike lengths ahead when a door in the right-hand wall abruptly opened and Tara Gallagher stepped out. She was breathing hard, having run through several buildings to get there, and she held the goo gun in her hands. She aimed it and fired – not at Kieron, but at the front wheel of his Harley. The sticky foam hit the spinning spokes and splattered in all directions, but some of it had stuck. As Kieron zoomed past and saw Tara swing the weapon like a club at his head, he also noticed that his bike was suddenly moving much slower than it should have been. It was like driving through thick mud.

Before Tara could fire at his back and incapacitate him, Kieron slammed on the brakes. The front wheels locked and he threw his weight forward, standing up on the foot supports. Momentum caused the rear end of the bike to rise up in the air, shielding Kieron from Tara's next shot but propelling him over the handlebars. For a long moment he hung in mid-air, but then gravity prevailed and he hit the ground, rolling over and over, feeling the skin on his hands and his back scraping against small stones.

To anyone standing outside, by the fence, it would have seemed as if Kieron had suddenly been fired out of the gap between the buildings like a bullet from a gun.

He lost count of the number of times he rolled, but one thought dominated his mind: the fence he was heading towards was electrified! If he hit it, he would die!

He twisted as he rolled, so that his feet were ahead of him, and then he dug his heels into the ground, slowing him, but not enough. The wires were just two metres away from him now. Desperately he splayed his hands and clawed his fingers into the earth.

He stopped with his face just inches from the deadly wire.

Exhausted, battered and mentally frozen, he took a breath to steady himself. All he wanted to do was lie down and rest, but something kept him going. It was the knowledge that he still had a job to do.

He suddenly realised that the tarmacked area where Bex had dropped him earlier was just off to his right, beyond the two fences. It was empty of cars. The security turnstiles and the cabin by the gates were there too, but the cabin's door swung open and he could see nobody inside. The guard had probably been called out to help in the chase. If Kieron could reach the turnstiles, he might be able to get through – *if* the ARCC glasses with Judith's iris image stored in their memory hadn't been broken in the crash and *if* the turnstiles hadn't been locked in a security crackdown.

His right hand pulled Bex's glasses from his jacket pocket and his legs twitched as his subconscious tried to persuade the rest of him to run towards the turnstiles, but in his conscious mind he knew that the game was up. Tara was clever: she would have locked the site down by now.

Which meant that Kieron needed to do something else.

He glanced over his shoulder. It had only been a few seconds since the crash, although it seemed much longer. Nobody else had emerged from the gap between the buildings, but they would, any moment now, he had no doubt.

Quickly checking that he'd pulled the correct pair out, and he wasn't about to throw the ones he thought of as 'his' set, Kieron flung the ARCC glasses with all his strength. They sailed above the first fence, but Kieron had always been terrible at cricket and rounders at school, and his lack of muscles and co-ordination showed. The glasses reached the top of their arc somewhere between the two fences and began their inevitable descent. He wasn't sure if they would make it over the second fence. If they didn't, they would be trapped between them.

'So, Ryan,' came Tara's voice from behind him, 'Todd will *not* be happy with you.'

Kieron turned. 'I take it the Lethal Insomnia trip is off?' he asked, loudly enough to disguise the sound of the glasses landing. He thought he heard them hit tarmac rather than sand, but he wasn't sure.

'Three Harley Davidsons totally wrecked,' Tara said. She walked towards him, keeping the huge weapon pointed at him. 'Quite a score.'

'I only counted one wrecked, and one goo-ed up,' he objected.

She grimaced. 'The one that you "goo-ed up" –' she started to say, but he interrupted her.

'*You* goo-ed it up, not me.'

'Children,' she muttered, then, louder: 'The one that was goo-ed up, by people yet to be established, will take a lot of restoration to get the scratches out. And the goo has an unfortunate corrosive effect on metal. A lot of the parts will need to be replaced. The second bike drove into a glass wall and burned up, while the third was driven into the security fence at the far side of the Institute by a guard who'd never ridden a bike before and didn't know what he was doing.'

'You can't blame me for that last one,' Kieron protested. 'And frankly the other two are a bit of a stretch.'

'It's not up to me,' she said, raising the goo gun so that

197

it pointed at his face. 'Todd will *not* be happy about this. One of them was a customised Hardtail Bobber, one was ridden by Steve McQueen in *The Great Escape* and one was ridden by Peter Fonda in *Easy Rider*. Those last two are the very definition of "irreplaceable".'

Things had got very confusing for Kieron. He felt as if he'd been pummelled all over his body; his head hurt, the scratches on his hands and his back stung, and he seemed to be expected to keep his end up in an increasingly bizarre conversation.

'I think I saw *The Great Escape* a few years ago, at Christmas,' he said weakly. 'I've never seen *Easy Rider*.'

'Of course you haven't,' Tara said dismissively. 'You're only a kid, and they haven't done a big-budget remake with CGI.' She sighed. 'Both films – all the good guys die. It's just like real life. Now brace yourself – this won't be pleasant.'

Kieron stared down the barrel of her weapon. 'You're not going to fire that at my face, are you? It's meant to incapacitate, not choke, surely?'

'Normally I'd aim it at your arms or legs,' Tara admitted, 'but you've annoyed me.'

'You said it corrodes metal! What about skin?'

'Let's find out,' she said. And pulled the trigger.

CHAPTER TEN

They parked up on the side of the interstate, in a lay-by that seemed to be set up for truckers who needed a break. Fortunately, they were the only ones there. Sitting in the hire car, listening to some bizarre American rock station whose name was composed of random-sounding initials – KVCG or KUJG or something – Bex was getting increasingly worried. She realised this because her fingers were drumming on the steering wheel, because she kept changing the radio station to see if there was anything better to listen to, and because Sam kept saying, 'Are you all right? You seem nervous.'

'Something's wrong,' she said eventually.

From where he sat in the back, Sam patted her shoulder reassuringly. 'Nothing's wrong. Kieron's intelligent. He's even fairly active. He'll complete the mission. OK, we've driven past the car park three times now and he's not been there, but all that means is that he hasn't got into the computers yet. He's fine. Trust me.'

'You don't know that,' Bex said.

After a few moments silence Sam said, in a small voice,

'You're right – I don't. I'm just trying to keep your spirits up. And mine.'

'You guys watch a lot of movies, don't you?' Bex asked.

'Yeah. Why?'

'You know that whenever a character says, "I'm sure everything's OK," it's about to go terribly wrong?'

'Yeah. It's a cliché. Or a trope, which is what we call it these days.'

'Yeah, thanks for that glimpse into teenage slang.' She took a breath. 'And you know whenever a character says, "Something's wrong," then something *is* actually wrong, and the audience is just about to find out how wrong it is?'

Sam's voice sounded like each word was being pulled from him with forceps. 'Yeah. I know films like that.'

'Well, something's wrong.'

'What do you want to do?'

'I don't know.' And it was true – she didn't. Her careful preparation of Kieron for this mission had covered everything that he might do, depending on a range of circumstances, but hadn't, she realised belatedly, addressed what she would do if she started getting worried. 'Let's drive back to the security gate again, just to see if anything's changed.'

Bex put the car in drive and pulled off. She'd chosen the waiting area carefully: just a little way ahead an intersection lay where she could turn around and go back to the Goldfinch Institute turn-off.

Thirteen minutes later they were heading back down the road to the Institute.

As they got closer, Bex noticed that the low clouds in the

sky seemed to be reflecting light from the Institute. Irregular, flashing light. Blue light.

'Someone's activated the alarms,' she said. 'I think Kieron's been discovered.' She pressed down hard on the accelerator.

'What will they do to him?' Sam asked.

'I don't know. It depends how guilty they are. If there's a simple explanation for the deaths of so many people in the same place for the same reason, then they'll probably call the police. If that's what's happened we can probably negotiate him out of custody fairly easily. Or break him out.' She took a deep breath. 'If, on the other hand, the Goldfinch Institute are at fault then they might just take him off for questioning.'

'And that means . . . ?'

'I'm not going to lie to you, Sam – it means they're going to hurt him.'

Silence from the back seat, then: 'We need to rescue him.'

'We do, but he's got both pairs of the glasses. We're literally and metaphorically going in blind.'

The Goldfinch Institute appeared over the horizon: a mass of blue glass buildings reflecting the light of the desert moon. As they approached it was obvious that alarm lights were flashing all over the complex, giving it the look of a macabre dance club.

'This is bad,' Sam whispered. 'This is really bad.'

'I'll do a slow drive-past of the parking area,' Bex said, as she approached the security cabin. 'If we're lucky, Kieron will have got out and will be waiting there.'

He wasn't. The tarmac square was empty. Bex didn't stop, but she made sure she drove through the area slowly enough that Kieron could make his presence known, if he was there.

The back of her neck itched. Someone was watching her careful drive-past. Maybe a security guard in the cabin; maybe someone else, somewhere else. And she didn't think it was Kieron.

'Stop!' Sam said urgently.

'Why?' Bex asked, but she was already slowing down.

'I saw something.'

She brought the car to a stop. As she tried to look casual, like a wife who'd come by to pick up a husband who was working late, she heard Sam move across the leather upholstery towards the driver's side back door. It opened and he slid out.

Bex noticed that across the tarmac, beyond the security fence, a guard had left the cabin and was staring at her.

'Hurry,' she said. 'Whatever you're doing, just hurry.'

The security guard started to walk towards her. Either he had a hidden remote control or there was someone else in the cabin, because the metal barriers started sliding down to allow him to exit.

'Sam?' she hissed.

'Got it!' he said, sliding back into the car and shutting the door.

Bex put the car back into drive and began to accelerate towards the one road that led to the Institute. In her rear-view mirror she kept watching the security guard. He stood there uncertainly, one hand on the butt of his gun.

'What have you got?' she asked as they sped away.

'Kieron's glasses,' Sam said bleakly. 'Either he dropped them, or he threw them over for us to find or because he didn't want to be caught with them.'

'Which pair are they?'

'Does it matter? They've got Kieron.'

'Yes, it matters. Which glasses?'

'The ones that Bradley was wearing when we first saw him, and Kieron used when you were in Mumbai and Pakistan, and you had on when he went into the Institute this morning. Those ones.'

'Thank heavens,' she said. 'Quick – put them on! See if you can see what Kieron's looking at!'

'Did you hear what I said?' Sam said, slipping the glasses on: '*They've got Kieron!*'

'Yes, but if *we've* got those glasses – if he managed to get those glasses to *us* – then we hopefully have a record of what's happened to him and what he found out. And that's the only thing that might help us to rescue him! Well done for spotting them. I could have driven right over them.'

'Nothing,' he said angrily. 'Just darkness.' He pulled the glasses off in disgust. 'They're switched off, or in a bag or something.' He shook his head. 'We have to get in there. We've got to get him out!'

Bex tried to keep her voice calm and level, even though she didn't feel in the slightest bit calm. 'The best thing we can do,' she said, 'is get out of here, so we don't get taken as well. We're no help to Kieron if we get captured. Once we're back, we can look at the glasses, see if he managed to record anything we can use. We can also talk to Bradley and see if he's got any ideas.'

'But you're employed by MI6!' Sam protested. 'Call them in to help!'

'That's not how it works, Sam. This is a deniable operation, which means MI6 won't even admit we exist. And remember – I'm not even supposed to have involved you and Kieron. No, we need to sort this out ourselves.' She sighed. 'Somehow.'

The tense and silent drive back to the hotel took half an hour, taking them from the desert isolation of the Goldfinch Institute to the perpetual lights and traffic of the centre of Albuquerque. Late though it was, cars, trucks and vans were heading in all directions, but Bex had never felt so alone. This had been her nightmare – getting Kieron into a dangerous, potentially lethal, situation just because he'd wanted to help. This was what she'd fought so hard to avoid. She should never have agreed to keep in contact with him. When she'd returned from India she should have taken the ARCC glasses and the earpiece from him, grabbed Bradley and relocated somewhere Kieron couldn't find her.

But beneath all that, beneath the professional guilt over getting an innocent member of the public involved in intelligence matters, there was something else. She *liked* Kieron. She'd come to really appreciate his attitude, his resilience, his intelligence and even his taste in music. Sometimes. If anything bad should happen to him, she didn't know how she'd be able to cope.

'Bex . . .'

'Yes,' she said softly.

'I'm sorry I got angry. It's not your fault.'

'It *is* my fault.'

'Kieron made his own choices, and I've never seen him happier than he's been this past month. It's like he's found something to believe in.' Sam hesitated for a moment. 'We're greebs. We don't believe in anything apart from darkness and the ultimate futility of human existence.'

'And ice cream,' Bex pointed out.

'And ice cream,' Sam conceded. 'But we've both discovered there's something bigger than ourselves that we can help with. That we can make a *difference* to. Kieron isn't here by accident – he made a choice. And so did I. You should respect that.'

Arriving in the hotel car park, Bex chose a spot away from other cars and in the shade of a desert tree with wide, spreading leaves. At least that meant the car would be slightly cooler when they came back to it. She checked the time. Sunrise would be occurring in maybe an hour or so. She needed sleep, but she had to keep going. She had to find Kieron.

As she opened the door to get out of the car, her mobile rang. Getting back in, she pulled it from her pocket. Probably Bradley, she thought – it was mid-afternoon in the UK. She quailed slightly at the prospect of telling him what had happened, but he might be able to help, and he had to know that things had gone wrong.

The ringing continued, but not from the mobile she held. It still came from her pocket.

She pulled out her *other* mobile – the one that she'd bought back in England to use as part of her undercover identity.

'Hello?' No mention of her name – that was standard practice for agents. Just an acknowledgement that she was there, listening.

'Hello?' A woman's voice. She recognised it, but couldn't place it. 'Is that Chloe Gibbons?'

Chloe Gibbons – the supposed publicist for the Lethal Insomnia competition. Her current cover identity. And now she recognised the voice – it was Kieron's mother.

'Yes,' she said, feeling her heart race. A tight band seemed to be gripping her chest, stopping her from breathing properly. 'Who is this?' She knew perfectly well, but she had to buy a few moments to get herself under control.

'This is Veronica – Veronica Mellor. I've been trying to phone Kieron to see how he is. Everything's OK, isn't it? It's just – I haven't heard from him.'

'Everything's fine, Mrs Mellor,' Bex said, trying to sound as reassuring as she could. 'The boys crashed out after the flight. They were exhausted, poor things. That's probably why Kieron hasn't called you.'

'Could you put him on – just for a second. I want to hear his voice, just to reassure myself.'

'Oh, I'm really sorry but I'm afraid he's in the studio with the band right now,' Bex said. She mentally crossed her fingers. 'I could drag him out, if you like.'

'No – don't do that,' Kieron's mother said hurriedly. 'He'd never forgive me. Is he eating properly?'

'Like a horse.'

'Not crap food – *good* food. Not chips and burgers and stuff.'

Bex remembered back to the ice creams, but said, 'I'm making sure they're both getting fresh vegetables and proper steaks. They seem to like the food here.'

'And Sam – is he having fun?'

She glanced over at Sam and put a finger to her lips, just in case he was going to say something. 'Yes, he's having a great time too.'

'And they're not too much for you to cope with?'

'They're both great boys.' She hesitated. 'Kieron's a credit to you, Mrs Mellor. He's been brought up really well.'

'Thank you. It's been . . . hard. Especially since his dad left. Look, I don't want to waste your time. Just, you know, get him to ring his mum, will you? And tell him I love him.'

'I will. And don't worry – he's having the time of his life.'

'Thank you.' She rang off, and Bex just sat there for a moment, holding the phone up to her ear. Those last seven words had been the hardest lie she'd ever had to tell.

'You should phone *your* mum,' she said eventually to Sam.

'Oh, she's probably forgotten I'm abroad,' he said levelly, looking away out of the car window. 'She probably thinks I'm down at the local youth club or something.' He paused for a moment. 'It's a big family,' he went on. 'Easy to lose track of a child or two.'

Bex wanted to say something reassuring, but she couldn't think of anything that might help. Instead she pushed her door open, intending to leave the car, but something made her stay where she was. It took her a moment to work out what had triggered her mental alarm bells.

'Sam?'

'Yeah?'

'Your room overlooks this car park, doesn't it?'

He thought for a second. 'Yeah, it does. I'd hoped for, like, a desert view or something, or maybe a panoramic view of the city, but all I get is tarmac, trees, cars and white lines. Why?'

'Which one is your room?'

He craned his neck, gazing up at the concrete edifice of the hotel. 'Third floor, two windows along from the end . . . oh. That's odd.'

'What do you see?'

'There's someone at the window. They're looking down here. Maybe I got it wrong.' He thought for a moment. 'Maybe there's another car park.'

'There isn't another car park, and there *is* someone in your room. And probably in mine as well. They've realised that Kieron isn't all he seems, and so they've come to take us prisoner.'

'They've stepped back,' Sam said. 'They've let the curtains fall back.'

'Then they've seen us, and probably alerted their people. They'll be coming for us.' Bex turned the key in the ignition. 'We need to get out of here.'

As Sam scrabbled to get his seat belt back on she reversed rapidly out of the bay, nearly hitting a black SUV that had appeared out of nowhere and which seemed determined to block their path. She managed to weave around it like a drunk driver spotting an obstruction just in time, then slam the car into drive and accelerate away.

Across the car park, people wearing black had appeared from all the hotel entrances. Two other black SUVs had leaped out of their parking spots and were converging on them.

Rather than crash into the SUV directly ahead of her, Bex veered left, heading diagonally across the parking lot and through the gap between a lemon-yellow sports car and a battered pick-up truck that was only a few centimetres wider than their car. She made it with just a bump or two but without hearing any squealing metal.

'We may have lost a door handle,' Sam shouted over the roar of the engine. 'Just saying.'

The SUV that had tried to block their exit had followed them, almost bumper to bumper. Too late, the driver realised they were driving a wider vehicle as the SUV slammed into the sports car and the truck. The sports car spun round, glass smashing and alarm blaring. The truck just rocked back on its suspension. In her rear-view mirror Bex could see a sudden bloom of white in the SUV's windscreen as the airbags deployed.

One down; no idea how many to go.

'Head over there!' Sam shouted, pointing to a distant corner of the car park.

'Why?'

'Why do people always ask why when you tell them to do something? Just do it! Please!'

She plotted the quickest route in her head: straight along a row of cars, then left across a stretch of tarmac kept clear for access, then right again. As she manoeuvred to get into the right row she glanced around. The car park had two entrances – one on a main route and one on a side road. It looked to her as if both had been blocked off by black SUVs. Whatever Sam had in mind, she hoped it was good.

The rear windscreen suddenly crazed over. An instant later Bex thought she heard a *bang*! Effect before cause: that meant the bullet was travelling faster than the speed of sound. *That* meant the people trying to catch them were armed with high-power handguns – something like .44 Magnums. Either that or someone in the hotel had a rifle.

A person in a hotel with a rifle: that would be ironic, considering what had happened to her in Mumbai just a week ago.

Approaching the turn, Bex realised that an SUV was coming up behind her. It would probably use the standard car-takedown technique: come alongside and then nudge the rear bumper of her car with its front bumper, sending her into an uncontrolled spin. She had to stop them doing that, which meant she couldn't slow down too much as she approached the junction. Instead she kept up her speed and actually passed the entrance to the access route.

'You missed the turn!' Sam said.

Bex crossed her hands on the steering wheel – left hand on the right side and vice versa. 'No, I didn't,' she said.

'I know what you're going to do!' Sam shouted. 'I've seen it in movies.'

'Hang on!' she said. Reaching down quickly, she pulled the handbrake up. The rear wheels locked, dragging against the tarmac and sending up plumes of smoke. Both hands back on the wheel, she turned it quickly. The car slewed through 180 degrees, so that it was now facing back the way they'd come. She released the handbrake again and floored the accelerator. The car leaped forward, heading back for a junction that was now invisible behind a wall of smoke.

A wall of smoke broken by the SUV that had been behind them. Bex had a momentary flash of the surprised faces of the driver and his passengers – all dressed in black and all, strangely, with red hair – as she sped past. They were too busy staring at her to notice one of the concrete bars that separated the car spaces from the access roads. Their car hit it at speed. The front of the car stopped abruptly, while the back rose up into the air, wheels spinning. Bex didn't like to think about the chaos inside. The car seemed to stand impossibly on its nose, like some bizarre sculpture, but it couldn't stay there forever. Slowly it toppled back down, slamming against the tarmac and bouncing.

'Cat in a washing machine,' Sam said, grinning as Bex made it through the right-hand turn that moments before had been a left turn. She accelerated away.

'What?'

'That's what they probably feel like.'

She turned right again, heading alongside another row of parked cars. Somewhere over to her right she became dimly aware of another SUV, with a third to her left.

Ahead of them she saw the end of the car park: a two-metre high wall of hedge stretching away in both directions, with concrete bars along its base.

'What was your brilliant idea?' she asked as they raced towards the hedge.

'There's a gap, straight ahead. See – there's no concrete bar. The hedge has grown across the gap.'

Bex was amazed. 'How did you find that?'

Sam sounded shifty. 'Kieron and I came down for a quick vape earlier, before we left. We had to – the entire hotel's covered with smoke detectors. We noticed it then.'

They were travelling so fast that, in a few more seconds, it would be too late to brake.

'Just out of interest, what's on the other side?' Bex asked, trying to sound casual. In her imagination it was the side of a building.

'A disused car park,' Sam explained. 'All cracked and covered with weeds.'

Now it *was* too late to brake. They were committed. All Bex could do was hope Sam was right. She kept her foot on the accelerator and forced her eyes to stay open as the hedge filled the windshield.

Crunch! and they were through, in a storm of leaves and twigs. Just as Sam had said, the car park on the other side was like the evil twin of the pristine one they'd been chased through: cracked, broken and abandoned. But there was an exit on the far side, and Bex steered directly for it.

Once on the main road, she sped away, then turned off as soon as possible. She kept an eye on the rear-view mirror through two more turns, but nobody appeared to be following them.

'Where to now?' Sam asked breathlessly.

'Somewhere anonymous where we can rest up and look at what Kieron has left for us.'

She drove back towards the airport, on the basis that there would be hotels there she and Sam could hole up in. She ignored the first few they passed, eventually turning in to a motel-style place where rooms more like cabins were arranged around a parking area, meaning you could park your car right next to your room. She told Sam to stay in the car while she went and booked a single room from the cabin that operated as the motel's reception desk, reasoning that anyone looking for them would be searching for a woman and a boy, probably in two rooms. As far as the unshaven man in reception knew, she was a lone woman. And besides, she had no intention of being there long.

It was almost dawn. The sky to the east had taken on a rose-coloured blush, and the air was already beginning to heat up. Their car was reasonably anonymous, but while Sam caught some sleep she returned it to the airport, then walked to a different rental firm and hired a different car. She stopped off at a diner on the way back and picked up food for them both.

Sam was asleep on the bed when she got there, fully clothed and snoring. Bex sat down in the room's only chair, slipped the ARCC glasses on and began to scroll through the material Kieron had recorded.

An hour later she took the glasses off, massaged her temples and sighed deeply.

Sam turned over and looked at her muzzily. 'What is it?'

'Sorry – I didn't mean to disturb you. You should try and sleep some more.'

'I'd rather know.'

She sighed. 'Kieron found out a lot of stuff before he got caught – and yes, he did get caught. Those thirty-five employees – they all died of heart attacks, like we thought, but they didn't die here in Albuquerque – they died in Israel. Tel Aviv. The Goldfinch Institute has a branch out there apparently. They do a lot of work with the Israel Defense Forces. Oh, and all the people that died were of Eastern European heritage.'

'What?'

'You can tell from their names. They're all Polish, Czech, Romanian, Bosnian, Croatian . . .'

'What else?' Sam asked, sitting up.

'What do you mean?'

'I mean, I can see it in your eyes. There's something else.'

Bex gestured to the bags of food she'd got from the diner, which she'd left on the dressing table. 'There's breakfast over there, if you want some.'

'Tell me.'

She sighed, then flicked her way through the recorded material stored inside the glasses until she found the particular bit she'd tagged earlier. 'Take a look at this,' she said, throwing the glasses to him. 'Tell me what you think.'

Sam slipped the glasses on. 'OK, this is one of those fancy computers Kieron said they had in the Institute. He's looking at the screen, and those are his hands on the keyboard. He's accessed the personnel records. There's a handwritten list by the side of the computer – I'm guessing

214

he's cross-referencing the names of the dead staff members you got from the medical examiner with the list of people employed by Todd Zanderbergen.' He paused. 'How am I doing? Do I get a prize?'

'Look at the various divisions of the company where the staff were employed.'

'Administration,' Sam read, 'Finance, Non-Lethal Weapons, Computing, Genetics . . . All obvious stuff.'

'Yes,' Bex said, 'but the Genetics division didn't appear on the company information we researched before we came here. And it's not in the promotional material they showed Kieron either. As far as the rest of the world is concerned, the Goldfinch Institute doesn't do genetic research.'

'What's the problem? Genetics is the next big thing – being able to decode our DNA, make changes to it, cure diseases caused by defects in the genes. Any research institute worth the name would be looking into that kind of thing.'

'But why hide it?' Bex closed her eyes, hoping that the suspicion forming in her mind was wrong. 'Let me put it this way – a company involved in military research that has a secret genetics laboratory suffers a whole load of unexplained deaths, but only of employees with Eastern European heritage. Eastern European *genes*.'

The silence in the room went on for a long time after she said those words. Eventually she opened her eyes. Sam was staring at her. The expression on his face was one of shock.

'They're developing biological weapons designed to kill people with particular *DNA*?' he whispered. 'Why would they do that?'

'Why wouldn't they?' Bex shook her head. 'The history of the human race is a history of racial groups hating and fighting each other. Arabs against Jews in the Middle East. Hutu against Tutsi in Rwanda. Bosnians against Serbs in Eastern Europe. White against black everywhere you look. Go back a few hundred years and it was the British against the Dutch and the Spanish against the French. You've heard the word "genocide"? The United Nations defines genocide as "acts committed with intent to destroy, in whole or in part, a national, ethnic, racial or religious group". And how can you distinguish one national, ethnic or racial group from another? Genetic testing. Now, imagine that one racial group gets hold of a weapon, like a gas or a virus or something, that can destroy *only* people with a different genetic make-up. What would happen?'

'Carnage,' Sam whispered. 'Wholesale slaughter, until the only people left in the world are the people who have the same DNA as the people with the weapon.'

'And that,' Bex said, 'is what I think we're up against – a man who has developed a weapon exactly like that.'

'Can we stop him?'

Despite the seriousness of the situation, Bex felt a wave of affection wash over her for the scruffy little urchin she'd somehow ended up with. No thought of getting away, no suggestion that they pretend they didn't know anything. His first thought was how they could deal with the situation they'd discovered. 'You're a good kid, you know that?' she said.

His expression was serious, and a shadow darkened his

216

eyes. 'I'm a greeb,' he said. 'Kieron's a greeb. We get chased down the street by chavs wherever we go. If the chavs could get hold of a way to eradicate all greebs and all emos, they'd do it without a second thought. That's why we can't let this go. But first we have to get Kieron back.'

Bex nodded. 'I'll see what I can find out. Pass me the glasses, will you?'

Putting them back on, Bex pushed away the recording Kieron had uploaded and tried to get into the Goldfinch Institute's admin-level computers using the hacking tools built into the ARCC kit. All she wanted to know was whether the police had been called to the site last night or whether Kieron's illegal entry had been reported, but it was no good – the security clampdown meant that the Institute had ramped up their firewalls. No way in, even to the areas they'd been able to access the day before.

'If Kieron's still being held,' she said, more to herself than to Sam, 'then we're going to have problems. They'll be expecting us to try and rescue him. If we thought it was difficult to get in before, it'll be nigh-on impossible now.'

'If he's still there,' Sam mused.

'Actually, that's a point.' She frowned, thinking. 'Zanderbergen might decide to leave the area for a while, and he might take Kieron with him.' Quickly she accessed the Albuquerque airport computer, hacking in to the data on flights in and out. 'Damn – someone filed a flight plan for a jet belonging to the Goldfinch Institute. Destination is . . . yes, of course. Tel Aviv. Due to take off in . . . no! Half an hour!' She moved her hands, manipulating information.

217

'If I can get access to the airport's security cameras in the VIP area . . . yes, I've got a live feed!' Her triumph was short-lived, replaced with anger and despair as she found herself looking at a picture being taken probably by a camera on a pole. It showed an executive jet with its stairway extended. A limousine sat at the bottom of the stairs. Todd Zanderbergen stood halfway up the steps, looking back towards the terminal. And at the bottom of the stairs, Bex's old friend and colleague Tara Gallagher had her arms around someone as she helped them out of the back of the car.

The person's head hung low, but Bex knew who it was. She recognised the jacket, the shoes she'd bought, the hair. Everything about him.

It was Kieron.

CHAPTER ELEVEN

Kieron regained consciousness suddenly. One minute he was out cold, floating in a dark void, and the next he jerked awake in a comfortable seat, eyes open wide and hands clenched.

'Ah, you're back.' Todd Zanderbergen sat opposite Kieron. He had a glass of champagne in his hand. 'I know teenagers sleep a lot, but you were going for the record. Tara and I had a bet on it.' He took a sip of the champagne. 'I won.'

'Yeah, I suspect you usually do,' Kieron said. 'Doesn't it get boring?' His mouth was dry, and his eyes felt gritty. He tried to move, but he'd been restrained.

He looked around. He seemed to be on an aircraft, but a small one, upholstered in white leather and with mushroom-shaped wooden tables that looked like they'd been carved out of oak. Circular windows ran along each curved wall. Blue light spilled in from outside, but he didn't know what time it was. Several seats were scattered around the narrow cabin. Todd sat in one of them; Tara Gallagher sat in another. Both of them faced the seat where he'd been imprisoned.

'What's the last thing you remember?' Todd asked. 'It's a professional question: I'm not interested in the state of your health.'

'Your Head of Security firing some kind of blue goo at my head.' Kieron glanced at Tara. 'I thought that stuff was just meant to harden around people and stop them from moving – not stop them from *breathing*.'

Tara just raised an eyebrow. It was Todd who answered. 'Yes, Tara did exceed the usage specifications a bit, but it's all information we can feed into the research programme. Grist to the mill, as they say, although I have no idea what grist is or why it should go through a mill. Do people have grist mills? I should Google it.'

He paused and took another sip of champagne. 'You've been unconscious for about eight hours. Part of that was due to the immobilising foam hitting your head and knocking you out; part of it was due to your mouth being obstructed and you having problems breathing. Some of it might be down to you being a teenager and just needing to sleep a lot; I honestly don't know. You're lucky Tara scraped enough of the stuff off your face so that you could breathe.' He frowned in fake concern. 'You might want to run your tongue around your teeth when you get a moment, check for any of the hardened gel that might still be there. I don't think we've run the toxicology tests yet. Best not swallow it by accident.'

Tara held a hand up. 'I've still got some underneath my fingernails,' she said. 'It's hell to get out.'

'We're travelling somewhere,' Kieron said. He could

feel the vibration of the aircraft's engine through the seat, although the noise insulation in the cabin seemed very good. 'Is it somewhere I might have wanted to go?'

'I don't know.' Todd shrugged. 'Ever wanted to go to Israel?'

Israel, Kieron thought with a sense of impending panic. A long way from the USA. Not as far from the UK, but I wouldn't want to walk it. All he could hope was that Bex and Sam had found the ARCC glasses he'd thrown over the fence, that they were intact, and that somehow his friends had managed to trace where he was and where he was going and could follow. That was a lot of things to hope for, but if they didn't all come true then he was in trouble.

Actually, even if Bex and Sam *did* manage to trace where he was going, it might still all end badly. What were they going to do – two people against a corrupt massive international research and development company?

Thoughts of the ARCC glasses suddenly made him wonder about the *other* set, the ones Bex usually wore. He hadn't thrown those ones over the fence. Or the earpiece either. Impulsively he reached up and checked the inside pocket of his jacket, where he'd left them. Even if Bex and Sam found the VR set and followed him to Israel, they wouldn't be able to contact him unless he had them. A shiver of panic ran through him as his questing fingers didn't find anything. Had he been searched? Had all his things been confiscated?

He ran his hands through his hair and his fingertips touched something plastic, something that curved. The arms of the ARCC glasses. He slid his hand down and felt his fingernails brush against a hard lump. The earpiece.

He took a deep, relieved breath. At least he still had *his* kit.

Across the table, Tara stared at him curiously. He scratched in an exaggerated way at his chest.

'Itch,' he said to her. 'Have you checked this aircraft for fleas? I think you might have an infestation.'

Tara sneered and looked away.

'Oh, forgive me,' Todd said. 'I'm being a terrible host. Would you like a drink? Not champagne, I'm afraid.' He held up the glass and looked into it, at the tiny bubbles. 'One mouthful of this costs more than most people spend on a car. I wouldn't waste it on you.' He seemed calm, but Kieron sensed an undercurrent of anger. It reminded him of the times he and Sam had been confronted by chavs in the shopping centre or the local recreation ground: they'd ask nice questions, like 'What's your name?' and 'Where are you going?' but you knew it was just a precursor to them punching you in the gut and then laughing when you crumpled up in pain.

'You hear these stories,' Kieron said casually, 'of rich bankers in the City of London spending tens of thousands of pounds on a single bottle of wine. My mum once said she doesn't know what's worse – the idea that there's one less bottle of incredible wine in the world or the idea that the rich bankers just swilled it down without appreciating it properly. So, is that champagne worth the money you paid for it?'

'I say again that it costs more than most people spend on a car,' Todd said carefully, 'but I prefer motorcycles. I have a neat collection of Harleys. Or at least I did until you managed to destroy them during your rather pathetic attempt at escape. And it's not as if I can claim them on my insurance. I mean, I can hardly explain what really happened to them, can I?'

Kieron smiled. 'Maybe if you collect all the bits together you can rebuild one complete bike. OK, it might be a bit singed, but at least you'd have *something*.'

Todd's mouth twisted in fury, and suddenly cold liquid splashed across Kieron's face, running down his forehead, cheeks and nose and the lenses of the ARCC glasses.

Todd's hands clenched the empty champagne glass: the left hand grasping the flute, right hand on the stem. His knuckles went white and his lips twisted into a snarl as the glass abruptly snapped, flute and stem coming apart with a high-pitched *snap* and a strange ringing sound. His right hand closed around the base of the glass, leaving the stem projecting from between his fingers. Slowly he raised it up until the sharp, broken tip pointed straight at Kieron's right eye.

Tara stared, wide-eyed and white-faced, at her boss. It looked to Kieron as if she'd never seen him like this before.

'Once I've finished questioning you,' Todd snarled, 'I'm going to make you feel so much pain you'll *beg* me to kill you just so it ends.'

Kieron blinked until the drink had run out of his eyes, then very deliberately licked his lips. 'Not a fan of champagne,' he said. 'Do you do milkshakes? I really fancy one of those right now – a good one, made with ice cream. Or a bubble tea. I tell you what – have you ever tried cream soda poured over vanilla ice cream? It tastes *incredible*. Much better than this stuff, and so much cheaper.'

Todd closed his eyes and took a couple of deep breaths. His lips moved as if he was reciting a mantra, some calming phrase that would help his anger drain away. When he opened his eyes, the storm seemed to have passed. 'There's water,' he said as if nothing had happened, 'or juice. Or, if you want to live a healthier life, wheatgrass shots or perhaps coconut water.' He smiled, and Kieron could see that the storm *hadn't* passed. The anger still bubbled away, underneath. 'Frankly, given what's going to happen to you, living a healthy life is probably the lowest of your priorities at the moment.'

'Water, please.' Kieron glanced over at Tara, trying to judge her mood. Was she so worried about her boss's sudden flash of temper that she might do something to help Kieron, or was she just going to go along with it, accept the generous pay packet every month and keep quiet? She seemed tense but subdued.

'I take it that Lethal Insomnia are off the itinerary?' Kieron asked, trying to lighten the mood.

Todd laughed. 'Yes, you've blown your chances on that, I'm afraid.' He glanced at Tara. 'Could you get a water for our friend here?'

'Don't you have attendants for that kind of thing?' Kieron asked.

'Yes, but Tara's in the doghouse. Security has been allowed to get very lax under her control. I'm reminding her that she needs to be very, very good for a while, and do exactly as she's told.'

'You strike me as a very "hands-on" boss,' Kieron said as Tara got up out of her seat and headed for the back of the aircraft. 'I'm surprised you'd let someone else design a security system for you. That thing about the firewall and the two levels of security – the outward-facing one and the inward-facing one, with an air gap between them – that was your idea, wasn't it? Not Tara's.' He was consciously trying to provoke Todd a bit with all these digs. Maybe not a very good idea, but he'd never been the kind of kid to buckle under pressure. Even in those shopping mall or park 'conversations' with gangs of chavs, he'd always felt an irresistible urge to needle them, insult them a bit when he answered their questions. Stupid stuff, like he'd say something quietly, they'd say, 'What?' and he'd say, 'Oh, you're deaf as well as stupid.' It unsettled them. Maybe it was a small revenge for the inevitable punch in the stomach, but it made him feel less of a victim.

Todd's hand clenched on the two pieces of the champagne glass, which he still held. His knuckles went white again. His voice, however, was perfectly calm as he replied: 'It was meant to be the perfect system, balancing accessibility for everyone *inside* with a firewall separating them from *outside*. But you got in. Very clever, but you must have had help. We should talk about that.'

Tara spoke, finally, as she returned with a bottle of water for Kieron. She looked at Todd as she said, 'I checked the security records. Judith came in through the turnstiles late

225

last night, but I called her, and she was at home. Somehow this kid managed to fake her eye-print.'

'How did you do that?' Todd asked casually.

'With ease,' Kieron said. He took a sip, then deliberately held the bottle out to Todd. 'Would you like to check this for DNA and fingerprints as well?'

He shrugged and smiled. 'Already done that. Didn't find any trace of you in any system we have access to. You're an unknown quantity.' He waved a casual hand. 'We have your two friends, by the way. The woman and the other boy.'

'I don't think you do.' Kieron looked around theatrically. 'They'd be here if you did, and I only see the three of us, plus, say, a pilot and co-pilot in the cockpit. Unless you've shoved them in the toilets?'

Todd smiled. 'Maybe they're in the baggage hold, freezing to death and suffocating from the lack of oxygen. Who knows? We'll take a look when we land.' He shrugged. 'There are questions we need to ask you about how you got into our system, who you're working for and how much you – and your employers – know. We can either have that talk now, calmly and in a civilised way – or we can have it after we land. That latter course is, I need to tell you, going to be a lot more painful.'

Kieron stared at Todd. The man seemed genuinely unsure about what Kieron actually knew.

'You know what I accessed?' Kieron asked.

Todd nodded. 'Staff records. Of all the things you could have looked at, you looked at staff records. There are secrets on that system that could have earned you millions if you'd sold them on the dark web, or even openly to my competitors, but you were snuffling around in my personnel files. I just need to know – why?'

'You honestly don't know?'

Todd shook his head, seemingly genuinely puzzled. 'It makes no sense.'

Kieron closed his eyes for a moment. 'Doesn't it bother you that thirty-five people who worked for you died, apparently of heart attacks, and all at the Goldfinch premises in Tel Aviv?'

'Employees die all the time, despite everything I try to do to improve their health,' Todd said, frowning. 'It's regrettable – they're like pets: you get attached to them sometimes – but it happens. They get buried, we pay out on their pension schemes to their dependents, we recruit replacements and everyone moves on. Soon there's just a couple of photographs on the "Employee of the Month" wall to remind us all that they were ever there. I don't see the issue.'

'They all died at the same time, didn't they?' Kieron asked quietly. 'In the same place, at the same time and for the same reason.'

Todd glanced over questioningly at Tara.

'Project ANCIENT MARINER,' she prompted after a pause.

Todd nodded. 'Oh, that. Yes, that was just an industrial accident. A gas leak. These things happen. Sometimes, despite our best efforts, technology breaks down and something bad happens. Regrettable, but that's life. Can't be helped. We wanted to avoid an investigation so we just changed the cause of death to "heart attack".'

'Thirty-five members of your staff, each of whose family comes from Eastern Europe.' Kieron could feel the anger building within him, and tried to restrain it. 'What possible accidental gas leak could just kill people whose families came from one area of the world?'

Todd gazed into his empty glass as if the secrets of the universe could be found in there. 'I think you've already worked out the answer,' he said quietly.

'You work on non-lethal weapons. That's what your company is known for, primarily.' Kieron's thoughts were racing as he spoke, sorting out the facts and the suppositions and organising them into a coherent structure. 'The whole point about non-lethal weapons is that they *don't* kill innocent bystanders. But sometimes non-lethal weapons *do* kill people. That blue goo, for instance, could have suffocated me. Those big water pistols that transmit electric shocks through the water might give some people a heart attack. So, if you *really* want to avoid innocent casualties, why not develop a lethal weapon that *only* kills the people you want it to? People from a particular country, or one particular part of the world. One ethnic group.' The anger was bleeding through into his voice now, but he couldn't stop it. 'People with a particular skin colour, or eyes of a certain shape. What is it? A virus? A bacterium?'

'Project ANCIENT MARINER,' Todd repeated quietly, still staring into his glass. 'So called because of some old poem. Tara's idea. "It is an ancient Mariner, And he stoppeth one of three". That's what this thing does: it kills, but it

228

kills selectively. Just the people you want to die. Yes, it's a virus – one that's been modified so that it only affects people who carry certain genes in their DNA. It's possible to tell a person's race and their whole heritage from their DNA – did you know that? I've had my own sequenced, just to be sure.'

'Well,' Kieron murmured, 'it would be embarrassing if *you* had some Eastern European heritage, wouldn't it?'

'Exactly. Turns out I'm ninety per cent Nordic, with ten per cent Native American thrown in. All good news – nobody hates the Nordic peoples or the Native Americans, so I'm safe.'

'But why?' Kieron asked softly, although he thought he already knew the answer.

'A weapon like that could make a man rich,' Todd said. 'Every country in the world has a faction that wants to kill another faction because of some trivial difference between them. And if you wanted to test it, just to see if it worked, why not organise an accidental leak of gas in a conference room where half the people had Eastern European heritage and half didn't? And if half the people die – the *right* half – then you know it's worked.' He finally glanced over at Kieron. 'I tell you this now, here, because I want *someone* to know how clever I've been, and because you'll be dead within twenty-four hours, just as soon as you tell us who you're working for and who else knows.'

'You've got a gas that works against emos and greebs?' Kieron asked.

Todd grinned mirthlessly. 'Actually, I probably *could* find genetic markers for emotional sensitivity, a tendency towards depression, fondness for the colour black and a love of loud, repetitive music. The problem is that I'd share those markers as well, so I'll stay away from that line of research.'

The rumbling of the engine changed subtly, and Kieron felt a slight shift in his sense of balance.

'We're approaching Ben Gurion Airport,' Tara said, standing up. 'I suggest you prepare for landing.'

'I thought we had permission to land at the Goldfinch Institute facility?' Todd asked. 'I don't want to have to mix with ordinary people if I can help it.'

'It's Israeli air control,' Tara explained apologetically. 'They're insisting we go through the main airport. But don't worry – we'll get the VIP treatment.'

'Is there a genetic marker for "ordinary people"?' Kieron asked quietly. 'Perhaps you could just get rid of them all.'

Todd just stared at him darkly then turned away as the aircraft descended. Kieron felt the same pressure in his ears as he had when he, Bex and Sam had landed at Washington Dulles, and then again at Albuquerque.

Bex. Bex and Sam. Did they know where he was and what had happened? Were they on their way to rescue him? Or had they missed the ARCC glasses entirely, maybe even run them over and crushed them? Were they sitting in the hotel now, wondering where he was?

A dark thought wriggled into his conscious mind: maybe Tara had tracked him back to his hotel after his first visit and discovered that he had two other people with him. Maybe Bex and Sam *were* in the baggage hold, frozen and asphyxiated. Maybe they'd been killed back in Albuquerque.

He didn't know whether to feel scared, angry, tired, hungry . . . A thousand emotions swirled around in his brain.

He settled on one.

Anger. No, two: anger and revenge. He was going to get out of this situation and teach both Todd Zanderbergen and Tara Gallagher not to mess with a teenage greeb and his friends. Oh, and not to threaten the world with a weapon that targeted certain sections of the population. That as well.

Landing was just a slight bump of the wheels on the ground. Within ten minutes they were stationary and the main door was being opened to let in air that was as oven-hot and as fuel-scented as the air back in Albuquerque. It was as if he'd never left. Within moments Kieron felt sweat springing up on his hands and face, and down his spine.

'I'm going to release your restraints,' Tara said. She reached down and pulled up a weapon from beside her chair. It was the microwave-beam generator that Kieron had used against her and her guards back in Albuquerque. 'Remember this?' she asked. 'If you make the slightest move, or try to shout out to anyone, I'll be demonstrating what it feels like.'

'I thought weapons were frowned on in airports?' Kieron asked.

'Did I mention I play the cello?' Tara said. 'I've got a cello case in the back of this cabin. No cello – I must have left that back in Albuquerque – but this thing will sit very nicely inside. And, funnily enough, I can operate it remotely by flipping one of the catches on the case. The microwave beam doesn't care whether it's inside the case or not – it'll still cause you agonising pain.'

Walking out into the late-evening heat, Kieron saw that they'd landed near an enormous complex of airfield buildings. A limousine stood nearby on the tarmac with its engine idling. At the bottom of the steps were three Israeli immigration officials. They checked the paperwork Tara gave them, nodded and stamped it. They even made a joke about her cello case.

The limousine pulled away from the aircraft. Kieron and Todd sat in the back; Tara sat in the front.

The sky was blue, but it seemed like a *different* blue from Albuquerque, and very different from the grey British skies. Everything seemed new: the roads, the buildings, even the clothes that people wore. The buildings were mainly square and bold, with wide expanses of glass. Nothing complicated or ornate.

'I like the Israelis,' Todd said suddenly, as they drove in the air-conditioned car. 'They're an immensely practical people. Likely to be good customers as well, given their touchy relationship with Hamas and the Palestinians.'

Within fifteen minutes they had left Tel Aviv and were driving through a dusty arid landscape. They passed road signs for places with names like Kfar Truman, Shoham, Bareket and El'ad. Despite his anxiety Kieron noted the orange groves lining the roads: orchards full of orange trees growing out of the baked earth like something miraculous.

Just as Kieron could bear the tension no longer, the limousine turned off the highway onto an unmarked road. As in Albuquerque, the Goldfinch Institute here seemed to value its privacy. Five minutes later, over the horizon appeared a mass of glass-covered buildings, none of which went higher than two storeys. Antennas and aerials covered the roofs. The only difference between this complex and the one in Albuquerque was that here the glass was red whereas there it was blue.

'Nice place,' Kieron said.

'Enjoy the view,' Todd said lightly. 'You've already had your last night's sleep, eaten your last meal and drunk your last drink. This will be one of the last things you ever see. Make the most of it.'

The security guard at the gate must have recognised the limousine because the metal plates – identical to the ones in Albuquerque – slid into the ground as they drove towards it. Once inside the double fence, they slowed to a halt. The driver got out and opened the doors for Todd, Tara and then finally for Kieron. They all climbed out.

Kieron slid the ARCC glasses out of his pocket and put them on. He had no idea whether there was anyone on the other end watching, but he had to hope. Without hope he had nothing.

Tara stared suspiciously at him. 'Short-sighted,' he said, tapping the frame. 'I've never been to Israel before: I'd like at least to get a look at the place before I die.'

'Check him,' Todd said to Tara, nodding towards Kieron. 'He's clever. I want to make sure he hasn't got any transmitters on him.'

Tara strode across to the security booth and went inside. Moments later she came back out with a small black box the size of a mobile phone. She pressed a button on it and held it out towards Kieron as she walked quickly back. He winced slightly as he saw a red light come on.

'There's something on him,' she said, frowning. 'Do you want me to search him?'

Todd shook his head. 'That thing can jam any signal it detects, can't it?'

Tara nodded.

'OK then,' Todd continued. 'Just set it to jam any signal it detects coming from him. We'll worry about what it is later.'

Tara input some instructions into the device, then held it up and waved it at Kieron. 'Whatever you were transmitting, kid, nobody's going to hear it.'

'Right,' Todd said as a golf cart appeared from the direction of the red glass buildings. 'Let's start. Although for you, I'm sorry to say, it's going to be more of a finish. As in: an hour from now, you'll be dead.'

CHAPTER TWELVE

'We're too late,' Bex said grimly. 'They're carrying him on to the aircraft. We'll never get there in time to save him – even if we could somehow crash through the security fence, drive across the tarmac and ram the aircraft to stop them taking off. And there are laws against that.'

Sam's face was white with worry. 'What can we do? I mean – it's *Kieron*!'

'I know. I know.' She shut her eyes tight and clenched her fists, thinking hard. 'Right, if we can't save him now, we'll have to follow him until we can find a way. Grab whatever you need – we're heading for the airport!'

In moments they were outside the motel getting into the car. Bex pulled the ARCC glasses from her jacket pocket and threw them to Sam. 'Check flights. How quickly can we get to Tel Aviv?'

She started the car and reversed rapidly out of the parking space, scattering small stones and sand everywhere and causing a passing car to suddenly swerve out of the way. Meanwhile Sam slipped the glasses on and started interrogating the virtual screen that only he could see.

'Working on it.' His voice sounded tense. Tense and scared.

Bex shook her head as she slewed the car round and slammed it into drive. Her heart seemed to have coagulated into a cold black lump in her chest. If anything happened to Kieron, she didn't know what she'd do.

They were five minutes down the main north–south road through Albuquerque when Sam swore under his breath.

'What's the problem?' Bex asked, but she thought she knew.

'There's no direct flights. Best I've found is an El Al one, but it takes over twenty-four hours, with a twelve-hour stopover in New York. There isn't a flight that'll get us there in less than that, unless we're prepared to wait around for a day, and even that only cuts the flight down to seventeen hours. A lot of routes are even longer and have two stopovers.' Despair had crept into his voice. 'We just can't do it! If Kieron's on a private jet it'll get there direct, in –' his hands moved in the air – 'ten hours! We'll be days late!'

Bex nodded. Part of her brain was concentrating on weaving from lane to lane, taking advantage of momentary fluctuations in traffic speed, while another part tried to work out their options.

She reached into her jacket and pulled her mobile out. 'Call Bradley. His number is saved as "Friend 1", just in case anyone steals the phone. Put him on speaker.'

A massive truck zoomed past on her right. She glanced in her side mirror. Another truck was coming up behind it, but for a second there was a gap right beside their car. She swerved suddenly sideways and accelerated to match speed, her front bumper inches from the truck in front and her rear bumper only just ahead of the one behind. A horn blared like an angry dinosaur. All she could see ahead of her was a set of red doors with a sign saying: 'How's My Driving? Call 1-800-Kiss-My-Ass!' *Funny*, she thought darkly. Her rear-view mirror showed nothing but a massive radiator grille.

Sam had her mobile in one hand and was fiddling with the car stereo with the other.

'This is no time to look for emo rock stations,' she snapped.

'I'm Bluetoothing the phone to the car speakers,' he said, sounding offended. 'There's a microphone in the mirror. It's easier than using speakerphone.'

Looking right again, she saw that the next lane across was empty. She swerved again, sliding out from between the trucks and accelerating even more. As she drew alongside the cab of the front truck she deliberately didn't look at the driver.

Sam, however, did. 'He's not happy,' he said. 'It's a good thing I can't-lip read.' He paused, then added, 'No, it's OK, he's using sign language now, and they're not nice signs.'

'We're in a hurry,' Bex pointed out. 'I don't care about his hurt feelings.'

Bradley's voice suddenly filled the car, blaring out of the car stereo. 'Yes?' Calm, not giving away his name or his number. Good training.

'It's me,' she said, not giving her name either, just in case anyone happened to be listening in. Bradley would recognise the voice. That, and the fact that she was the only person who had the number of the burner phone he was using.

'How's things?'

'Bad. We need help.'

'Tell me.' Those two words were a cue to her that she could talk freely.

She thought for a second. How to phrase this without giving too much information to anybody who might be listening in? 'One greeb's been taken and is heading for Tel Aviv in a private jet. We need to follow, but the passenger jets are far too slow.'

'OK.' He paused. 'I can see where this is going, and I don't like it.'

'I need you to hire a private jet to take us from Albuquerque to Tel Aviv.'

She heard Bradley sigh. 'Do you actually know how much that will cost?'

She slid back into the left-hand lane, ahead of the massive radiator grille of the truck that had been in front of her moments earlier. It seemed to lurch forward towards them, as if the driver wanted to slam into them, but she floored the accelerator and zoomed ahead. For a moment, she thought she saw a waving fist and a furious expression in the truck's cab, but she looked away, concentrating on the road in front and to either side.

'Not precisely, no,' she said. 'But I'm guessing it's a lot.'

A sign for the airport passed by to their right. Next off-ramp.

'It's a huge amount. I mean, seriously vast.'

She drifted right, preparing to exit the interstate and head for the airport. Somewhere in the distance she thought she heard the wail of a police siren. She checked her speed. The last thing they needed now was to get pulled over.

'Yes, but can we afford it?'

A pause. Bradley was either checking their business account balance or sitting with his head in his hands, hyperventilating. 'We can,' he said eventually, 'but it means we're wiped out. We won't be able to afford anything else. Certainly not the rent for this fabulous apartment I'm sitting in. Probably not food either.'

'They've got "K",' she said simply. She didn't want to name Kieron, but Bradley would know who she meant. 'We have to get him back.'

Another sigh. 'You're right. I'll eat at Courtney's place from now on.'

'You will not,' Sam muttered.

'Drop the hire car off and head into the airport,' Bradley continued in a businesslike manner. 'I'll text you the details of where to go.'

'Thanks,' Bex said awkwardly. Bradley signed off just as the sign for the hire-car drop-off area came into sight.

Sam opened the door even before Bex had bought the car to a halt. 'Come on – we need to move!'

'If we just abandon a hire car here without completing the paperwork,' she pointed out, 'then someone will call us back. And it's not like there's a plane waiting for us – Bradley's still got to do his stuff.'

Sam growled under his breath, but he pulled the door closed again.

A few minutes later they were walking briskly towards the single terminal building.

As the glass doors slid shut behind them, encapsulating them in chilly air conditioning, a man with a short beard, wearing dark trousers, white shirt and a cap, moved towards them. Bex tensed, ready to punch him and run, but then noticed the epaulettes on his shirt. A pilot? Bradley must have acted quickly.

'Chloe Gibbons?' he asked. Her fake identity.

'Yes. You are?'

'I'm Dan. I work for a small local jet company: FalconAir. About thirty seconds ago we received a booking for an urgent flight to Tel Aviv. That's you, right? I was told to look out for a woman and a boy looking stressed.'

She tried to dredge up a smile. 'That's us. How quickly can we take off?'

'Payment's already cleared, and we've filed an urgent flight plan. Should be able to get you into the air within twenty minutes.' He raised an eyebrow. 'I have to admit, this is an unusual flight for us. We usually get hired to take business executives to New York or defence contractors to Washington, D.C., when they've missed their scheduled flight. What kind of business are you in, if you don't mind me asking?'

Bex's mind went blank. Her thoughts actually seemed to freeze. So much had happened so quickly, and she was feeling so stressed, that she literally had no idea what to say.

Sam came to her rescue. 'My dad's in the movie business,' he said casually. 'He's directing a movie in Israel – wants us to come out and see him.'

Dan nodded. 'That explains it. OK, I guess you have your passports? Good – we'll take you through the VIP security channel and get you onto the aircraft as quickly as we can.'

As Dan led them past queues of travellers who gazed at them with expressions ranging from blankness to jealousy, Bex murmured, 'Quick thinking.'

'I just wish it was true,' Sam replied. 'Actually my dad's a lifelong drifter who can't hold down a job for more than a week.' He glanced up at Bex. 'If there's a bar on this aircraft,' he whispered, 'can I have a drink? I mean, a proper, adult drink.'

'No,' Bex said firmly. 'A milkshake if you're lucky, then you need to sleep. We both do. We have to get as much rest as we can before we get to Israel.'

'What about food?'

She nodded. 'That's a good idea. Keep our strength up.'

'I wasn't thinking about my strength,' he muttered; 'I was thinking I'm hungry.'

Out on the tarmac stood a beautiful sleek white aircraft with a company logo stencilled on the side. Dan gestured to the steps leading up to the hatch. 'Please, make yourselves comfortable. Kristi will greet you and get you anything you need. Buckle yourselves in and we'll get in the air as quickly as we can.'

Everything after that was a strange mixture of urgency

and tedium: steaks and fries, ice cream, blankets and sleep, all while the aircraft was heading across America towards the Atlantic Ocean, towards Europe, towards the Middle East. In those interstitial moments when Bex found herself awake, not knowing what time it was, she tortured herself with attempts to divide the time it would take to get from Albuquerque to Tel Aviv by the number of pounds it had cost to book the aircraft, so she knew exactly how much of her and Bradley's business bank account was draining away every second.

She flashed back to a couple of weeks ago in Mumbai; getting an assassin to give her information by having Kieron take chunks of money from the woman's account. The assassin seeing her ill-gotten savings get smaller and smaller had worked better than torture; now Bex was going through the same experience.

Kristi, their young, blonde and bubbly stewardess, woke them gently after what seemed like an age of sleep. 'We're half an hour out,' she said. 'Can I get you some breakfast: juice and croissants?'

'Sausage, eggs and bacon?' Sam asked sleepily.

Security at Ben Gurion Airport was much tighter than in Albuquerque, and the armed soldiers walking around the terminal seemed much more tense. Many of the men wore skullcaps, while many of the women had headscarves. She also saw several Orthodox Jews in their severe black suits and wide-brimmed black hats, from which long corkscrews of curls hung down.

'Have you been here before?' Sam asked.

Bex shook her head. 'Never, but I have some friends out here. I did some work with Shin Bet.' At his blank look she added: 'They're the Israeli internal security organisation, like MI5 in the UK and the FBI in America.'

Sam frowned. 'I thought that was Mossad.'

'No,' she explained patiently, 'Mossad are *external* security. They're the equivalent of MI6 or the CIA.'

'Right,' he nodded, impressed, 'I'll try to remember that.'

'Can you access the local airport computer network with the ARCC glasses and see if you can find out when the Goldfinch Institute jet touched down?'

Sam glanced around nervously. 'If I start waving my hands here, someone's going to think I'm acting suspiciously and shoot me. There are a lot of guns around.' He grinned suddenly. 'Although there's a lot of gorgeous women in uniform carrying those guns, which is kind of attractive.'

'Easy, tiger,' Bex said. 'Let's go across to the window. If anyone looks, they'll think you're describing the scene outside to me.'

Moments later, Bex was gazing out across the harsh Israeli landscape while Sam used the ARCC glasses. His lips moved, giving a running commentary of what he was doing. 'Right, I'm in. Very good security, but your kit has some seriously good hacking tools. Looking for recent arrivals. No, no, no . . . yes! Got them. The Goldfinch Institute jet landed about twenty minutes ago.'

'We have to find them *now*,' muttered Bex.

'I've got an address for their facility. It's out in the desert. Probably about a half-hour drive.'

'Then we need to get a fast hire car and follow them.'

'When you say "fast",' Sam asked carefully, 'do you mean, like, a sports car? Because that would be cool.'

'If we can afford one. Given how much it cost to get us here, we might be limited to mopeds.'

In fact, Bex managed to negotiate a good rate for a BMW Z3 from a specialist car-hire booth that didn't seem to be doing much business and was glad to see a customer.

As they walked out of the main terminal building of Ben Gurion Airport and headed towards the multi-storey car park where the hire cars were located, she said to Sam, 'I need you to check the route that will take us to the Goldfinch Institute premises. We have to assume that's where they're taking Kieron. If it's not then we've wasted a phenomenal amount of money – not that I care, as long as we get him back.'

The BMW was small, but streamlined: bright red and open-top. Judging by his expression, Sam fell in love with it the minute he saw it.

'When all this is over,' he begged, 'and we've got Kieron back, can we find a stretch of deserted road and let me drive it? Please?'

'No.'

'Can I at least sit behind the wheel?'

'Yes – when we get Kieron back.'

A noise behind them sent a shiver of tension up her spine. It sounded like someone's shoe scraping against the ground. She turned quickly, stepping to one side to avoid any attack that might be coming.

An Israeli woman stood just a few metres away. She didn't have a headscarf, like many of the other women Bex had seen in and around the airport, but her hair was so full and glossy it was pretty obviously a wig. Married women who followed the Jewish faith strictly were required to cover their hair in public, she'd heard. She carried a small hard-shell suitcase in her hand.

'Wombat,' the woman said.

Bex relaxed slightly. She and Bradley had established a series of coded exchanges when they'd first started working together, so that if they had to pass messages through other people they would know that those messages were genuine. They'd chosen to use pairs of animals. It had seemed funny at the time. This woman knew the system, which meant she'd been sent by Bradley. He'd arranged something while Bex and Sam were in the air. Good thinking. The woman probably didn't even know what she was carrying; she was just following instructions.

'Anteater,' Bex said. It was the response to 'Wombat' that she and Bradley had agreed, all that time ago.

The woman nodded. She put the small suitcase on the floor, then turned and left.

'Pick that up,' Bex said to Sam, 'and get in the car.'

'Wombat? Anteater?'

'It's code. Bradley's sent us some stuff. Probably fresh clothes. Maybe some kit we can use. Anyway, get in the car and work out our route.'

While she familiarised herself with the controls and gingerly drove the car out of the car park and onto the road, Sam checked the ARCC glasses. He had the suitcase perched uncomfortably on his lap.

'Take a left at the next junction, then drive straight for five miles.'

The BMW leaped ahead as Bex pushed the accelerator down as far as it would go. The road was clear, and she couldn't see any sign of speed cameras. Time to push the car to its limits.

She kept an eye out for anything that looked like a limousine. Tara Gallagher had carried Kieron out of a limousine back in Albuquerque, and Bex suspected that was how Todd Zanderbergen preferred to travel. She saw nothing. Either the car taking Kieron was further ahead of them or it was on a different route entirely and they were screwed.

'I'm going to see what's in the suitcase,' Sam said. 'Maybe Bradley's sent us some snacks. A few cans of drink, maybe.'

Bex sped up, enjoying at least for the moment the way the morning air seemed to blow the cobwebs from her brain.

Sam flipped the latches and pulled up the hard top. 'Oh my God!'

'*What?*'

'It's guns! He's sent us guns!'

Bex smiled. 'That's very thoughtful. What kind of guns?'

'A couple of automatic handguns and what looks like a disassembled sniper rifle!' He glanced at her, wide-eyed. 'Can I –'

'No. Close the case.'

He sighed. 'You never let me have any fun.' He paused for a moment, distracted. 'Take a right at the junction in one mile. Then it's straight for twenty miles until we turn off on a side road. Looks like the same kind of set-up they had in Albuquerque.' He frowned and shook his head. 'Were we really in Albuquerque? It all feels like a dream.'

'I wish it was,' Bex muttered, slowing for the turn.

She floored the accelerator again, guiltily enjoying the sheer power of the car, but no matter how fast they went they didn't catch up with anything that looked remotely like a limousine. Once or twice they zoomed past another car, but they were small enough and dusty enough that she ignored them.

'Side road coming up,' Sam pointed out.

Bex slowed, but the turn was so sharp that she skidded the car sideways for a hundred yards or so, swan-necking and having to accelerate back along the side of the road in reverse before she could get on to it.

'That was impressive,' Sam said, brushing dust from his eyes.

She took the access road more slowly. It was rutted and untended, looking like it headed to a farm rather than a research institute. It was all in keeping with the way Zanderbergen had disguised his place in the USA. He was apparently a man of habit.

Something came into view over the horizon: a forest of antennas, followed by the top of a cluster of buildings clad in red glass.

When the bottom of the buildings came into sight, along with a familiar-looking double fence and security cabin, she pulled over and stopped the car.

She concentrated on what was happening down at the security gate. A black limousine had just passed through the gap, and the metal plates were sliding back up to block the way.

'We're too late,' she said dejectedly. 'They've gone inside.' Although what she had planned to do if they had caught up with the limousine, she realised she hadn't exactly thought through.

'Then we go inside,' Sam said firmly. 'If that's what we have to do to get him back, that's what we do.'

'Hang on a second.' Bex watched as a driverless golf cart made its way from the nearest red glass building down towards where the limousine had parked. The driver of the limousine got out and opened the doors, one after the other. Todd Zanderbergen stepped out of one side and Tara Gallagher from the other. Moments later, Kieron joined them.

He was alive! She felt her heart leap.

Kieron reached into his jacket pocket and pulled his ARCC glasses out. Casually he slipped them on and looked around. Bex grinned. That kid reacted instinctively in a way that some agents took years to learn. He must be scared, probably terrified, but he was still thinking about the mission, and keeping his head.

'Check the link to Kieron's glasses,' Bex murmured to Sam. 'He's just put them on.'

As Sam made gestures in the air, Bex watched as Kieron said something to Tara. Todd said something to her as well, and she walked over to the security cabin. Moments later she came back holding something in her hand. She waved it at Kieron, then said something to Todd. He answered, and Tara appeared to be typing something into the device she held.

'That's strange,' Sam muttered.

'What's strange?'

'The glasses – for a few seconds there I could see what Kieron was seeing, but all I'm getting now is static.'

'Static?'

'It's like they're being jammed.'

Bex sighed. 'Tara's holding some kind of electronic gadget. It must have detected the signal and countered it. We're back to square one.' She sank down to the ground, the adrenalin and anxiety of the past hours catching up with her.

Then a sudden thought occurred to her, a shaft of light in the darkness that was threatening to engulf her. 'Sam – slide that suitcase over.'

'We're going in armed?' Sam sounded simultaneously scared and enthralled.

'No.' She opened the case. Ignoring the two Glock handguns, she focused on what she recognised immediately as a disassembled M24 sniper rifle. The various parts – bolt, assembly rod, operating rod, trigger block and firing assembly, stock and barrel nestled in foam rubber, along with a Leupold Ultra M3A 10×40mm fixed-power scope.

It took her fifty-five seconds to assemble the whole thing.

'What are you going to do with that?' Sam asked nervously. 'Kill someone?'

Bex aimed the gun at the three people inside the wire fences.

CHAPTER THIRTEEN

Kieron stared bleakly out at the Israeli landscape beyond the security fence. This might be the last bit of the real world he ever saw. Shame it was mainly rocks, dust and scrappy little plants. If he was going to die on an espionage mission – as was looking increasingly likely – then why couldn't it be in Hawaii?

A flash of light at the top of a nearby hill caught his attention. The sun glinting off something? Maybe a bit of broken glass. Nothing that was going to help save his life, unfortunately.

'Come on,' Tara said, shoving Kieron from behind. 'You've got an appointment with agonising pain. We wouldn't want you to be late.'

Kieron turned to glare at her. It was the only way he had of showing resistance; well, that and snarky comments. He was just about to speak when he saw another flash of light over Todd's shoulder.

Todd and Tara were both facing forward, towards the buildings. They couldn't see the flashes.

A tiny bud of hope began to unfurl in his heart.

251

'Dammit!' Tara snapped. There was a sudden *crack!* and a clatter as something hard hit the ground. Kieron turned, and saw that the jamming unit she had been holding was now on the ground a few steps away from her. She looked confused.

'You clumsy idiot,' Todd shouted. 'Check that the thing's OK!'

'It slipped from my fingers,' Tara said as she walked over and bent to retrieve it. 'I don't know what happened.'

'What happened was that you were paying too much attention to pushing the kid around and not enough to keeping hold of the jammer. Is it broken?'

Tara had picked the jammer up and was staring at it bleakly. 'Smashed. Must have hit a stone when it fell. Sorry, boss.'

Looking at it, Kieron could see that the screen had broken, and a corner was torn off. He glanced back at the hilltop where he'd seen the flashes of light. Coincidence? Perhaps not.

'Do we have another one? Tell me we have another one.'

Tara's expression gave Kieron hope that there weren't any spares.

'I think so,' she said hurriedly. 'I'll get someone to check.'

'Why is it that I'm surrounded by incompetents?' Todd snarled. 'Seriously, someone – tell me.'

'Because you hire them,' Kieron pointed out helpfully.

For a moment Todd looked as if he was going to backhand Kieron, but instead he pushed him towards the golf cart.

'That,' a voice in Kieron's ear said, 'was possibly the most difficult shot I've ever had to take.'

Bex!

The bud of hope in Kieron's heart suddenly bloomed. Yes, he was still a prisoner, and, yes, he was inside a double-layered security fence while his friends were outside, but at least he had friends, and they were nearer than he'd dared to hope. They'd followed him!

'So, what's the plan?' he asked as they sat in the golf cart and it started to move off. He made it look like he was speaking to Todd and Tara, but really he was asking Bex.

'Not sure yet,' Bex said. 'We're kind of playing this by ear. The first step was breaking that jammer and getting in contact with you. I can't read lips at this range, but it didn't look as if they spotted anything suspicious – did they? Answer me if you can, but don't act suspiciously.'

'You do talk a lot, don't you?' Todd said as they headed into a red glass canyon between two of the buildings of the Goldfinch Institute. 'That's an annoying habit generally, but it'll come in useful when we're interrogating you.'

'No,' Kieron said firmly, answering Bex but making it sound like he was defiantly rejecting Todd's threatening words.

'That's good,' Bex said. 'I was using a silencer and I tried to clip the corner to knock it out of her hand. A fraction lower and there'd be a bullet hole through it, and that would have given the game away straight away.' She paused. 'Sam's fine, by the way, and he's with me. And we're going to do everything we can to get you out safely. Don't worry Kieron – we're here for you.'

'Do whatever you need to,' Kieron said.

'We will,' Bex and Todd said at the same time, and Kieron felt a shiver run up his spine. This was going to be tricky: communicating with Bex while making it look like he was making comments about what was going on. He'd been getting used to it, but now his life was at stake.

'We need to get you away from them before they can get that replacement jammer Tara mentioned,' Bex said in his ear as the golf cart turned a corner and continued driving between the red glass buildings. 'And I can't shoot it out of her hand again once you're inside. We haven't got long to think of something. The problem is, I haven't got access to the plans of the Institute's buildings here in Tel Aviv, so I can't guide you. They'll be on the internal server, not the external one.'

'This place,' Kieron said, turning to Todd, 'it looks just like the one in Albuquerque, except it's a different colour. What is it – are you obsessive-compulsive or something? Do you like having everything exactly the same? Is that why you only hire redheads?'

Todd just snorted, as if the question was too trivial to answer, but in Kieron's ear Bex murmured, 'Good question, well presented. I'll call up the plans of the Albuquerque complex – you downloaded them from the internal server when you were in there, didn't you? Let's assume for the moment that this facility is the same as that one.'

'Yes,' Kieron went on, then added, this time to Todd, 'that must be it. Obsessive-compulsive.' He shrugged. 'Not that there's anything wrong with that. I cut the labels out of any clothes I buy, because I don't like the feeling that I'm being identified as part of some big company's advertising strategy. I like to be anonymous.'

'If you don't shut up,' Todd said wearily, 'I'll get Tara to cut off the little finger of your left hand. She carries a special device, you know, just to do that. She modified it from one of those things businessmen use to slice the ends off cigars.'

They were approaching one of the red glass buildings now, and ahead of the driverless golf cart Kieron saw a sliding glass door opening to let them in.

'Right,' Bex said, 'I've got the plans up. From what I can see, the footprint is identical, but what's inside might be different.'

The golf cart swept in through the doors. The space inside was huge: occupying most of the building as far as Kieron could see. The cart was driving down a curved corridor made of plain glass, like a tunnel that ran from one side of the building to a position in the middle. The glass was so clean that it almost seemed as though it wasn't there. Only that slight distortion when Kieron tried to look through it at an angle, rather than straight on, gave away its presence. It also gave away its thickness: that glass had to be nearly three centimetres thick!

That wasn't the most impressive thing, however. Kieron stared, amazed, at what was on his left and right, beyond the glass. Satellites! Real satellites, designed to go into orbit around the Earth! They ranged from the size of a small car to the size of a coach. Some of them were unique, but others had similar siblings, differentiated only by numbers painted on their sides. Each one had shiny blue solar panels that unfolded around them like wings, and each one bristled with antennae. As he looked more carefully, and as the cart raced past them, he saw that some of them were based around vast, tube-like telescopes with lenses the size of a dustbin lid, while others ended in massive dish antennae that were probably designed to transmit, or scoop up, radio waves. It was like driving through an exhibit of props from some science fiction movie, except that this was real.

'I didn't,' he said, 'know that the Goldfinch Institute was into satellites.'

'Oh, we do a lot of things,' Todd replied. 'Basically, if I get an idea then I sketch it out on a napkin, give it to my people and they build it.'

'Everyone needs a hobby.'

Todd shook his head. 'Not a hobby. I don't think I've sketched anything that hasn't earned me less than ten million dollars. It's a business. A very profitable business.'

'You should put those napkins in an art gallery,' Kieron observed.

Todd stared at him pityingly. 'I already have,' he said.

Kieron opened his mouth to answer, but closed it again. Best not to aggravate Todd *too* much. The man was threatening to torture and kill him, after all.

Then again, if he was going to be tortured and killed, why not just go for wall-to-wall insults?

Oh, he thought, but then he might decide to torture me worse. Or for longer.

Instead, he said, 'I guess this is a construction facility. Is that a clean room the other side of the glass? All dust and contaminants removed?'

Todd nodded. 'Not my favourite part of the Institute. The overheads are high, but the risk of something breaking down in orbit is too great, and you can't send a technician out into space to repair it. No, non-lethal weapons are far better.' He paused. 'And lethal ones of course. I do those too.'

The cart got to the far point of the glass tunnel, halfway across the enormous room, and Kieron gazed around in awe. The centre of the room was effectively an octagonal glass tube running right up to the ceiling. Several massive doors set into thick rubber seals allowed access to and from the satellite area. Right in the middle of the tube was something that looked a bit like a high-tech oven made out of white metal, except that it was the size of a house. Well, *larger* than Kieron's house. You could drive a double-decker bus through the door. Cables and corrugated pipes emerged from the top and curved away to the ceiling, where they seemed to join what Kieron had thought was a giant air-conditioning system: square metal trunking that led away towards the walls.

The golf cart came to a stop near to the huge door.

'Right,' said Tara, 'get out.'

As Kieron stepped onto the white-tiled floor he gazed at the oven-thing. It seemed to loom over him like some kind of gigantic gargoyle. It looked *dangerous*, like some industrial incinerator. The sight of it did not fill him with pleasant thoughts or confidence.

Tara walked around the oven-thing, to a control console

that emerged from the floor like a high-tech mushroom. She pressed a series of buttons.

'So what's this?' Kieron asked, pointing. 'Are you genetically engineering really, really big people here? Is this where they live?'

'Space is a very harsh environment,' Todd said, waving a hand at the myriad of satellites in the clean zone beyond the glass walls. 'That's why building these is so expensive. There's pretty much zero pressure in orbit, which means not only that any sealed container, like a fuel tank, has to have really thick walls so it doesn't burst like a balloon, but also that substances like rubber and plastic, and even some metals and some types of glass, release atoms and molecules dissolved in them or trapped in microscopic cracks, and those atoms and molecules can spray over optics and solar panels and reduce their efficiency. Also, people think that space is cold, but that's not necessarily true. In Earth's orbit, in direct sunlight, things can heat up to 260 degrees Celsius. Of course, if they're not in direct sunlight then they can cool down to below minus 100. So, obviously we have to test our satellites before we launch them to make sure they can withstand the conditions, and that's what this thing does. We put a satellite inside, reduce the pressure and then change the temperature from really cold to really hot and back again. That's what the really big door is for, obviously.'

Tara pressed a button on the control console. A normal-sized door that Kieron hadn't even noticed swung open in the bottom of the much larger door.

'So,' Todd went on calmly, 'I can't offer you much choice

258

in the pressure department, but do you want to be frozen or cooked? Either way it's going to be really, really unpleasant.'

'You choose,' Kieron said, equally calmly although he felt sick. 'I'm not going to let you make me part of this. You're the one with his finger on the button. Well, *she* is, but you're telling her what to do. I'm just an innocent bystander.'

Todd shrugged. 'Cold it is then. We can always turn the temperature up later.'

'Hold on, Kieron,' Bex's voice said in his ear. 'I'm working to get you out. Just be brave.'

'If you're going to do anything,' Kieron muttered, 'then now might be a good time.'

'Thanks for the advice,' Todd said. 'Tara – if you could?'

Tara had left the console without Kieron realising. She pushed him from behind. Surprised, he staggered towards the massive environmental chamber, almost tripping. She pushed him again. He grabbed hold of the door so he didn't sprawl inside.

'Hang on,' Todd called. 'In all the fun, I almost forgot to ask: who *are* you working for?'

'I had a summer job in a cafe once.' Kieron had to force the words past a throat that seemed to have swelled up in panic. 'I got fired because I couldn't remember the daily specials, or make a decent cappuccino. Does that count?'

Todd nodded at Tara. She knocked Kieron's hands away from the door and then shoved him between the shoulder blades. He fell inside the chamber. He twisted around, trying to climb back to his feet and get outside, but the door was already swinging closed against its rubber seal. A small window set into the door gave him a view of Tara's grimly smiling face.

'There's a microphone in here,' Todd's voice crackled. 'Just tell me who you're working for and I'll open the door. You'll maybe lose a toe or a finger to frostbite, depending how long you resist for, but that's OK. You're not a golfer, are you? Losing a finger will ruin your swing. Tennis too.'

'I've known people like you all my life,' Kieron shouted. 'You're just like the bullies at school, only you're richer. They always said they'd give my packed lunch or my schoolbooks back if only I asked nicely, but they never did. So – I can either tell you what you want to know and then die, or I can keep the information to myself and still die. One means I give in, the other means I die fighting. Guess which one I'm choosing?'

'I'll ask again once your fingers are so frozen you'd be able to snap them off like icicles,' Todd's voice said, 'and when your breath starts turning to ice in your throat.'

A throbbing sound started up. Kieron could feel the vibration through the soles of his feet. Some kind of device that would reduce the temperature in the chamber? It had to be.

He looked around wildly. The chamber was maybe twice his height, with white metal walls and a white tiled floor marred by scuffs and scratches. Light came in through narrow but long vertical strips of glass running up to the ceiling, which was almost hidden by various pipes and vents. The glass strips had scorch marks on them, which didn't make Kieron feel any better at all.

A shiver ran through him. Was it getting colder, or was he just scared? Actually, it might be both.

He could see his breath forming clouds in front of his face. He wrapped his arms around his chest. Should he sit down? Would the floor retain heat, or were there cooling elements built into it?

Actually, he could feel his feet getting colder. He started stamping them, moving around, trying to keep one foot off the ground as much as possible.

'You look like you're skipping!' Todd's voice crowed. So he had cameras in there as well. 'Just like a girl in the playground!'

'I said you were a bully,' Kieron shouted. Gusts of vapour drifted away from him and towards the ceiling.

'Still working on something,' Bex said. She sounded strained.

'No hurry,' Kieron murmured, and then louder: 'I live in Newcastle. I'm used to the cold.'

His fingers had started to tingle, and every breath hurt his lungs. Looking around he could see drips of condensed water vapour running down the chamber's walls. Most of them froze before they got to the floor, leaving trails like wax running down a candle in those small Italian trattorias his mum took him to for a treat.

His mum. A sob threatened to erupt from his chest, stopping his breathing. He was never going to see her again! And Bex would disappear to another town, with another identity. His mum would never know what happened.

'Anything to tell us?' Todd's crackly voice asked. 'If you're too cold I can turn the heat up. Right up.'

'Tell my mum,' he said to Bex, forcing the words past jaw muscles that had clenched against the cold. 'Don't leave her in the dark.'

'No need,' Bex's voice said. She sounded . . . not defeated. Not strained.

She sounded confident.

Something went *crash* outside, and the lights flickered. The rumbling engine sound cut out completely. Warmth enveloped him like a duvet, making him realise just how cold the chamber had got, and how quickly. What had happened?

The door he'd come through – well, been thrown through – suddenly clicked open. He didn't know why, but before anyone could change their mind, he staggered towards it and fell back out.

From his sprawled position he saw that a second golf cart had appeared. This one was just as driverless as the first, but it had crashed into the mushroom-shaped control console. The console itself now canted heavily to one side. It had been half pulled from the ground, and wires dangled from its base, dripping sparks. The cart itself lay on its side, wheels still spinning pointlessly.

Todd and Tara had apparently been in the way when the cart drove into the central area. They both lay on the floor, looking dazed.

'Not as easy to drive as you might think, mate,' Sam said in his ear.

'Sam – that was *you*?'

'Of course. Bex accessed the central robotic cart area on

262

the external server and took one over, then she got me to drive it.'

'You begged me to let you drive it,' Bex shouted in the background.

'There's five different cameras on the front of each cart, plus infra-red and microwave sensors. It's like playing a video game. Right – now we have to get you out of there. Get in the cart.'

Kieron stared at the scene before him. 'I don't know what your five cameras are telling you, but you crashed it. Just like you crash vehicles in any computer game you play.'

'Not *that* cart, idiot. *This* cart.'

Something went *beep!* behind Kieron, making him jump. Turning, he saw a third driverless robotic cart right approaching. He climbed in, still feeling shaky from the stress of the environmental chamber.

'We're just outside the main gate,' Sam said. 'I'll get the cart to take you right there.'

Either Bex or Sam must have hacked the cart software, because the one Kieron was in took off with such rapid acceleration he was thrown backwards and almost fell out. He grabbed onto the frame and hung on as the cart raced back along the glass tunnel.

'A few minutes and you'll be safe,' Sam said in his ear, just as something exploded against the wall of the tunnel. The smoothly curved walls suddenly changed into a jigsaw of sharp glass shards the size of Kieron's head. They fell like fragments of a frozen waterfall, embedding themselves into the ground.

'What the hell?' Sam yelled.

Kieron glanced back over his shoulder. Todd had got up off the floor and was pointing a weapon at him. Maybe he kept it in the golf cart that had brought them here. It looked something like a revolver.

The expression on Todd's face was as close to insanity as Kieron ever wanted to see.

As Kieron watched, Todd aimed at him again and pulled the trigger.

A line of fire etched itself through the air towards Kieron's head. A small black dot at the front of the fiery line, growing larger with every microsecond, had to be a projectile. Some kind of miniature missile, maybe, propelled by hot exhaust gases from burning fuel. Even as part of Kieron's mind wondered what kind of fool would fire what was effectively a small rocket launcher in a vastly expensive satellite construction and testing facility, another part tried to tell him that in less than a second that small rocket and his head would occupy the same space. And he couldn't seem to make his body move out of the way. Time had slowed down massively, but so had his reactions. He couldn't move.

The cart swerved sideways, taking it into the area where the satellites sat like high-tech monoliths. The rocket *swish*ed right past Kieron's face, so close that the heat from its exhaust burned his cheek. It smashed through the still-falling chunks of curved glass, bouncing off them and deflecting sideways, into the construction space.

Where it hit a huge satellite, passing right through its solar panels and smashing directly into the main body before exploding.

The satellite began to topple.

'Go left!' Kieron called. Sam must have heard him, because the cart suddenly veered again.

The exit lay just ahead. The floor between the cart and the exit was covered in shards of glass from the smashed tunnel.

'Drive straight ahead!' Kieron shouted. 'If you do that, we'll get through the door.'

The cart sprang forward. Kieron heard the crunch of glass beneath its wheels. He looked sideways, to see the massive satellite falling sideways and crashing into the next one in line. That one began to topple as well. It was like watching dominoes fall, one after the other, except these were multi-million pound pieces of astronomical technology.

The first satellite hit the floor. Its solar panels seemed to explode upwards in thousands of fragments of blue while its body crumpled and cracked.

Fascinated, Kieron would have liked to watch the next one go down, but he had more important things to do. He glanced behind him, searching for Todd Zanderbergen as the cart sped towards the door to the outside world. For a moment he couldn't see where the man had gone, but then he spotted him standing at the shattered end of the glass tunnel, halfway between the giant environmental chamber and where Kieron's cart had reached. He was aiming his weapon again, but not at Kieron. He was aiming off to the left.

At the nearest satellite to the door – the one on the other side of the one that had fallen and smashed so completely.

Kieron immediately saw what Todd intended. He wanted

265

to bring the satellite crashing down like a tree, blocking Kieron's path out.

Or crushing him. Kieron suspected that either result would please Todd.

'Stop!' he shouted.

'Why?' Sam sounded confused. 'We're nearly there!'

'Just do it!'

The cart came to a skidding stop just as Todd fired. The tiny missile *whoosh*ed past him and hit the base of the satellite. This one was taller and narrower, made of several sections linked by thinner bits, like an extended wasp. Fire splashed around its base, and slowly, majestically, it started to fall. Just as Todd had intended, it hit the ground where the glass tunnel had been, crumpling and cracking into several sections at the joints. There must have been fuel in a tank inside, because the small fire caused by the missile suddenly became swamped by a much bigger explosion so hot and so bright that Kieron had to throw his arm up to protect his eyes. A wave of heat washed over him.

Kieron leaped out of the cart and ran towards the door to the outside, but it was no good. The blazing, crumpled satellite completely blocked the way.

'Find me another way out of here!' he shouted to Sam.

'Working on it,' Sam said.

Kieron looked back towards the centre of the building. Todd was stalking towards him, murder in his eyes.

Kieron glanced around desperately, looking for something, anything, he could use to fight Todd or escape, but there was nothing.

266

Except . . . except the gun that Todd held.

Kieron ran sideways until he was clear of the crashed satellite, standing in front of the thick red glass wall of the building. He turned. Trying to look as casually defiant as possible, he put his hands on his hips.

'How much damage have I caused?' he shouted at the approaching Todd. 'Must be millions of dollars' worth by now. Tens of millions. *Hundreds* of millions?'

'I'll get it all back,' Todd shouted. 'ANCIENT MARINER will make me *billions*!'

'And kill billions,' Kieron pointed out.

'Ordinary people.' Todd raised his gun. 'People like you, not extraordinary people like me. The world will be less cluttered and better off.'

'You're a psychopath,' Kieron said.

Todd stopped about twenty metres away. 'Yes,' he said, 'I know. Mom and Dad sent me to a psychologist. He made that diagnosis. Didn't tell me anything I didn't already know, but I killed him anyway, for his attitude. He thought I needed treatment. He didn't know what I know – it's people like me who are successful in this world. So, yes, I am a psychopath. And you're dead.'

He fired the weapon.

Before the projectile had even left the stocky barrel of the gun, Kieron had dived sideways. His shoulder hit the ground hard, sending a lightning spike of pain through him, but he rolled clumsily and scrambled back to his feet as the projectile hit the building's glass wall. Massive cracks propagated in all directions. The missile exploded, and the blast pushed the glass fragments *outwards*, into the open air. Kieron ran through the flames and through the gap that had been opened, shielding his eyes with his arm.

The heat of the fiery explosion gave way to the heat of Tel Aviv's climate. The blue sky above seemed like the most beautiful thing Kieron had ever seen after the red-tinged, sterile building interior. He ran along the side of the building, desperately trying to get ahead of Todd. Left at a junction between buildings, then right at another junction, breath rasping in his chest all the time. He thought he could hear Todd's footsteps behind him all the while. The centre of his back, right between his shoulder blades, itched, waiting for the next missile to hit his spine.

The maze-like configuration of the buildings confused him, and the long stretches of glass wall meant that Todd could come around a corner behind him at any time while he was running for the *next* corner, and that would be fatal.

He got to yet another junction, a crossroads this time. He was about to turn right when Sam's voice in his ear said, 'Go straight on!'

'I can't!' he virtually screamed; 'Todd will see me!'

'There's a door just ahead, on the left. It's your closest route into a building.'

Kieron ran, stumbling now rather than sprinting. He wasn't sure how much more of this he could do. He felt as if he was right on the edge of collapse.

Just as Sam had said, there was a doorway in the left-hand wall just ten steps past the crossroads. It opened silently as he approached.

He ran inside, and the door closed again behind him.

This building seemed to be a storage area. Yellow lines on the floor delineated separate zones. The first one on Kieron's right had wooden crates stacked up almost to the ceiling high above; the one on his left had hard plastic boxes in military camouflage colours arranged on racks of shelving. He ran along an aisle, then turned down another one lined with large metal containers so that he couldn't be seen from the doorway.

'There's a way out on the far side,' Bex said suddenly. She seemed to have taken over from Sam on the ARCC kit. 'Keep on going straight, then turn left at the end.'

He got to the end of the row of containers, and stopped.

'Keep going,' Bex said. 'What's the matter?'

'Can you see what I see?' Kieron asked, staring straight ahead.

He was looking at an area in the centre of the room, surrounded by high walls of metal containers. Right in the middle were around forty barrel-shaped canisters, bright orange in colour. Each one had a stark yellow-and-black biohazard symbol stuck on the side. And each one had the words 'Project ANCIENT MARINER' stencilled in black letters above the symbol.

'That's the virus,' he said grimly. 'It's ready to send out.'

'Leave it,' Bex said urgently. 'We can alert someone as soon as we get you out of there.'

'Like who?'

'Don't worry about that now. Just get out!'

'The police? The army? For all we know, the Israeli

government might be one of the Goldfinch Institute's customers. Even if they're not, by the time they do anything, Todd will have shipped all these canisters out, and then what will happen? People will die. *Lots* of people.'

'There's nothing you can do. Just get away from there. We'll worry about Project ANCIENT MARINER once you're safe.'

Kieron felt torn. He wanted to *do* something about the virus, but he didn't know *what*. If he had more time he might think of something, but he couldn't have more than a few seconds before Todd caught up with him.

Todd? Could he get the man to fire his missile gun at the canisters, blow them up by accident?

'Would fire destroy the virus?' he asked, glancing around to see if Todd was near.

'Yes,' Bex said after a few seconds, 'as long as it's hot enough. I can see what you're thinking, but the explosion might just disperse the virus before the heat destroys it. Unless –'

'Unless *what*?'

'Unless I close the building's door from here and turn off the ventilation system and the fire-suppression system. That way the fire would keep burning until everything inside was destroyed.'

Kieron shook his head angrily. 'Wouldn't work anyway. The gun's not got enough missiles to destroy all these canisters.'

'Then get out – we'll think of something else.'

Kieron started to move again, heading for the far side of the building. When he was two-thirds of the way along a row of empty metal shelves, something *ping*ed off a strut.

He turned. Tara stood at the end of the row. She held a nasty-looking gun with a silencer on the end of the barrel.

She fired again.

Kieron dived to the ground and rolled beneath the lowest shelf. There was barely enough clearance for him: he had to lie on his back and haul himself along by grabbing hold of metal struts. The bottom shelf was so close to his face that he had to turn his head sideways. The ground beneath him scraped his ear as he pulled and slid his way to the other side of the rack. He heard footsteps as Tara ran towards where she thought he was going to emerge. Quickly he reversed course, wriggling back to where he'd entered. He got to his feet and quickly pulled his shoes off, then ran soundlessly along to the nearest corner and went in the opposite direction.

Tara and Todd, both searching for him. He didn't stand a chance.

His lungs burned with exertion and his muscles ached. Blood trickled down his neck from his scraped ear. His two pursuers were wearing him down, and they didn't seem to care how much damage they did to the Goldfinch Institute, just as long as their precious ANCIENT MARINER survived.

He stopped and bent over, hands on his knees, desperately trying to find some last reserves of energy he could use.

'I think this is it, Bex,' he said. 'I can't go any further.'

He expected Bex to shout at him, give him a pep talk, tell him that he had to fight on, but she didn't. All she said was: 'Look to your right.'

He looked. Ten containers, like large military suitcases, were lined up on the floor between two piles of wooden crates.

'What?' he asked.

'Look at what it says on them.'

He looked. The stencilled lettering said: 'ICARUS'.

For a moment the word made no sense, and then he remembered. The *other* Goldfinch Institute, in Albuquerque. The tour of the buildings. The video showing a man strapped to a device that had a tiny jet engine, a fuel tank and a wing about as wide as the man was tall.

'You're kidding,' he said. 'I don't know how to fly one of those things!'

'I'll get hold of the specs,' Bex said. 'You put it on.'

He glanced quickly around. No sign of Todd or Tara. With the last of his strength he pulled one of the suitcases out and opened it. The device inside looked like a metal rucksack with rubber straps. The wings had folded down into a shape like a surfboard. He struggled into the straps. The folded wings dragged along the floor, and a circular plate with various controls pressed against his chest.

'What now?' he asked. He felt like he had no willpower left, no energy, no ability to do anything apart from follow instructions.

'You're not going to like the next bit.'

'I don't like it already,' he said quietly, feeling the rubber straps dig into his chest and the weight of the folded wings pull against his shoulders.

'You're going to have to get as high as possible so you can launch yourself.'

'What?' he said, confused. 'You mean go up to the *roof*? I can't do that! I can hardly even *walk*!'

'No, I mean you've got to climb those shelves behind you and jump off.'

'Bex, I –'

'Do it,' she said, like a PE teacher telling him to climb a rope in the gym.

He was too tired to argue. He grabbed a high shelf with both hands, put his right foot on a low shelf, and started to climb.

It seemed to take forever, and his muscles kept screaming at him to stop. The folded wings dragged him backwards relentlessly. Several times his fingers slipped or lost their grip and he almost fell, but eventually he pulled himself onto the empty top shelf. He gazed up into the space around him, between the top of the shelving and the cables and ventilation tubes attached to the ceiling high above.

'That was the easy bit,' Bex said firmly. 'Now you have to jump.'

'I really –'

A bullet flashed past him, clipping the top of his ear and cutting through a lock of his hair. Hot blood splattered across his forehead. Calling on energy he didn't even know he had, Kieron scrambled to his feet and stumbled towards the edge of the shelf.

'Red button, dead centre of the control plate –' Bex's voice reminded him of all the teachers he'd ever hated at school – 'that'll activate the jets. Then there are two joysticks, one on either side. The left one takes you up and down; the right one takes you side to side. Now . . . *run*!'

Several holes suddenly appeared in the metal surface ahead of him, sharp edges reaching up like tiny claws. Bullet holes.

The edge of the shelf was coming up fast. He fumbled for the control plate and pressed the button in the centre. It might have been red, it might not; he couldn't see it.

Something seemed to kick him hard in the middle of his back. He staggered and almost fell, but somehow he kept on running, running . . . until he launched himself off the shelf and into empty space.

He assumed he was going to drop straight to the ground. He was *convinced* of it, but behind him, the wings snapped out, unfolding into the graceful curves he'd seen in the video back in Albuquerque. Instead of shielding his head protectively, his arms tucked back so his hands could grasp the controls.

He felt the heat of the jet exhaust against his legs. The kick became a push, the push became a shove, and he was flying! He was really flying! Beneath him he saw shelves, crates, boxes and canisters sliding past like the landscapes he'd seen from the windows of the aircraft as he, Bex and Sam had flown in to Albuquerque.

No difficulties for him. He tested the controls: swooping right and swooping left, then up and down. It was so easy!

Except, he suddenly realised, he was fast running out of building.

'Can you see the door ahead of you and to the right?' Bex's voice asked.

'No!' he shouted.

'Look *down*, near the ground.'

'Oh yes, I see it now.'

'Aim for that. I'll make sure the door stays open.'

Kieron jinked down towards the ground, then levelled out. He was heading along one of the aisles between the crates, shelves and boxes. He thought he saw Todd Zanderbergen's face flash past, contorted in comical surprise, but that was behind him now and the doors were ahead of him, getting closer really fast.

His hands jerked the controls, and suddenly his path curved upwards. The doors disappeared below him, and the wall above them flashed past so close he could have reached out and touched it.

'What do you think you're *doing*?' Bex's voice was a frustrated shout, like the PE teacher's voice when he'd struggled up her damned gym rope then pulled the end up after him and refused to come down.

He altered his path again, so that he was flying upside-down along the ceiling, away from the doors and back into the building. Pipes, cables and vents formed a bleak cityscape. For a second he imagined that he was flying along the surface of the Death Star out of Star Wars and he laughed joyfully. Then a quick twist of the controls and he was the right way up again.

'I'm doing what has to be done,' he shouted, hoping that Bex could hear him over the rushing of air and the roar of the jet engine. 'This thing is armed. I remember seeing it on the video. How do I fire the missiles?'

'Kieron –'

'Just tell me!'

275

He looked around, trying to get some sense of where he was. The ANCIENT MARINER canisters were stored in the centre of the building, he remembered. He adjusted his course into a spiral, and gazed down intently, looking for them.

Bright orange. Yes, there they were.

Todd Zanderbergen stood beside them protectively. He raised his missile gun and fired it. A line of bright orange and yellow flame headed straight for Kieron, but he adjusted his flight controls gently and moved slightly out of the way. The missile passed beneath him. He thought he heard the *boom!* as it hit the roof.

'There are two buttons, one on each of the directional controls. They fire the left and right rockets. Kieron –'

'Yes, I'm sure,' he said.

He adjusted his course, straightening and dipping so he was heading right for the bright orange canisters. His fingers touched the buttons on top of the flight controls, and suddenly, from beneath the wings behind him, two small, pencil-like objects flashed ahead of him and towards the crates of Project ANCIENT MARINER. Todd – a small figure on the ground – saw what was happening and raised his hands desperately, like King Canute trying to hold back the inevitable tide. Kieron steered his course off to one side, but a tall stack of shelving was in the way. He spotted a gap between two stacks of crates and aimed for it. The crates flashed past him, then he was in the open again.

He couldn't see what was happening behind him, but he felt a wall of heat pass over him. The air itself seemed to ripple.

'I'm keeping the doors open,' Bex said, 'and I've disabled the fire-suppression system. Are you going to get out *now*, or hang around and do some sightseeing?'

'Time to leave,' he said, pulling the jet wings around and heading for where he thought the doors were located. 'I don't know how much fuel I've got left.'

The approaching wall was alive now with dancing orange and red light. Whatever was happening behind him, it was big and it was impressive and it was spreading rapidly. He just wished he could see it.

'Can I keep this thing?' he asked as he swooped through the doorway. The brightness of the clear blue sky blinded him for a moment, but the hot Israeli air was cool in contrast to the burning building behind him.

'If you're not careful,' Bex said, 'I'll make you fly back to England in it.' She paused. 'But good work, kid. *Really* good work.'

CHAPTER FOURTEEN

They flew back to England first class. Bex thought the boys deserved it, after everything that had happened. The business couldn't really afford it, but that's what credit cards and overdrafts were for. They'd get the money back – somehow.

'Did you report what happened, back there?' Kieron asked. He had the remains of a lobster thermidor on the plate in front of him, along with a glass of champagne Bex had allowed him to order. Sam, beside him, had discovered that his seat could go completely flat. He was lying down, covered with a blanket, playing a game on the tablet he'd been handed when they boarded. Bex suspected he might never want to get off.

'I've briefed Bradley about everything,' she said, 'and he'll pass it on to MI6. They need to know what Todd Zanderbergen was up to. They'll liaise with Shin Bet and the FBI to close the company down.'

'And we just go home and pretend nothing happened?'

She nodded. 'That's right. Nothing *did* happen. Remember that. Or, rather, *don't* remember that.'

He took another sip of his champagne and glanced around

the first-class cabin. 'I could get used to this lifestyle,' he said appreciatively, settling back in his seat. 'I swear there are movies on these tablets that haven't even been released in the *cinema* yet.'

Bex closed her eyes briefly. Mention of MI6 had caused a seed of concern to germinate in her mind. They weren't any closer to finding out who the traitor was in the organisation – the one who was working with the neo-fascist Blood and Soil thugs in the UK. That was next on her agenda. As soon as she got back, she and Bradley needed to investigate that.

And make some money, quickly.

Kieron suddenly seemed to perk up. He sat up straight, gazing intently ahead of him.

'Sam,' he said urgently. 'Sam!' He hit Sam's leg underneath the blanket.

Sam emerged like a tortoise coming out of hibernation. '*What?*' he asked, blinking. 'I'm on level twenty!'

'See those blokes on the other side of the cabin?' Kieron pointed, and Sam turned his head to look. 'Do they look familiar to you?'

Bex looked as well, feeling a slight twinge of concern.

'Dunno,' Sam said. 'They look pretty radical.'

'That,' Kieron said firmly, 'is Lethal Insomnia.'

'You're kidding!'

Bex settled back in her seat and closed her eyes. The boys were fine. She'd be fine too, with a bit of sleep.

Look out for more spy action from A·W·⊕·L·

Someone is trying to kill Bex and Bradley, but they don't know about Kieron and Sam. That may be their only saving grace. But how were the explosions triggered? And who wants them dead?

LAST BOY STANDING

Coming in 2019

Turn the page for more . . .

CHAPTER ONE

'What's your name?' the red-haired girl asked, smiling at Kieron.

'K-Kieron,' he stammered. 'What's yours?'

She sighed and tapped the name badge pinned to her shirt. 'Beth. And I just needed your name so we can call you when your coffee's ready.' She ostentatiously wrote *Keiron* on a post-it note and stuck it on the side of a cup with a Sharpie. 'Like, when it's ready, you know?'

'Oh. OK.' He wondered whether to mention that she'd spelled it wrong, but decided to keep quiet. Everybody got his name wrong. Either they spelled it the way the girl had, or they put an 'a' instead of the 'o' at the end. He'd got used to it. Once he'd asked his mum why she and his dad had given him the most unusual spelling of his name they could manage. 'Oh,' she'd said vaguely, 'did we? I think it was the name of one of your dad's friends. He might have been at the wedding.'

'Anything else?' the red-haired barista asked brightly. 'Something to eat, maybe?'

Kieron scanned the shelves of the refrigerated area to his right. 'Er . . . what do you recommend?'

'The gluten-free lemon drizzle cake is very nice.'

Which means they're not selling enough of it and want to shift some more slices, he thought cynically.

'Just the coffee, please,' he said.

He handed over a five-pound note, grimly surprised at how little change he got, then moved to the end of the counter where the coffee would magically appear with his name on it. Spelled wrong. Well, as long as they *pronounced* it correctly, he didn't really care.

He glanced around. The cafe was new, in a side street close to the shopping mall he usually went to. Bex had taken him there a couple of weeks ago, when they'd got back from America. This was where the more unusual shops lurked – the ones selling black or purple women's clothing with a lot of lace or embroidery on it, or men's clothes that seemed far too tight and probably required you to have a hipster beard before you even tried it on. Oh, and there was a comics and gaming shop. Someone he knew from school worked there. Sometimes Kieron managed to score a staff discount, if the manager wasn't watching.

'Kieron?'

'Yes?' He glanced around.

It was Beth. 'Your coffee is ready.'

'Thanks.'

He'd put his stuff on a small two-person table, just to secure it. His bag was there, with his laptop inside. And his schoolbooks.

As he sat down, his gaze slipped to his rucksack. In there, in a hard case, were the ARCC glasses that he'd found, months ago now, on a table in the food court of the shopping mall. Those glasses had opened up a world of adventure, excitement and danger for him. They'd also introduced him to Bex and Bradley – the two MI6 agents (well, freelance contractors, Bex would always point out) who had changed his life. Given him confidence. Trusted him with their lives. And those ARCC glasses could access any computer anywhere in the world – not just the obvious ones, like the Internet, but secure databases as well. Secret ones.

So why did he have to painstakingly prove a mathematical equation when the sum of all human knowledge was right there, in his bag? Why did *anybody* have to learn how to do *anything* when they could just ask about it and get an answer in a few seconds?

He sighed. He knew why – kind of. Because intelligence came from knowing these things and being able to apply them and extend them, or at least that's what his teachers would have said. What if he was on a desert island or, God forbid, the Internet had failed because of a zombie apocalypse? How would he be able to survive then?

Still, if his survival during a zombie apocalypse depended on his being able to prove the derivation of a magnetic field of a solenoid from a current loop, then he was in serious trouble.

He opened up his laptop, sighed, leaned back in his chair and took a sip of his coffee. Just a few weeks ago he'd been flying through the air with what could only be called a high-tech military jet pack, risking his life in order to stop an insane billionaire from selling biologically engineered viruses that could target particular *types* of person based on their DNA.

A few weeks before *that* he'd been helping Bex prevent the detonation of a series of neutron bombs around the world. And now, here he was, sitting in a cafe that smelled of burnt coffee beans trying not to look at the cute red-haired barista.

Life sucked. And he couldn't tell anyone apart from Sam *why* it sucked. It wasn't the bullying per se. It wasn't the fact that he felt like a loner, an outsider – he was quite proud of that. No, it was the huge gulf between the life that he'd *experienced* over those weeks and the life that, for want of a better word, *life* seemed to want to push him back towards.

Helping Bex and Bradley wasn't sustainable. He knew that. He was a temporary solution, a last resort while Bradley was medically unable to use the ARCC kit. Bradley was meant to support Bex while she was on missions by passing her useful information, like blueprints of buildings or identities of people she was looking at. Once Bradley had recovered sufficiently to work again, and once he and Bex had discovered who in their MI6 parent organisation was working with the neo-fascist group Blood and Soil, they wouldn't need him any longer. *That* was why he didn't want to go into school any more. *That* was why he was depressed. It was like being in a car on a motorway and seeing the exit ramp you wanted to take, *needed* to take, passing by, and knowing that the road you were stuck on just kept on going into the distance, monotonously, forever.

'A horse goes into a bar,' a voice said from behind him, 'and the barman says, "Why the long face?"'

He recognised Sam's voice instantly. Without turning around, he reached out with a foot and pushed the other chair away from the table so his friend could sit down.

'So, *why* the long face?' Sam asked, sitting. 'It's long even from behind.'

Kieron shrugged.

'A white horse walks into a bar,' Sam went on. 'The barman says, "We've got a whisky here named after you!" and the horse says, "What – *Brian*?"'

'Shouldn't you be in school?' Kieron asked.

Sam shrugged. 'You know what – I probably should.' He sniffed. 'They've burned the coffee beans. You can tell. My mum's into all that. She's been watching videos on YouTube on how to make the perfect cup of coffee, from selecting the right bean from the right country all the way up to choosing the absolutely optimal steam pressure on the machine. And she's got one of those fancy machines as well. Dad bought it for her for Christmas last year.' He nodded his head at the counter. 'Like the one they've got. Well, I say *bought*, but it might have come out of the back of some van in a pub car park. You can never tell with my dad.'

'That joke, by the way,' Kieron pointed out, 'only works if you know that there's a brand of whisky called White Horse.'

'I thought everyone knew that.'

'In your world, maybe.'

Sam shrugged. 'It's all my Uncle Bill drinks. He gets a bottle for Christmas from everyone in the family – I mean, a bottle from each person, not just one bottle from everyone. Same on his birthday. That pretty much sets him up for the year.' He paused. 'OK, a horse walks into a bar and says, "Pour me a pint of beer, will you?" The barman rubs his eyes in disbelief and says, "Did . . . did you just talk?" The horse says, "Yes, why?" and the barman goes, "It's amazing! I've never seen a talking horse! You know, you should really go talk to the local circus – they would *love* to have someone with your skills!" The horse replies, "Why? Are they short of plumbers?"'

This time Kieron sniggered. 'Yeah, OK, that's good. I like that.'

'I'm thinking of setting up a website – all the best "horse walks into a bar" jokes in the world.'

'How many have you got?'

Sam winced. 'You've heard them.'

'Just three?'

'I could expand the website to other animals. "A bear goes into a bar –"'

'Don't,' Kieron interrupted. 'Just . . . don't.'

'Just let me do this one. A bear goes into a bar, right, and says, "I'd like a pint of . . . beer," and the barman goes, "Why the big paws?"' He stared at Kieron. '*Big paws*. Like, bears have got big paws. And he *paused* before finishing the sentence.'

'Yes, it was funny when you told it and it was funny when you explained it.' Kieron looked properly at Sam for the first time, and sat up straighter in his chair. 'What's wrong?'

'Nothing's wrong.'

'Yes, it is.'

'No, really. Nothing's wrong.'

'I can tell. I know you, and I know the way your face goes when there's something wrong, and it's gone there now. It's gone there so much it might just as well pitch a tent and stay there for the night. So, come on – what's wrong?'

Sam sighed. 'Get me an iced latte and I'll tell you.'

On his way up to the counter Kieron surreptitiously counted the change in his pocket and checked the price on the board fastened to the wall. He just about had enough.

'What's your name?' the barista – Beth – asked him brightly.

'Still Kieron,' he said. Her smile faltered slightly.

After a lot of faffing about with a blender, ice cubes and a double shot of coffee, Kieron took the drink and returned to the table. 'So?' he asked, putting it down in front of his friend.

'So . . .' Sam sighed. 'You know my dad, right?'

'Yeah. You described him to Bex once as, "a lifelong drifter who can't hold down a job for more than a week". I think those were your exact words.'

'Yeah, that sounds about right. I counted up once: he's had just under a hundred different jobs, some of them overlapping. Longest he's ever stayed at one is three months; shortest is three days.' Sam stared out of the front door of the cafe at the bright street outside. 'Thing is, he's actually found himself a real job now. A proper job.'

'That's good, isn't it?'

'It's in Southampton. Loading stuff onto the cruise ships before they leave – food and drink and stuff. Still, at least that means we'll be OK for lobster and champagne at Christmas.'

'Oh.' Kieron frowned, trying to work out where this was going. 'How does your mum feel about that? I mean, I know she gets irritated at him – I've heard the arguments from halfway down the street when I go round to your place – but I don't think she'd want him to go away for weeks on end.'

'She doesn't – mainly because she doesn't trust him not to

find a girlfriend down there and spend all his money in the pub.'
Sam hesitated. 'That's why she's talking about all of us moving
down there with him. "Make a new start," she says; "All of
us, together. It'll be wonderful." But the thing is – it won't.'

'*All* of you? Including Courtney?'

Sam shook his head. 'No, not Courtney. She's sorted. She's
got a good job and her own flat. And a boyfriend, although
Mum doesn't know about Bradley yet. But Caitlin and Amber
still live at home, so they'd go down to Southampton. And
so would I.'

Kieron suddenly felt as if he was standing in the middle
of a minefield. Whichever way he stepped, something might
explode. 'How do *you* feel about that?' he asked carefully.

'I think it's stupid.' Sam took a gulp of his iced coffee. 'I
mean, yes, it's a new place, and if anyone could do with a new
start, it's us, but –' he shook his head – 'I don't *want* a new
start. I may not love Newcastle, but I'm used to it. I know
where everything is. And –'

He stopped, but Kieron thought he knew what Sam had
been going to say. *And you're here.*

He felt a lump in his throat, and he had to blink quickly to
get rid of the prickle in his eyes.

That feeling he'd had earlier, of life being like sitting in a car
going nowhere forever? That landscape the car was driving into
was looking bleaker and bleaker now. Just dry earth and the
occasional cactus. He only had one real friend in the world –
Sam. Bex and Bradley felt like friends, but they were older and
he knew in his heart of hearts they were temporary. In a few
weeks, or months at the most, they'd be gone. But Sam – he'd

assumed he and Sam would go on and on, to the end of their schooldays and beyond.

'Maybe,' he said carefully, 'your mum would let you come and stay at my flat. I mean, changing school at this late stage is bound to affect your grades. There's space on my floor, and I'm sure my mum won't mind.'

'Do you think that's an actual possibility?' Sam asked plaintively.

'Yeah, course. Do you want me to ask her?'

'Please.' Kieron noticed that Sam's throat was working, as if he needed to swallow. He handed his friend his glass and Sam took a grateful gulp.

'Just bear in mind,' Sam said, 'I'm not going into school and leaving you studying at home.'

'Don't worry – we'll find a way around that.'

'When school's over,' Sam asked suddenly, 'what do you want to do?'

'I dunno. Just hang out.' Kieron suddenly caught up with the conversation. 'Oh, you mean, after we *leave* school!'

'Yeah.' Sam shrugged casually. 'You ever thought about going to college?'

'Kinda. Difficult to think of any subject I'd want to do though. I wondered about film studies. Or maybe psychology.'

'Psychology – good idea. Try to explain our dark teenage thought-processes.'

'Why are you asking?'

'I've been thinking . . .' Sam sounded unusually hesitant, '. . . maybe we could, like, set up a company together. Do something that'll make us some money.'

'Secret agents?' Kieron laughed. 'Or maybe private detectives.'

Sam scowled. 'I was thinking more like website design, or repairing computers and tablets and mobile phones, but if you're just going to laugh –'

'No.' Kieron forced himself to sound serious. 'Actually, that's not a bad idea. We could get ourselves a little unit on an industrial estate maybe.' A vision of how all this might work started unfolding in his mind. 'We'd need to learn to drive, at least on a moped, so we could pick up the broken stuff and bring it back for repair. No, scratch that – we'd definitely need a car. We might just get a small PC CPU on the back of a moped, but definitely not any of the high-end gaming machines. We'd need some money, to set up and buy circuit boards and tools and stuff. Maybe we could apply for a loan. I'll ask my mum about that.'

'Actually,' Sam said, '*my* mum's got all the information. You can get things called Enterprise Loans.'

Kieron nodded. 'Sorted. We'll get one of those.'

'Sorted,' Sam said, and extended a fist. Kieron bumped his own fist against it.

They chatted for a while, reminding each other of things that had happened to them over the past few months and marvelling at how their lives had changed so much while apparently, to anybody else, having stayed the same. Eventually Kieron's macchiato was as cold as Sam's iced latte and he couldn't in all conscience keep sipping at it, so they left.

'You want to come back with me?' Kieron asked. 'We can get some lunch. There should be something in the fridge.'

'Might as well,' Sam replied. 'It's not as if there's any pressing need to save the world today, as far as I know.'

Kieron punched him on the arm. Hard.

The walk took them three-quarters of an hour. It would have been quicker, but they had to divert twice to avoid gangs of chavvy teenagers standing outside the off-licences. They both knew from harsh experience that they'd get called names, shoved and spat on if they went too close. Bitterly, Kieron thought the kids ought to have signs around their necks, like in a zoo: *Please do not provoke the chavs – they are liable to bite without warning.*

'We're nearly grown-up,' Sam pointed out darkly as they headed down a side street on one of their detours. 'We shouldn't have to be scared of them!'

'You adopt the moral and logical high ground,' Kieron replied, glancing back over his shoulder to see if they were being followed. 'I'll visit you in hospital and bring you grapes.'

'Why do people always bring you grapes when you're in hospital?' Sam frowned. 'When I broke my arm, I had so many bags of grapes by the side of my bed there wasn't room for anything else. What I wanted more than anything else was a Chinese takeaway, but nobody thought to bring one. Just grapes.'

'Something to do with the European Union,' Kieron said vaguely. 'I think there's, like, some kind of rule about fruit and hospitals – only grapes are allowed. And maybe tangerines.'

When they got to Kieron's flat, he noticed that his mum's car was outside. 'That's unusual – she should be at work.' He checked his watch. 'She's not due back for another couple of hours.'

Sam shifted uneasily. 'If you want me to go . . .'

'No, come in. It's probably fine.'

He slid his key into the lock and pushed the door open.

'Mum – I'm home!' he called. 'I've got Sam with me.'

'I'm in the living room,' his mum called. It sounded like there was something wrong with her voice, as if she was choking on something.

'You go to my room,' Kieron said to Sam. 'I'll check on Mum.'

'All right if I get a can of drink from your mini-fridge?'

'Yeah – just make sure there's one in there for me.'

As Sam headed along the corridor to Kieron's room, Kieron stared at the doorway into the living room. He felt suddenly sick. Something had changed, and not, he thought, for the better. It was as if his life had suddenly lurched sideways, unbalancing him, but he didn't know how or why. An emotional earthquake with no obvious cause.

He took a deep breath and headed into the living room.

His mum was sitting on the sofa, staring at the TV screen. Well, not so much *sitting* as *slumping*. The TV was off, but she was staring at the screen anyway. Two bottles sat on the table beside her, next to a half-full glass, but they weren't the usual prosecco or red wine. One of them was a bottle of gin; the other a bottle of tonic water.

Well, at least she's not drinking the gin neat, he thought.

'Hi, Mum.'

'I thought you were supposed to be doing your schoolwork today?' she said, staring at him and frowning.

'I went to the library,' he said automatically. It was a lie, but if he told her he'd gone to a coffee shop to work she would have asked why, and the explanation would have taken far too long. Better just to avoid the truth entirely.

'The library?' she repeated. 'Can't you find out whatever information you need on the Internet?'

Fine time for her to become technologically literate! he thought.

'The Internet's great for superficial stuff, like names and dates and equations, but if you want to get into a subject in-depth you need books.'

'Oh. OK. Good to know that libraries are still useful for something.' She reached out for her glass and seemed surprised to discover that it was empty.

'Mum – what's wrong?'

'Nothing. Nothing at all.' She wriggled around on the sofa so she could reach out for the gin bottle and poured a substantial amount into her glass. Then, putting the bottle back, she picked up the glass and took a gulp without bothering to dilute it with any tonic water.

'There is something wrong. Please – will you tell me what it is?'

She sighed. 'OK. Sit down.'

He sat in the armchair facing her. Suddenly he didn't want her to say anything. He didn't what to know what was wrong. If he didn't *know*, then nothing was wrong. It wasn't logical, but that was how he felt. Knowing would make it real.

'Sam's here,' he said. 'He's gone to my room.'

'Sam? Sam Rosenfelt?'

'Yeah.'

'I saw a post from his mum on social media. She said they might be moving to Southampton. Is that right? Southampton?'

He nodded, wincing inside. 'It's . . . a possibility. I want to talk to you about that, but –' he took a deep breath – 'first you need to tell me what's happened. It's something bad, isn't it?' A sudden thought grabbed him by the heart and squeezed. 'Is it Dad? Is he . . . is he dead?'

'Not as far as I know.' She took another gulp of straight gin. 'Although I wouldn't put it past him to die without telling us.' She shook her head. 'Sorry – that was uncalled for. No, as far as I know he's fine.' She seemed to realise that there was something wrong with her drink, and reached for the tonic bottle. 'It's work,' she said, topping her glass up until it was in danger of overflowing.

It's called a meniscus, Kieron thought, staring at the way the gin and tonic mixture clung to the rim of the glass all the way round the edge but rose up slightly towards the middle. It's to do with surface tension. I learned that last year. At school.

'I've been – made redundant,' his mum said, not looking at him. 'Laid off. Fired. I am officially "surplus to requirements".' Her face seemed to be twisting more and more with each phrase. 'I have been "downsized". Dismissed. Sacked. Given the boot.'

Kieron felt like he'd suddenly been hollowed out. 'What happened?'

'I can't remember if I told you at the time, but we merged with another company a few months back. We were given all kinds of assurances that nothing would change and that our jobs were secure, but it was all crap. They've decided to let the human resources department in the other company handle all the HR issues, and they're were fully staffed. So – they've had to "let me go".'

Kieron watched her for a few moments, but she stayed that way – eyes closed and head back. Eventually he got up, moved across to her and took the glass from her fingers. She didn't even seem to notice. He put it on the table beside her, then picked up the bottle of gin and took it out into the kitchen. After a moment's thought he put it in the fridge. It wasn't exactly hiding it, but then again it wasn't in plain sight either.

Sighing, he went down the corridor to his room.

Sam was playing on Kieron's PC. He glanced up when Kieron entered. 'Everything all right?'

'Mum's lost her job.'

Sam shrugged. 'Like I said: my dad's lost loads of jobs. It got to the stage where he'd come in the house and say, "I've lost my job," and we'd say, "Have you looked behind the fridge?" like it was a ritual or something.' He paused. 'Things'll work out. Don't worry.'

Kieron shook his head. 'She's been in this job for years – not days, like your dad. This has never happened to her before. I've never seen her like this.'

'Maybe this is life telling her that it's time for a change.'

Kieron held up his hand. 'Maybe this is me telling you to shut up before I slap you.'

'Fair point. Grab a spare controller and join me on this thing – I'll put it on two-player mode.'

Kieron was about to pull up a chair and join Sam when his mobile *beep*ed. He pulled it from his pocket and glanced at the screen. 'Message from Bex,' he said. 'Give me a minute.'

'I haven't seen her for a while. How's Bradley?'

'I'll find out. Hang on.' He checked the message.

Kieron – can we meet up? We need to have a serious talk. That cafe in Hooley Street, 4 this afternoon?

The cafe he'd been in just a few hours ago. Funny, the way life seemed to loop back around on itself sometimes.

'Everything OK?' Sam asked, eyes still fixed on the screen.

'I don't know,' Kieron said carefully. 'I think I'm about to be dumped.'

Piccadilly
P R E S S

Thank you for choosing a Piccadilly Press book.

If you would like to know more about our
authors, our books or if you'd just like to know
what we're up to, you can find us online.

www.piccadillypress.co.uk

And you can also find us on:

We hope to see you soon!